BECKY BERNSTEIN
GOES BERLIN

BECKY BERNSTEIN GOES BERLIN

Holly-Jane Rahlens

Arcade Publishing • *New York*

First English-language Edition 1997

The characters and events in this book are fictitious. Any similarity to real persons, living or dead, is coincidental and not intended by the author.

Library of Congress Cataloging-in-Publication Data

Rahlens, Holly-Jane
    Becky Bernstein goes Berlin / by Holly-Jane Rahlens. —1st English-language ed.
        p.   cm.
    ISBN 1-55970-381-4
    I. Title.
PS3568.A43B43   1997
813'.54—dc21   97-9453

Published in the United States by Arcade Publishing, Inc., New York
Distributed by Little, Brown and Company

Designed by API

10 9 8 7 6 5 4 3 2 1

BP

Printed in the United States of America

For my two and only, Eberhard and Noah

Contents

BECKY BERNSTEIN
GOES BERLIN

Prologue

Sunday, September 27, 1992
Evening

Felix was a lousy bastard. To say the least. And believe me, I'd love to say more. I'm dying to let you know in very exact, precise terms what I really think of him. But I won't. I'd rather not run the risk of alienating you in my very first paragraph with the vulgar vocabulary I would need to capture the details of his character. So I'll leave his description at a pithy "lousy bastard."

Of course I should have known better. Did anything distinguish him from the dozens of other unworthy, insensitive men who had drifted in and out of my life while I dwelled in that desert land called Singledom? No, nothing. Nothing save the x at the end of his name — which made it especially tedious to speak of him in the genitive — his striking head of red hair, his freckles, and the angora longjohns he wore to protect his weak bladder. I should have known better than to expend my energy on a genitively challenged, frisky, freckle-faced bunny eight years my junior. Granted, he was a charming young thing, with and especially without the longjohns. But when you come right down to it, who needs a Pippi Longstocking with a weak bladder for a boyfriend, anyway?

Listen, I knew there wasn't a serious future for us in the cards. It's not like I'm stupid. I'm a New Yorker. But all along I thought I was calling the shots. I thought I, Rebecca Lee Bernstein, was sitting at the controls and inventing the plot. And then what happened the evening before we were to drive to Venice?

I'd never been to Italy. I'd never swooned in a gondola, seen the moon rise over a lagoon, or spent an afternoon with the pigeons in the Piazza San Marco. And besides, I'd thought, a squirt of Mediterranean *allegria* might work wonders. I was in something of a crisis and needed a perk-me-up.

My career had fallen into a rut. No one else seemed to notice, but I was beginning to feel careless and cynical about my biweekly TV talk show *Breakfast at Becky's*. (Actually, who *can't* be cynical these days about yet another babble show? Let alone one on a *local* Berlin station?) My interviews were becoming predictable. I needed a rest from the show, a rest from broadcast journalism, a rest from having my nails manicured every time I went on. Manicures are so fatiguing. You can't even read a book while they're being performed on you. But they were a necessary evil. I like to keep my hands looking halfway decent, since on *Breakfast at Becky's* the camera is forever zooming in on me holding up some guest's best-selling book, shaking hands with Sylvester Stallone, or petting Siegfried's and Roy's favorite tiger cub.

When I think back on it now, two years later, the only successes I'd had that summer were the aforesaid Felix, an ambitious investment broker who had sold me some securities that turned out — thank God! — to be far more faithful than he was, and "Bingo Berlin," a short story I'd written about two American women seeking their destiny in the New Germany. It was my third meek attempt at writing fiction, but the first that seemed to work. I sold it to this highbrow literary German radio

program and in the heat of the moment sent it off to a friend
of a friend who works at *Mademoiselle*. I was so pleased with
the piece I even toyed with the idea of leaving television and
taking up the life of a struggling writer — a romantic notion
from my college days. Unfortunately I didn't have any more
inspiring ideas for fiction, and in my heart of hearts I knew
that I was far too timid to give up my bread and butter, stale
and rancid though it sometimes was.

So things that summer were a bit on shaky ground.
Small wonder I was thrilled with the prospect of Venice. But
then what happened? This pup, this Pippi, this lousy weak-
bladdered bastardex Felix with his inflated ego calls me up
and tells me he's sorry but he needs his space, he needs time to
think, and anyway, his ex-girlfriend Hildburg has come back.

His ex-girlfriend Hildburg? Since when did he have an ex-
girlfriend? Let alone one named Hildburg? He never told me
about her. I'm sure of it. How could I ever forget a name like
Hildburg?

There I was, right in the midst of smearing gorgonzola
on some rolls I was preparing for our trip, and there he was,
rubbing it in about how terribly sorry he was, but he'd have to
postpone, it was one of those things, and why wasn't I saying
anything?

"I can't. My mouth is full. I'm getting rid of the gorgonzola
sandwich I just made for you," I said, not without some
bite.

"I didn't think you'd take it so personally. And you
shouldn't always eat when something upsets you. You ought
to watch your weight."

I almost choked on the roll. I ought to watch my *weight?*
Since when was my weight an issue? Was this going to be his
last piece of advice before he fell back into Hildburg's anorexic
arms?

"Not that you're fat," he added quickly. "And not that I mind. You're very attractive. Really. But it wouldn't hurt you to lose a few pounds around the hips. You're a public figure. People expect a certain look."

It wouldn't hurt me to lose a few pounds around my hips? Tell me, is this a tactful human being? The return of an old girlfriend was to some degree understandable, but to be tossed aside as if I were a piece of gristle was unforgivable.

"Say something," he said. "Or did you hang up on me?"

"No, I did not hang up on you. But what I *will* do is put the receiver back in the cradle. It's not the same as hanging up, but it accomplishes the same thing and is not as rude, you LOUSY BASTARD!" Whereupon I replaced the receiver in its cradle and proceeded to devour the rest of the gorgonzola sandwich.

Wait a minute. Don't start thinking that this is going to be a story about Felix. He just happened to be around wreaking havoc and clogging up my heart the evening my life changed. I'm merely exploiting him as expository material. It's my way of getting back at him, the lousy bastard.

And don't for a second think that this is going to be yet another tale about yet another not-so-young woman with spreading hips, failing vision, and an apartment infested with dust and memories who whiles the evening away sipping raspberry schnapps, wondering if this is just a passing midlife crisis or, heaven forbid, her life, period.

Granted, after hanging up on Felix and downing the gorgonzola sandwich I turned to the mirror and did, indeed, see a not-so-young woman with spreading hips and an apartment infested with dust and memories. My eyes weren't failing but they were red with tears, my lips encrusted with crumbs and cheese mold. My lover, a puppy, a pipsqueak, a babe, had had the gall, the sheer nerve to dump me on the eve of our vacation. Yes, I *was* wondering if this was, heaven forbid, my *life*.

But no, I did not lunge for the raspberry schnapps. Instead, I blew my nose on my shirttail, inhaled deeply, raised my fist at the mirror, and swore to myself to clean up my act. "This will never ever happen to me again!" I cried out, vowing right then and there that instead of leaving town, I'd use my ten-day vacation to straighten out my life, to begin to rid myself of all my excess baggage, of all the extraneous pounds of junk and cellulite that had been weighing me down for years. Who needed that creep Felix to tutor me in the evils of gorgonzola? For months I'd been planning to go on a diet. Yet that was nothing compared to the years I'd been meaning to steamroll through my apartment, flatten out its bulk, take inventory, and rearrange its innards utterly and completely. Undetectable to the naked eye, clutter reigned all about me, hidden cleverly behind apparent neatness and tidiness, lurking in the far depths of locked closets, dark drawers, stuffed wardrobes, hard-to-reach shelves, out-of-the-way cabinets. But I knew it was there. Somewhere in me was the belief that, as with shedding the excess fat on my bones, de-junking all that chaos would also usher in a new epoch, a chance for redemption, a fresh beginning. Oh, how I longed for the perfect body in the perfect space. It was time to go for it.

"This will never ever happen to me again!" I raged at the mirror one last time like some demented Scarlett O'Hara. "As God is my witness, this will never happen to me again!"

And *that's* when I lunged for the raspberry schnapps.

Two years have come and gone since then, but I remember clearly that I slept surprisingly well that night. And early the following morning, keeping to my promise, I put myself and then my apartment on a strict diet. This is our story. And no one else's. Especially not Felix'x. The lousy bastard. To say the *very* least.

Chapter One

Monday, September 28, 1992
Diet Week: 1
Day: 1
Weight Loss: 0
Afternoon

"Sex!" Barry said to me. "And that's the only thing. Sex. Trust me on this one. It's the only thing men want. Sex. Sex. Sex." Each time Barry pronounced the word his voice grew louder, deeper, more expressive. With each intonation his hands seemed to knead an ever-growing pair of buttocks.

Barry was an actor, originally from Detroit, presently of Kreuzberg, Berlin. He worked with an immensely popular, artsy Russian-German theater ensemble that stamped and stomped around the stage making huge gestures, a good deal of noise, and very little sense. Theatrics had become Barry's personal style too.

"But he *was* getting it," I protested. "Sex in all variations."

"Sideways? From behind?"

"Yes!" I cried. "Front. Back. On top. Sideways."

"Upside down too?"

"Him or me?"

Barry chuckled and took a bite out of the gorgonzola sandwich I'd given him. "Accept it," he said. "Hildegard gave him more."

"Hild*burg*."

"And you'll never know why. And it doesn't matter."

I frowned.

"Does that upset you?" he asked.

"A little. Yes."

"What's your IQ?"

"One-forty-eight. But what does that have to do with this?"

"Because for someone with an IQ of 148 you're pretty stupid, that's why!" Barry headed toward the bathroom where his laundry was waiting for him. "What was it? A couple of weeks? Write him off and go on to the next one. Leave Felix to his Hildkraut."

"*Burg*. Hild*burg*. But you're right. Heike already told me to forget the moron. Who even knows what *his* IQ is?"

"Take it easy. He can't help it if his IQ is lower than yours. Give the guy a break."

"A break? I should give him a break?" I screeched. I hate it when men let other men get away with murder. "I'll break his lousy arm when I see him, the cretin."

"Hey, you've got a little mean streak there, you know."

"So?"

"Just screw the moron. Heike gives you sensible advice. How's she doing?"

"She's not on the market, if that's what you want to know."

"Great tits."

I rolled my eyes. How could you carry on a serious conversation with this guy? "Do you have nothing else to say about my oldest friend except 'great tits'?" I asked.

"Great ass."

Barry Sonnenberg was incorrigible. But cute.

"Don't ever say to a man that you think he's cute," cute little megastar Rich Matell once told me in an interview. "Men want to think they're *virile*."

"Well, Rich," I had said, "take me on a date and *then* I'll tell you if you're virile too."

Rich and I never went out, but the line got a good laugh and secured my position with the station, and with my feminist colleagues.

Barry and I never dated either. Thank God for that. What a randy heartbreaker he was! Every Monday he'd drop over to do his laundry, and you wouldn't believe all the soiled sheets he could accumulate in a single week. But we were good friends, two Americans among ogres, and in exchange for some detergent, a few scandalously expensive kilowatt hours of electricity, and a six-pack of beer, he'd shed light for me on the world according to a cute, male, Neanderthal stud.

He reappeared at the kitchen door wearing imitation Ray•Ban sunglasses and a backpack containing all his folded, laundered sheets.

"You know, I was just thinking," he began. "That Hildlinde must really have had a strong hold on Freckle-Face. I can't imagine someone truly wanting to leave you."

"Why, thank you, Barry. That's very sweet of you."

"I can't imagine anyone voluntarily leaving a woman who has a Miéle washing machine with fifteen programmable cycles and a dryer with automatic shrinkguard."

The first thing that caught my eye was the gorgonzola sandwich. I scooped it up and aimed it at his head. "I'll give you exactly five seconds to get the hell out of here!"

"I'm going. I'm going," he said, giving me a peck on the cheek. He turned toward the door.

"Hey, wait a second!" I said. "Take your sandwich."

"No, you finish it."

"I can't. I'm on a diet."

Barry raised his eyebrows.

Since my resolution of the night before, it was the first time I had actually said those words out loud. They sounded foreign and, frankly, not very convincing. I hadn't even mentioned the diet to Heike, although we had talked on the phone for at least an hour. Carrying not an ounce of fat on her sinewy, athletic body, Heike was not the type to empathize with anyone's struggle to pare off a few pounds. "You want to lose weight?" she once said to me. "Fill your plate as you always do, and then get rid of half of it." As I say, she was not a big help when it came to diets.

"You're on a diet?" Barry asked. "Forget it. You like food too much. You'll never stick to it. And anyway, didn't you try something like this last year?"

I made a face. "Last year is not this year."

"And didn't you try something like this the year before that too?"

I nodded peevishly.

"Quit while you're still ahead. Trust me on this one. It won't work."

"Yes it will."

"How long do you want to torture yourself?"

"Twenty pounds or size seven/eight. Whatever comes first."

"Twenty pounds?!" He smirked. "I'd say you have a chance at losing five. No more."

"You're wrong."

Barry adjusted his backpack. "Well, don't go overboard. Men like a little meat." And then, grabbing my buttocks, he lasciviously whispered in my ear, "Sex. Sex. Sex."

I jabbed him in the ribs.

"But I'll tell you something," he said, his hands squeezing my bottom. "It wouldn't hurt you to lose a few pounds around the hips."

While my four-hundred-calorie lunch of stewed tomatoes, basil, and potatoes was simmering on the stove, I spread the paper out on the kitchen table.

For a journalist, I'm a pretty crummy newspaper reader. Taking in more than the headlines is too much of a chore for me. If prodded, I'm quick to admit that I'm an ignoramus when it comes to politics. But rarely do we invite politicians to *Breakfast at Becky's*. And if Karla Menzel, my producer, in a sudden fit of bravado decides to do so, she and our assistants are *very* good at briefing me.

I surveyed the front page: Uta Pippig wins the Berlin Marathon; thousands demonstrate in Germany against growing anti-foreign sentiment; heavy fighting in Bosnia. My eyes began to droop. What the hell, I was on vacation. I folded the paper, tossed it aside, and began charting my apartment's six-week reduction plan instead.

A bathroom, a kitchen, one bedroom, an office, and a living room were to be reduced to their bare essentials. It was a mammoth task. I ought to begin with something simple, a chore that would give me an impetus to carry on. The worst clutter should be tackled somewhere in the middle, when I still had enough energy to pull me through the muck and mire. Trying to take on the worst at the very beginning might make me lose spirit, but if I left it to the very end, it would haunt me throughout and spoil the fun. The ring binders would be a fine task for Week Three. Sifting through the hundred-odd binders stuffed with almost twenty years of work-related articles, papers, and reports in first, second, third, and up to tenth draft, all of it hidden within four pull-out drawers under my platform bed, was sure to be the most untempting job of all. My record collection was a pest, but it wouldn't require too much thought. A Rickie Lee Jones on the cover would mean "save," a Tom Jones "terminate." It would be tedious, but a cinch. Yes, I'd leave the records for the end, for Week Six.

I set about scrutinizing the whole apartment, inspecting each room like a finicky summer camp counselor the day before Parents' Weekend. Systematically I opened and closed drawers, looked behind doors, jotted down the major clutter zones, and plotted their demise.

It was a fifth-floor walk-up in Berlin's posh Wilmersdorf neighborhood, warm and sunny, my very own bachelorette pad and a far cry from the dark and mildewy apartment I used to share with four lovable slobs and that I had moved out of seven years before. Here, apparent orderliness soothed the critical eye. Indeed, I was quite a neat and tidy person, although some of my friends might think that was too pleasant a way of putting it. They might find the words *fastidious, finicky, methodical, obsessive,* or *compulsive* — take your pick — a bit closer to the truth.

I wasn't always like this. When I was younger I was only obsessive and compulsive. It wasn't until I lived alone in my very own apartment that I became fastidious, finicky, and methodical. And now, finally, I was the perfect example of a perfect neurotic. I'm the type of person, for instance, who can *always* find what I need around the house. Immediately and without fail. If a blackout were to descend upon us by surprise, not only would I know where the flashlights were, but they'd have fresh batteries in them as well. The cabinet under my kitchen sink is a picture of orderliness, my skirts and blouses are hung according to color, the novels on my bookshelves are arranged alphabetically. My files are kept up to date, and my

slides, slipped into gray cases labeled with subject and date,
are neatly stacked in a cool, dark place.

But to me, it still wasn't enough. My orderliness had a
tragic flaw. I wasn't nearly as neat as it seemed. I was a sneaky
one: I hid my disorder. I pushed things out of sight, shelved
the chaos, shifted articles from the light of day to the dark-
ness of a cramped hall closet or a folder marked "miscellane-
ous." My home had long been invaded by objects that lived
for a moment and then disappeared into a forgotten space under my bed, behind a bookshelf, inside the broom closet, in a
shopping bag on my pantry floor. And it haunted me. I had
recurring nightmares in which I was attacked by worms that
had been drilling through the clothes I'd packed away for the
Red Cross and never delivered. Or of being knocked dead by a
bowling ball, my roller skates, and the vacuum cleaner, all of
them tumbling out of my hall closet when I opened the door.

I sat down on my old, lumpy double bed. Germans call it
a French bed. I wonder why? To praise the French for being so
ingenious as to create a bed for lovers, or to deny the fact that
they, the Germans, ever actually sleep together? In any case,
as soon as I got rid of all this surplus stuff, I would begin to redecorate, exchange this mastodon of a bed for a healthy queen-
sized latex mattress and a subtle, simple bed frame, get rid of
the old pinewood shelving in my office and add streamlined
up-to-the-ceiling black bookcases, discard the dirty off-white
carpeting, the floral design sofa, the fluffy cushions. I wanted
new sleek lines to match my new sleek looks.

The last time I'd done anything for the apartment was
years before, when I had converted the generous pantry behind the kitchen into a walk-in closet. The armoire in my bedroom was ready to split in two and looked increasingly like a
rack at the flea market, so my army of dresses and skirts and
blouses invaded the pantry, which I had equipped with shelves

and rods. It was an excellent solution, although I often had the sneaking suspicion that their close proximity to the kitchen was infusing my clothes with the subtle odor of garlic.

I glanced at my watch. I had a full five hours before the professor and Martin were to come over for our weekly skat session. I needed a simple, constructive, motivating task for starters. I looked back up at the pantry door. Behind it was my answer.

But first I would eat.

I was shocked. There was no way I could ever have fit into this skirt. Not even a Barbie doll could have wriggled into it. Where was its waist?

I threw the brown mini on the kitchen table, raced to my bedroom dresser, pulled out a measuring tape, and galloped back into the kitchen. The skirt's waist measured in at twenty-five inches. I wound the tape measure around my waist. Was twenty-nine inches possible? No. Impossible.

I raced back into my bedroom and took a good square look in the mirror. Yes, it *was* possible. And besides that, my hair was sprouting gray. I'd have to do something about that too.

I returned to the kitchen, picked up the twenty-year-old mini, and sniffed at it. It smelled of the insect-resistant cedar block that had been resting between its folds. I held it up to the light, scrutinizing it, searching for telltale signs of decay. No, it was in perfect condition, which was all the more discouraging, for would I *ever* be able to wear it again?

The next few weeks suddenly seemed overwhelming. Maybe Barry was right. Maybe I shouldn't torture myself. Maybe I should give up before disappointment set in. But I shuddered at the thought. No, I'll prove it to him. And Felix. I'll show them all that I can do it.

"Okay, six weeks. I'll give myself six weeks to fit into this thing," I said out loud, flinging the brown skirt onto my "save" pile. It would be my incentive.

I reached for the next item. In the corner of the closet behind a roll of leftover carpeting from my living room something glittery caught my eye. I bent down and pulled at it. Out came my red-and-gold-brocaded Maharishi love-and-peace dress.

The Red-and-Gold-Brocaded Maharishi Love-and-Peace Dress (August 1971)

It was a hot summer night. Inside the Museum of Modern Art it was even hotter.

"Look at *him* over there," I whispered to Marsha, pointing to a full-bearded, long-haired, sunglassed, love-beaded someone. "Near the *Drowning Girl.*"

Marsha turned slightly and gave a cursory glance at the exhibition crowd. Her eyes fell for a moment near the Lichtenstein, but since she didn't put her glasses on, I could tell her heart wasn't really in it.

"Where?" she murmured, followed by a soft burp.

I was getting impatient. "The guy in the purple tie-dye shirt and the Mexican vest! Over there, with all the hair. Isn't that Bobby Katz? Terry's sister's ex-boyfriend? The Columbia premed?"

Marsha felt obligated to look again.

"What do you think?" I drilled away, whipping off my wire-rims and throwing them back into my bag. "My type or yours? I think yours. I'm not too keen on the beard. What do you say?"

"Becky, I don't think I feel well," Marsha said. "What

exactly is a Salisbury steak? What's it made of? Can those frozen dinners go bad?"

"How do I know what a Salisbury steak is? I offered you the glazed ham with the macaroni and cheese, didn't I?"

Marsha looked at me reproachfully.

"All right," I said, "do you want to go out in the sculpture garden for some fresh air?"

She nodded.

"Too bad," I said, gesturing toward hirsute Bobby Katz as we headed for the back doors. "I'm sure we could have had him."

Marsha burped again. God, she was such a hypochondriac, such a neurotic — really quite typical for a psychology major. Of course she wouldn't hesitate to say that I was such an egocentric, such a narcissist — really quite typical for a drama major. Nonetheless, we'd both agree that we were the best of friends. That's what we'd been ever since 1963 when we were in the eighth grade and shared a locker in gym class. Later, both our families moved to Forest Hills where we went to Kaiser's Diner every day after school for the best vanilla egg cream in the state of New York. It was there that Marsha disclosed to me that her secret wish was to buy contact lenses, lose twenty pounds, get married, live on a farm in the country, and have five children. My secret wish was to buy contact lenses, lose twenty pounds, stay single, live in a duplex off Central Park, and have five lovers. We were a perfect match, and had been for eight years, so of course I had invited her to be my guest at the exhibition preview at the museum that evening.

Just that afternoon, when I got back from shopping downtown, I had found my brand-new Museum of Modern Art student membership card in the mail. It was my entrance to the adult world of art, adventure, and excitement. I loved museums, ever since I fell in love with the brontosaurus in the

Museum of Natural History on a nursery school trip. But this past year I'd been especially drawn to the Museum of Modern Art. Its hallowed halls seemed to be charged with a solemn energy I found particularly irresistible.

After I called Marsha, I put two TV dinners in the oven, pulled off my brown mini, unpacked the dress I had bought, slipped into it, and pranced up to the full-length mirror in my parents' bedroom.

I wouldn't quite say it was *the* most beautiful dress I had ever seen — Audrey Hepburn's Edwardian black-and-white Ascot ensemble in *My Fair Lady* was really quite a mind-blower — but my latest acquisition was certainly the most beautiful dress I had ever seen that I could *almost* afford.

Since early morning I'd been rummaging through the racks at the Macy's Herald Square pre-Labor Day sale. Then suddenly it was there: a lovely, flowing, midi-length patchwork floral print granny of various pink-reddish hues, trimmed at the sleeves, the collar, and under its empire bust with gold and red brocade. At $69.99 it cost two-thirds of my weekly salary from the notions store in Cambridge where I had worked that summer, but still, it was a real bargain. I'd just have to be careful and not buy anything else until Christmas. In fact, I wouldn't *need* anything else, for now I, too, had my very own flower power dress. What it was doing at Macy's I'll never know. The store was not known for its counterculture Junior Department. But then again, I hadn't gone there with that in mind. If I had wanted a bona fide, made-in-India, far-out, good-vibrations, blow-your-mind granny, I would have gone all the way down to one of those stores in the Village that smelled of incense and tea and coconut candles. But I didn't. I didn't want anything junky. If there was one thing I had learned at that stuffy notions store near Harvard Square, it was how to judge quality fabrics. And my new dress was quality. It was a dress that even poor dead Janis Joplin would have been proud to wear, in spite of its being from Macy's Herald Square.

Actually, I *liked* Macy's. I knew my way around that store like a cop his beat. I knew where the cleanest rest rooms were, the fastest checkout lines, the best cup of coffee, the smartest bargains, the quickest escalator. It was where I spent almost every one of my lunch hours during the three summers I worked for my aunt Mabel at Daisy Dee, Inc. Daisy Dee was a children's fashion manufacturer and Aunt Mabel was the office manager. For years she'd been training me to be her summer slave. And I had been a willing victim.

When I was eighteen Aunt Mabel inflicted all the humdrum office work on me: typing and telexing, filing checks, and adding up long columns of numbers. But it was easy and left me ample time to fantasize about Mickey Baines, one of the designers who sat in the back cutting room.

The summer I was nineteen, I was taught to work the switchboard, a Medusa-type contraption with dozens of snakelike cables attached to it, requiring my utmost concentration and the sweetest answering voice I could muster. Whenever Spencer Heatherstone, the new and *very* attractive junior partner, buzzed me to put him through to the factory in South Carolina, I was sure he could hear my heartbeat over the buzz in the line.

When I was twenty, I was assigned to the showroom. It was my job to assist the salespeople when they were working with customers. "Becky, dear," saleslady Janet Rosenthal would call out to me, "please bring us the Rosebud sunsuit in the yellow and pink cotton, size 6X, with the matching sunbonnet and tulip carryall. *Tout de suite.*"

I was also responsible for keeping the showroom clean, neat, and uncluttered. I sorted out the old dresses from the new, hanging the reds next to the oranges and the pinks, putting the blues with the purples and the greens. Everything had its place: the shorts beside the bermudas next to the pedal pushers which came just before the pants; the velvets first, then the wools, the linens, the cottons, and the rayons. It wasn't an easy task for me. My closet at home was a war zone, and it took a great deal of self-discipline to keep the showroom in line.

"Someday you'll be grateful to me that I made you respect orderliness. Just you wait and see," said my aunt Mabel. "And watch those feet," she added, pointing to my Pappagallos. (I was still a bit pigeon-toed, a holdover from childhood, and Aunt Mabel was forever reminding me of this past affliction.)

On a slow day, I would sit in the far corner of the showroom, read *Gone with the Wind* or Jane Austen, wonder if maybe I should become a writer instead of an actress, and dream of Vito Spinetti, Daisy Dee's top salesman. Once a week I worked with him and his customers. He never missed an opportunity to make me blush, especially when the showroom was empty and he had nothing to do. "Becky, dear," he would call out, pretending to be with a customer, "please bring us the Midnight Surprise push-up corselette in black leather, size 36D, with the matching leather whip. *Avanti!*"

But the best part of my summers at Daisy Dee was lunchtime. When the clock struck 12:30, I'd punch out my card, break out of my slave's chains, and get out of the joint as fast as I could. Gulping down my tuna on rye or egg salad on white, I would dash to the elevator and race across the street into the anonymous, cool, perfumed halls of the World's Largest Department Store. For an hour I could pretend I was a Roman princess on a New York holiday, a model in *Seventeen* magazine, a debutante the day before the cotillion. Or Janis Joplin's successor getting ready for a concert.

"You got *that* hippie number in *Macy's?*" Marsha said incredulously, shaking her dyed platinum-blond hair. "Just goes to show you how establishment flower power has become. Before you know it, marijuana'll be legal."

We were now out in the sculpture garden at the Museum of Modern Art where a jazz concert was in progress. I was sitting on top of the cool marble steps, my back leaning against Pablo Picasso's goat, pretending to understand the complexities of the free jazz composition being performed. Marsha was seated next to me, burping. I had conned a guard into allowing us to sneak in without paying. Conning was a technique I'd learned from my salesman father, and something I was rather good at.

"That guard at the entrance is really cute," I said. "I can't believe he let us in for free. We saved five bucks each."

"You know, I think it's the sauce, not the Salisbury steak. I taste the sauce in my mouth."

"Do you think he's really a guard? Or do you think it's just a summer job that — omigod!"

Was I dreaming? Who was that standing not more than twenty feet away from me?

"Marsha, omigod!" I sputtered out. "I can't believe it, omigod! This can't be happening. Is this —"

"What? What? What's the matter?"

"Ssshhh," I said. "Not so loud."

"What's the matter, for Christ's sake?" she whispered.

"Marsha, look over there, leaning against Rodin's *Balzac*. Do you see? It's Dustin Hoffman. My God, it's Dustin Hoffman and he's *looking* at me."

As I spoke, I realized that the actor Dustin Hoffman was not only looking at me but, believe it or not, *smiling* at me too. My heart turned to lead and plopped down into my stomach.

"Did you see? Did you see?" I whispered feverishly. "It's Dustin Hoffman. And he smiled at me. Did you see?"

"What am I, blind or something?" Marsha replied disdainfully. But she was only feigning disinterest. I very distinctly saw her squint to get a better look. "But what's —" Marsha was interrupted for a moment by her TV dinner sauce. "Oh, I'll never eat that stuff again!"

"Ssshhh!"

"But what's he doing here?" she whispered. "I thought he lived in Hollywood?"

"Not at all. Just this morning I happened to read in the *Enquirer* that he has this luxury duplex apartment right here in New York, in Manhattan, off Central Park West and —"

"Since when does a Phi Beta Kappa English and drama major read trash like the *National Enquirer?*"

The concert was over and the crowd was applauding.

"It was on the rack while I was standing on line in the supermarket," I replied, raising my voice above the din. "And since when does an intelligent psychology student make herself sick over a silly frozen Salisbury —"

I stopped speaking in midsentence. Was I going to faint? None other than Dustin Hoffman, the star himself, was walking toward me.

"Omigod, Marsha, look. He's coming. He's coming here."

It took a few seconds for Dustin to reach us, several fleeting moments in history, freeze-dried into my mind. If I were ever to write a screenplay of the story of my life, this particular sequence would surely be shot in slow motion:

> In total silence, save for the racing beat of Becky's heart, the camera follows Dustin's feet in white rubber thongs moving step by step toward Marsha and Becky. Inch by inch, ever so slowly, the camera pans upward, caressing his legs. Through the fabric of the beige corduroy jeans we can almost see, yes, almost feel the actor's taut leg muscles thrusting forward toward their new destiny. The camera picks up Dustin's shirttails slipping sloppily out of his pants. A pair

of sunglasses hangs precariously from a breast pocket. And then we see The Grin. We are witness to the most amazing grin anyone has ever encountered in a museum sculpture garden.

"Hello," Dustin said to me.

I was in shock. I cannot remember what I said. I assume I said nothing.

"Hello," Dustin repeated.

"Hello," I said, rising, my voice cracking.

"Good evening," said Marsha, far away on a distant planet.

"I am wery sorry," Dustin said, grinning sheepishly. "I am wery sorry, but I do not speak wery vell English."

"You don't speak wery vell English?" I replied witlessly.

"Oh, I am sorry," said Dustin, giving me his hand. "Jürgen Markowski."

"What?" I said, shaking his hand, ever so slowly suspecting that something might possibly be awry.

"Jürgen," he said. "My name. Jürgen Markowski. I have seen you in the exhibition before."

"Oh," I said, my hand reaching into my bag, fumbling for my glasses. "Oh, that's your name. What was that again?"

"I have seen you in the exhibition before."

"No, I mean the *name*."

"Jürgen," he said. "Jürgen Markowski."

"Your-gan Mar-cuff-sky?"

He nodded, grinning.

"I'm Becky. Rebecca Lee Bernstein," I replied, slipping on my glasses and taking a good, solid look.

Omigod! What a blunder! Here was most definitely *not* my favorite actor. Here was most definitely *not* anyone I had ever seen on a movie screen. Here was most definitely just someone who in the dark shadows of a hot August night simply happened to look very much like my very favorite actor.

But — and for this I was very grateful — here was most definitely someone who most decidedly was interested in me, me, me.

"And this is my friend Marsha Lipschitz," I said gaily, turning to Marsha. She too now had her glasses on.

"Nice to meet you," Marsha said.

For a moment my brain searched desperately for something intelligent to say. "And this is Picasso's goat," I managed to come up with, gesturing toward the sculpture.

"Nice to know you, too," Jürgen replied, patting its head. Hey, he had a sense of humor. For that, too, I was very thankful.

"Do you often come to the museum?" Marsha ventured to ask our new friend.

"No, this is my first time."

His first time in New York's finest museum?

"I do not live here," he continued. "I live in Berlin."

"In Berlin?" I said. "You mean the Berlin in *Germany?*"

Jürgen nodded.

"The Berlin in *Europe?*"

Jürgen nodded again.

"Oh," Marsha said, a look of triumph in her eyes, "so I suppose you don't live in a luxury duplex apartment off Central Park?"

If looks could kill, Marsha would already have been in the morgue.

"What is that — a 'lachsery duplechs'?" Jürgen asked.

I'm going to make a Marshbury steak out of her, I thought.

"A luxury duplex is a — well, it's a — uuhh —" Marsha was having a hard time.

"It's a *special* apartment," I said.

"A special apartment? Lachsery duplechs? I see," Jürgen

replied, still grinning. "In Berlin I live in a lachsery duplechs, too. It is a special apartment called a *Wohngemeinschaft.*"

My eyes grew wide. Not only did he have a sense of humor but, as it now seemed, a duplex too.

"A voan-ga-mine-shaft," I repeated tentatively.

"Yes," he went on. "A special apartment for many people."

"Many people?"

"I live with four people. What is it called when all have a part of all?"

"All have a part of all?"

"You mean sharing?" Marsha put in.

"Yes, we share everything."

"Everything?" I said. "Even . . ." My eyes grew wider than they already were.

"You mean a commune?" said Marsha.

My eyes began to pop out of their sockets. A luxury duplex *commune?*

"Oh, no no," said Jürgen, blushing. "Something is not right in the understanding. We are just friends. We share because we have no money."

"No money?" I murmured.

"Love and peace," said a voice.

We whipped around and were face to face with bearded, long-haired, sunglassed, love-beaded Bobby Katz in the purple tie-dye shirt and Mexican vest. He smiled at me innocuously, glassy-eyed, holding up his index and middle fingers. "Great dress," he said, hovering on a cloud of oblivion. "Love and peace Maharishi."

If I ignored him, he would go away.

"You live in Berlin?" I said to Jürgen, returning to the subject at hand.

Jürgen nodded.

Marsha burped.

Of all the places to live, he lived in Germany? *Germany?*

"Love and peace," said Bobby Katz. "You're Becky, aren't you?"

In the hot summer night I could feel sweat beads forming on the nape of my neck. My head was heavy, dizzy, and I was in the throes of making the most important decision of my life. To my left stood my destiny: my best friend getting sick over a TV dinner. To my right stood my destiny: a premed hippie high on tie-dye. In front of me stood my destiny: a young Berliner with no money, sloppy shirttails, and the nicest, warmest grin of anyone I had ever met, a killer grin that melted my tumbling heart to goo.

"That's really a groovy dress," Bobby said.

I turned my back to Bobby. "I've never been to Germany," I said cheerfully to Jürgen. "Just the other day, I was telling Marsha I should take a trip there soon."

And before I knew it, I wasn't buying my red-and-gold-brocaded Maharishi love-and-peace dresses downtown at Macy's Herald Square but at Karstadt's Hermannplatz in West Berlin.

Chapter Two

Monday, September 28, 1992
Diet Week: 1
Day: 1
Weight Loss: Still 0
Later that evening

I was losing. I was hungry. And my back was killing me.

"Eighteen," I bid hesitantly.

"Pass," said the professor forcefully.

"Ugh," I said, looking at Martin expectantly. "Bid higher, pleeease."

"Pass."

"What? You're holding back!"

"I am not! You should see my hand. Nothing. A pittance. Just sevens and eights." Martin paused for a moment and then added, "And a smattering of royalty."

"A 'smattering of royalty'?" I made a face. "I'm sure you have five bowers at least!"

I picked up the skat — a meager queen and a nine. "Forget it. I definitely lose this one." I slapped my cards down on the table and noticed for the first time that evening how dirty my fingernails had gotten groping about the dusty corners of the pantry. The red-and-gold-brocaded bodice of the Maharishi peace dress had been covered with sticky dustballs.

What a thrill the sight of that dress had given me! It evoked the sounds and shape of an age I had lived and loved and claimed as my own. Maybe that's why we have such a hard time throwing things out. They remind us that *we were there.* Like the words we carve in a neighborhood tree or a park bench (BECKY WAS HERE, AUGUST 1971), they say, "Look, that was me, and that's the way it was. And wasn't it wonderful?"

But if it was so wonderful, why had the dress made me feel so wretched?

Because it also had a flip side. It was proof that the past had gone, that twenty years ago was really twenty long-gone years ago. Things remind us that we're not here forever.

The whole afternoon had been one reminder followed by the next. After the dress, I had pulled another potential discard out of the closet. Although its breast pocket was blemished, I couldn't bear to part with my Brownie uniform from the fourth grade. It was still ripped where Phyllis Jefferson, the class bully, had tried to grab a box of Girl Scout cookies out of my hand. I folded it carefully, tenderly placing its matching brown pixie cap on top. I reached up and put it on my memory shelf next to the blue poncho. My mother had spent months knitting the poncho. She had arthritis, and it was quite an accomplishment. Although I never wore it, I could never throw it out. That would have been sacrilege, and would have caused my mother far more pain than her arthritis. I looked at the label. It was the kind anyone could get from a mail-order catalogue. MADE ESPE-CIALLY FOR YOU BY was embroidered on the top, and below it was a smudged GLORIA BERNSTEIN ink stamp. My mother used to sew those labels into everything she knit: jackets, berets, scarves with hanging pompoms, even the thick wool socks my father wore when he sold encyclopedias door-to-door in midwinter.

"For Christ's sake, Gloria," I can still hear him hollering. "They itch!"

Maybe these labels were my mother's way of saying *Gloria was here.*

And the yellow herring-bone dress with the purple-red stains I kept too. I wore it on my first date with Jürgen, the day after we met. We had walked from Fifty-ninth Street all the way down to Ratner's on the Lower East Side where Jürgen ordered the famous borscht and I the blueberry blintzes with sour cream. Some of the filling must have spilled onto my lap. I didn't discover it until it was too late, a few hours and ten cups of coffee later. Who could have guessed that that walk would end much further east than the Lower East Side, on the other side of the Atlantic, in Berlin?

Needless to say, the blueberry-beaten dress wound up on the "save" pile too, an ever-growing muddle of bright wools and fantastic prints. By midafternoon the pile had gotten so high it almost reached my thighs. The "terminate" mound was far smaller, composed of just two pairs of limp, tattered bell-bottomed hiphuggers and one pair of white satin boxer shorts featuring a boxing glove emblem with the words THE FIGHTER. It had been a freebie from a record company during my radio deejay days.

This was not what I had intended. I *had* to get rid of more stuff. How was I ever going to get on with my life if I couldn't sort out my past?

I found a few rusty Greek drachmas in the front breast pocket of my purple overalls from the late 1970s. I owned better-fitting memories of that era. I zipped the coins back up and gave the garment one last affectionate hug before I shoved it aside for my Red Cross sack. It was joined by ruffled, flouncy peasant skirts from the early 1980s, cotton hot pants from who-knows-when, worn-out velvet midis, and

conservative accordion-pleated maxis. I threw out anything
synthetic, polyester, nibbled by moths, pilled, faded, or flawed.
I got down on my knees to check for unaccounted odds
and ends underneath the wardrobe. My fingers tapped around
a bit in the dusty muck and did, in fact, encounter a metallic object. I pulled, and out came my ergonomic, one-legged,
height-adjustable, swivel-seat fold-up chair, dragging a pair
of longjohns along with it. I snatched up the undergarment. It
was angora. It must have been Felix'x. How in the world did a
pair of his longjohns ever get in *here?* This was as baffling to
me as to why I ever got involved with the lousy bastard in the
first place.

I marched into the kitchen. I flung open the sink cabinet
and threw the angora longjohns into a pail. I'd cut them up for
rags. Dirty windows would be their destiny, the kitchen floor,
the toilet bowl. . . .

I was losing. I was hungry. My back was killing me. And now
my fingernails were dirty too.

I scrutinized my cards. There was no way I could win.
"Spades are trump," I announced with a sigh. "I wish we could
play Doppelkopf instead of skat. Doppelkopf is so much more
civil. It's simpler, and you get a partner, too. If you lose, you're
not alone."

"Find a fourth player, my lovely," said the professor, "and
I'll play every night. I've been telling you this for years."

Professor Kurt Bloch, my next-door neighbor, widower,
retired *chef de cuisine* and author of the cookbook series *Intelligent Cooking with Professor Bloch*, was the most attractive man over seventy I have ever encountered. He was also
a health nut par excellence, having not too long ago run the
Berlin Marathon in just over four hours.

I sat up straight in my chair, hoping to reduce the back pains.

"Too bad it didn't work out with your yuppie," Martin said to me. "He could have played Doppelkopf with us. Investment brokers are supposedly excellent cardplayers. They know how to take risks. Don't you think, doll-face?"

"I asked you please not to allude to that person in my presence," I said.

"You told me not to mention his *name*."

"The lousy bastard," I said under my breath.

"To say the least," Martin added, smiling wryly. He poured himself some more beer. "You're not drinking. Is something wrong, doll-face?"

Martin Peters worked up the block at the ergonomic furniture store, but in his real life he was a gay sociology student with a "helper complex." He was a great guy with only one bad habit. He was always calling me "doll-face," in English no less, something a friend of his in San Francisco once taught him.

"Hey, are you okay, doll-face?" he asked again.

"I'm dieting," I told him.

"How many more times must I tell you, my lovely," said the professor, "that if you jogged, you wouldn't have to diet?"

"Tell me at least three hundred and eighty-seven more times."

"And what happens then?"

"By then I'll have lost so much weight dieting, I might get up the courage to put on those skimpy shorts and do a few laps."

"A deal," he said.

"Can we play cards now?" I asked.

Professor Bloch wasn't ready to play yet. "Frankly, I don't know what your problem is," he said. He took a shot of vodka. "You know how to choose good friends, why not good lovers?"

"She's only interested in men with glamour and power and wealth and looks," said Martin.

"That's not true!" I banged my fist on the table. "I don't give a shit about looks. Only glamour and power and wealth."

The two men laughed.

"In any case, men are not my top priority," I went on. "First I fix up me and my apartment. Then I work on my career and on earning big money. Then, maybe, I'll —"

"You worry too much about money, doll-face," Martin said.

"A girl's gotta make a living," I replied glibly. "And quit calling me doll-face! Come on, let's get this game on the road."

"You make at least ten times as much as most people from the East," said the social worker in Martin.

"Don't exaggerate. And anyway, I'm *not* from the East, thank God."

"You're a snob."

"You're right, I *am* a snob. It depresses me there. It's dull and dowdy, it has no glitter and too many spies. I need more."

"Glamour and power and wealth?" he said.

"Exacto! Put my show on national TV and I'd stop complaining, plus I'd have time to write ten more 'Bingo Berlins' if I wanted to. And I could sleep late. Which reminds me, Martin, I need a new bed. Something sleek and simple. And cheap."

"Becky, good beds are expensive."

"You can give me a special price, can't you?"

"Stop talking about money!" he protested.

"What are you so touchy about?"

"You walk by my store ten times a day and you only come in to visit when you want to buy something on the cheap. When was the last time you came by just for a cup of coffee?"

"Martin, I'm busy," I answered lamely.

"What you need, my lovely," said the professor, taking a good slug of beer, "is stability in your life, a quiet harbor to come home to, not another asinine young sprig like" — he paused a moment for dramatic effect — "like what's-his-name."

"Could we play cards already?" I asked.

"He dressed a little too snazzy for me," Martin went on. "But he had excellent biceps."

"Let me be the judge of that," said Professor Bloch, the marathon runner.

"No, let *me* be the judge of that," said Martin, the gay activist.

"No, let *me* be the judge of that," said I, the thwarted girlfriend. "And I'm telling you, his biceps were not nearly as good as his gluteus muscles. Now, enough! Let's play."

It was a comfort having two friendly neighbors around. Indeed, I felt quite safe with Martin and the professor, especially playing cards. Unlike the Germans, who learn to play skat in nursery school, I wasn't introduced to the game until I was over twenty-one, so Martin and the professor were inherently better players than I. But they drank too much beer, and far too quickly, which spoiled their winning chances. Beer (and then vodka) on Skat Monday was the professor's only vice, as far as I knew. Although it relieved me to know he wasn't perfect, his drinking often seemed excessive. Whereas alcohol made Martin a careless player, it made the professor intrepid, even a bit cocky. He'd play a *grand* when he should have been considering a *nullo*. He'd announce a *contra* although he had all but two trumps. But after three years of Skat Monday, I had it all figured out: if I was careful, nursed my wine, was dealt a halfway decent hand, and made sure my partners' beer glasses were always full, by 9:45 I would be able to win a few games by default, catch up to the men, and often come out ahead.

But it was only 9:38. Needless to say, I lost the game.

The professor gathered up the cards.

"Becky, I want you to meet someone," he began.

"Oh, that's sweet of you, professor," I replied pleasantly, taking a sip of my mineral water. My stomach growled with hunger. "I want to meet someone too."

"No, I mean someone special."

"Well, I want that someone to be special too."

"I mean I have someone special in mind. A friend of mine."

"A friend of yours?" I was shocked. I adored Professor Bloch, but there was no way the man of my dreams ran around in his crowd. I didn't necessarily gravitate toward pups like Felix, but grandpas, even ones like the professor who looked like Paul Newman and cooked better than Uncle Ben, weren't really my thing. "Forget it," I said. "I'm not ready to date again yet."

He must have known what I was thinking. "Sometimes you're pretty simple-minded," he said testily. "Not all my friends are ready to kick the bucket, you know. Do you even know who my friends are?"

I blushed. "I'm sorry. I'm a little out of kilter. My back hurts."

"Who is it?" Martin asked gaily.

"Egon," Professor Bloch answered.

"Egon? Egads! With a name like Egon I should set him up with Hildburg," I said.

The professor chuckled, and we were friends again.

"And may I ask," I said with a twinkle in my eye, "how old this stud is?"

"He's forty-four and a friend of Manni's. Relieved?"

Manni was the professor's oldest son.

"He's been separated from his wife for a year, and they're getting a divorce," he went on. "He's a biochemist in cancer research and a nice guy. I could tell you more, but you might have more fun finding out for yourself."

Professor Bloch was set on getting me together with this Egon. I couldn't hurt his feelings. "All right," I relented. "Give him my number."

Martin began dealing the cards.

I excused myself, rushed to the bathroom to scrub the grime out from under my nails, grabbed an apple to still my appetite, and dutifully sat back down at the table. I was losing. I was hungry. I was being set up on a blind date. My back was killing me.

As I sighed, an idea suddenly occurred to me. I jumped from the table, jerked open the pantry door, knelt down in front of my wardrobe, and pulled out the ergonomic, one-legged, height-adjustable, swivel-seat fold-up chair.

"Remember this?" I said to Martin. "Remember I bought this chair in your store about three years ago?"

I set the chair up at the kitchen table and sat down. It was actually quite comfortable. I could already feel my back relaxing. I looked at my watch. It was 9:45 P.M. on the dot. Finally. It was time to start winning.

"Yes, I do remember," Martin said. "But if I remember correctly, we later found out there was something wr —"

"Okay," I sang out, taking a juicy bite of my apple, "let's go for it!"

And that's when the chair collapsed. With me in it, of course.

The Ergonomic, One-Legged, Height-Adjustable, Swivel-Seat Fold-Up Chair
(Summer 1989)

"Do you know what Heinrich Heine once said?" Hannes asked me.

I shook my head.

"He said, '*Heimat ist dort, wo man sich nicht erklären muß.*' Home is where you owe no explanations."

We were standing in the middle of a museum, at a photo exhibition of contemporary Jewish portraits. Dozens upon dozens of German and Eastern European writers, scientists, scholars, and plain old grandmas and grandpas peered down at us from the walls of the Martin Gropius Building. They were the faces of men and women who some fifty years before were discriminated against, condemned to extermination, forced to leave their homes and homeland. They were ancient faces with skin as hard and scaly as desert reptiles', scarred, wrinkled, and marred with age and illness. Here were all kinds of faces: intelligent, thoughtful, coquette, wise, melancholic. Yet at the heart of every photograph, at its very core, were the eyes: breathtakingly grand eyes of indescribable vitality.

I stood there and felt so very proud to be one of the family.

So there we were, Hannes and I, standing in the middle of a museum in Kreuzberg, Berlin. It was a Wednesday in late July. It was noon. It was our second date. And I was on the verge of falling in love. Hannes already had. At least that's what he told me a few days later while sitting in front of the replica of an Eskimo igloo in the Völkerkunde Museum in Dahlem. Sitting in front of the igloo, he told me that he fell in love with me and my red lipstick on our very first date. And the first date was on Monday, two days before our noonday interlude in the Martin Gropius museum.

Prior to that Monday I knew very little about Hannes, just that he was 1) friendly and outgoing — a rather rare trait among German male folk, 2) a writer of solid talent and grand ambition, 3) losing his hair rapidly, and 4) at least a foot taller than me. We had met briefly at a party Heike had schlepped me to, and we had agreed to meet again that following Monday evening on neutral territory, in a café.

I remember that on the afternoon before that first date, Barry Sonnenberg had dropped by to do his laundry and to borrow two hundred marks.

"But this is only a hundred and ninety," he said after I handed him the money.

"I took ten off for the salami sandwich you'll be making in five minutes, for the two beers you're going to drink within the next hour, for the long-distance call you'll probably make to some girlfriend in Hamburg, and for the detergent and electricity you'll be using to do your laundry. It's a bargain."

"You never cease to amaze me," he said, shaking his head.

"Look, I'll make a deal with you. If you help me figure out what to wear tonight on my date, I'll throw the detergent in for free, okay?"

"It's a deal," Barry said. "Be a tart. I don't care what men say, they want tarts. Red lipstick. Rouge. Mascara. High heels and big tits. And don't be pushy. Men don't like pushy broads."

At the time I possessed neither high heels nor "big tits." My Maidenform trainer in the sixth grade was my first and last bra, and ever since I sprained my ankle at age thirteen dancing to *hava nagila* at Melvin Minsky's bar mitzvah, I've shied away from heels. I opted for the lipstick — Scarlet Passion, the deepest shade of red I could find in my collection, a leftover from a trip to Spain a few years earlier — and added a tinge of rouge, and then mascara as a final touch.

A few hours later, Hannes and I were sitting in a café sipping white wine spritzers and giving our own answers to a VIP questionnaire in the *Frankfurter Allgemeine* newspaper — one of those what's-your-favorite-food-favorite-book-favorite-color-favorite-place-to-die deals that famous personalities feel honored to be asked to answer. What they don't know is that it is also a very handy tool on a first date. If you play it right, by the end of the evening both dating parties more or less know what they'll be getting into if they dare to meet again. Which is exactly what Hannes and I decided to do. We had no other choice, for it turned out that we had the same favorite artist (Edward Hopper), the same favorite Hopper painting *(Chop Suey)*, and the same favorite food (gorgonzola on Italian white). Furthermore, we discovered we had the same computer, the same word processing program, and even the same brand of diskettes (No Name). And what a coincidence: we also had the same favorite card game — Doppelkopf.

"What?" he roared, reaching out over the table to hug me, almost spilling his wine. "What? An American who plays Doppelkopf? Now that's really something!"

"Don't get so excited. I've almost forgotten how. We only play skat. But we're looking for a fourth man to play Doppelkopf."

"You just found him," said Hannes, popping up out of his chair like a jack-in-the-box.

It struck me that it might actually have been worth my while putting on all that heavy lipstick.

And when to my utter surprise I heard that Hannes and I had the same favorite pastime — museum hopping — well, I was almost certain that for this fellow I might even slip on a pair of high heels.

"My greatest experience was *Mona Lisa* in the Louvre," Hannes said.

"Mine was Dustin Hoffman in the MOMA," I replied, smiling as mysteriously as Mona.

Although we had problems deciding on a favorite museum (Hannes's was the Galleria degli Uffizi in Florence, and mine was my aunt Ethel's apartment on Central Park West) we had no trouble agreeing that ever since Brian DePalma's movie *Dressed to Kill,* the Metropolitan Museum of Art in New York undoubtedly took first place as the sexiest museum on the silver screen. That's the movie where Angie Dickinson is sitting in an art exhibition minding her own business when this very attractive, dark-haired, European-looking fellow begins to flirt with her. I hate the movie — there's too much unnecessary blood and splattered brain matter in it — but that scene is quite a showstopper.

And here was someone who understood my fervor!

Indeed, there was no denying that Hannes was the best boyfriend material I had come across in ages, but — uh-oh — he was yawning. I had to make a move.

"Would you like to go for a walk and get some ice cream?" I asked. And he nodded.

It was one of those gorgeous, warm nights that steal your heart away, one of those rare nights people write songs about. It was a night you'd be crazy not to let seduce you.

The Kurfürstendamm — West Berlin's Fifth Avenue — was cluttered with humanity. Chubby tourists were stampeding down the street like elephants, cameras bouncing ferociously on their chests. Hordes of teens in blue jeans were gathered out in front of the discos, the boys guzzling beer and James-Deaning their cigarettes, the girls giggling and squealing and running their fingers through their hair self-consciously. Silver-haired, buxom ladies streamed out of the theaters, dressed in their silky best, all tangled up in pearls and ruffles, pretending not to notice the parading whores in high black patent-leather boots far too hot for July.

The smell of pizza for one mark fifty was in the air, bratwurst, exhaust fumes, egg rolls from the Chinese snackbar, Hannes's *Egoïste* cologne. . . .

What a delicious night! It was a night with the whiff of a promise lingering on every corner, a promise that the summer would last forever. Or at least until early morning.

In any case, according to what Hannes told me a few days later in front of the igloo, he fell in love with me (and my Scarlet Passion lipstick) right there on the south side of the Kurfürstendamm, somewhere between Knesebeckstraße and Joachimstaler Straße, on a late Monday evening in midsummer. I held out for another thirty-six hours. But then it happened with the Heinrich Heine quote.

I have always had a weakness and a great respect for walking dictionaries, for well-read, learned people who can come up with the right phrase at the right time. I don't care who they quote — William Shakespeare, Spiro T. Agnew, Dow Jones — it's a gift I myself do not possess and find exceedingly charming in others. This goes all the way back to my childhood when I first read the saga of King Arthur. I was particularly enchanted by Arthur's brilliant and erudite magician-mentor-friend Merlin the Wizard, the Wise One Who Knew All, the man who was always there to answer Arthur's questions. What bliss to have someone like that around the house on a steady basis! But since I couldn't, I went out and got myself an *Encyclopedia Britannica* instead.

Now, certainly I don't mean to compare Hannes to Merlin. He couldn't hold a candle to him. But at least he was more fun than any old encyclopedia could ever be, right? Why not go for it?

So there we were, Hannes and I. It was our second date. We were in a museum in Kreuzberg in the middle of a photo exhibition of contemporary Jewish portraits, near a large placard that read WHAT IS HOME? and standing directly in front of a huge photograph of Jewish literary critic and Heine expert Marcel Reich-Ranicki. He was featured leaning against a well-stocked bookcase with his right hand raised to his head in rare perplexity, as if to say, "Gee, I'm afraid I can't give you an answer to that question."

And that's when it happened, when Hannes quoted Heine.

Well well, I thought, here's someone who not only comes up with the right quote at the right time, but it's in the right place too.

I was looking at Hannes while he quoted Heine, and for the first time I noticed that he was unshaven. Now, not only do I have a weakness for people who can quote from memory, but I also have a soft spot for men with anything from a five o'clock shadow to a two-day stubble. I don't like beards or goatees, and I'm not particularly keen on moustaches and whiskers either, but I find an ever so subtle, dark, scratchy bristle quite appealing. And when I noticed his, I felt a tug, a twinge in my chest, a twist in the immediate region of my heart. Our eyes met and locked — click! — and stayed that way.

The spell was broken when I noticed a tiny droplet of caked toothpaste on his horn-rimmed glasses. My hand jerked forward and for a moment I wasn't quite sure what it was going to do. Was it going to reach up to the horn-rims and scratch off the speck of toothpaste, or would it aim lower and stroke Hannes's unshaven cheek? In the end, what it did do was dive into my handbag and pull out a pen and a pad.

"Say that again," I said.

Hannes repeated Heine's words while I wrote them down:
Home is where you owe no explanations.

"Well put," I said. "Well put."*

And then I looked back up at Hannes — all those twelve inches up. Our eyes met again, locked again, clicked again. And I felt my heart tug away again at a most rapid pace, and finally tumble down, down, deep down into my stomach. My hand jerked forward again, dived back into my handbag, but surfaced this time with a pack of chewing gum. I was on the verge of falling in love and my throat was suddenly quite dry. I took a stick.

"And you," Hannes asked. "Is this home for you, or are you always explaining yourself?"

"I'm always explaining myself. Always," I answered. "You want a piece of gum? Peppermint."

He nodded.

---

* A Note from the Author:

Forgive me, dear reader, for asking you to come all the way down here to the bottom of the page and read this microscopically tiny print. But it's my duty to let you know that Heinrich Heine never really said the wise words Becky has attributed to him here. Our apologies. Let me explain:

In the late 1980s an ex-lover of mine named Anton, a fellow not unlike the Hannes of this tale, quoted that *Heimat* phrase while we were viewing an exhibition similar to the one described. I immediately wrote it down, asking the source, but Anton said he only knew it was from Heine. His quoting talent, like his basic emotional makeup, only went so far. Anton Schulze had a bon mot for every occasion, and I would eagerly record it, but he rarely knew the source. (Months after we split up I was still discovering homeless witticisms on crumpled scraps of paper in drawers, in pockets, in the nooks and crannies of my handbags. It was very irksome and resulted in a good deal of heartache.)

At any rate, I was smitten with Heine's supposed words and thought about integrating them into my own work. I set about finding the source myself.

As I gave him the gum our fingers touched ever so slightly and I felt the damp heat of the palm of his hand. I wondered what it would feel like to have those fingers caress my hair, my lips, the nape of my neck. . . . Once again, I felt my heart begin to tumble. It plunged down from my stomach, down, down, this time down so deep, I'm too shy to tell you where it landed.

And just as if Hannes had read my thoughts, he took a step toward me. Omigod, was he going to kiss me? Right here in front of Marcel Reich-Ranicki? He took another step toward me. He was so close now, I could smell the peppermint gum in his mouth.

"I wish we could sit down. There's no place to sit down here," he said without taking his eyes from mine.

Frankly, I wished we could *lie* down — my knees were about to buckle from all that tension.

But Heine was quite a prolific writer, and I must admit I simply did not have the stamina to track the quote down to the bitter end. Oh, I scanned his collected poems, leafed through his letters, x-rayed his essays, traveled with him to Paris and back, attacked famous quotation reference books, but nowhere did I even come close to spying the phrase "Home is where you owe no explanations."

In the meantime, though, the quote had become a part of me, a part of my thinking, my philosophy, so how could it not become a part of this book? I opted to place it in this chapter. But then a colleague of mine, Freimut Mecklinghaus, a fine editor and connoisseur of German literature, read the manuscript and had half a heart attack. "No, no," he wrote in the margin with his fat red pen, "I am sure it is not Heine. The sentence construction is too modern." He encouraged me to call the Heinrich Heine Gesellschaft in Düsseldorf to confirm his suspicion. I did. Alas, the quote was not from Heine. And I thought it best to share this with you.

What a blockhead that Anton Schulze was!

(To find your place again in the main text, just look for the **And** printed in Futura boldface on the preceding page.)

"Yes, it would be nice to sit down," I managed to say without taking my eyes from his. "Museums never seem to have seating accommodations when and where you want them."

"Yes," he said.

"Well," I said.

Silence.

I cleared my throat.

Silence.

"You have some toothpaste on your glasses," I said.

And *then*, finally, he kissed me.

Hannes and I were an item for about three and a half weeks, twenty-five action-packed days full of wet kisses, white wine spritzers, and mushy museum visits.

The very afternoon after our second date and our first kiss, heady and clearly in love again, I floated into Martin Peters's ergonomic furniture store. A chair in the window display had caught my attention.

"It's called the Anywhere Chair," Martin told me once I was inside. "You can set it up anywhere. On the ground, on concrete, on wooden floors or carpeting. It's height-adjustable, it swivels and swerves. It's light, practical, stylish, affordable, and only has one leg. And when it folds up, it fits right into any handbag larger than twelve by sixteen."

Martin, whose real aim in life was to work with poor, disadvantaged street kids, had a very strong ethical code. When he knit his brows, I knew his morals were getting the better of him. "The only problem," he continued in a whisper, "is that it's not really as ergonomic as it looks. One customer actually complained that it exploded on him. Of course, it's more comfortable than other fold-up chairs, but no collapsible chair can fully comply to ergonomic principles."

"I'm more interested in the economics than the ergonomics," I said. "What does it cost?"

"A hundred and twenty-nine marks. But for you eighty-five."

Now *this* was the perfect gift. "I'll take two."

Martin pricked up his ears. "Two?" he said.

"Martin," I said, beaming from cheek to cheek, "I think we've got our fourth Doppelkopf player."

"*That* was your mistake," said Barry Sonnenberg a few weeks later, several days after Hannes had backed out of my life. Barry was folding his laundry on my kitchen table. "That chair was a big, big, big mistake," he said.

"It was the perfect gift," I retorted.

"No it wasn't. It was pushy. Must I repeat? If there's one thing men can't stand, it's pushy broads. And that was puuuushy."

"How so? He complained about the lack of seating in museums, so I gave him a seat. Come on, it was a cute idea."

"Exactly! Number one, the idea was too original. You were sending out signals that you were smarter than him. Men don't like that. Especially writers. Number two, the chairs were not cheap. You were letting him know you felt he was a good investment. Never let a man know how important he is to you after just one date —"

"It was the *second* date."

"I don't care. Too early. When you get all clingy and desperate on the second date, you don't just scare off the buttheads. Even the nice guys go running. So remember, the male does the hunting. The female gets hunted. Number three, the guy's six feet four and you go and put him onto a milking stool. Do you know how ludicrous that looks?"

"It was height-adjustable! He could have made it into a bar stool if he wanted to."

"And number four, a *chair!* A stupid *chair!* How domestic can you get? He probably thought you were about to redecorate his apartment."

"Bullshit."

"He left you because of that chair. Mark my words."

"You're wrong!"

"Than why did he leave you?"

This, of course, was a question to which I had given a good deal of thought.

"I think it was the Scarlet Passion," I replied.

Barry looked confused.

"My lipstick," I said. "I ran out of my red lipstick. I was positive I had two, but I ran out and couldn't find the other one."

Barry shook his head. "Lame. Lame. Lame. Becky, the chair was a mistake. Accept it. The Secret Passion —"

"Scarlet. Scarlet Passion."

"Running out of his favorite red added insult to injury, yes, but still, it was the chair. Trust me on this one," he said. He gulped down the last of his beer, lit a cigarette, and gave me a peck on the cheek. "I've got to go to rehearsal. Just remember for next time, no chairs and stock up on the Harlot Passion."

"*Scarlet!*"

"Better luck next time," he said, swinging his backpack over his shoulder and closing the door behind him.

The Anywhere Chair was *not* a mistake, although if pressed I might at the time have admitted that it had two slight draw-backs. Firstly, Hannes, unlike me, did not go around Berlin carrying an oversized handbag. Neither did he own a car in which he could stash the thing when it wasn't in use. In the end, *I* was the one who got stuck carrying our Anywhere Chairs everywhere — which I didn't really mind at the time but which, when I think about it now, somehow did render our relationship, as well as my posture, somewhat lopsided.

Secondly, who would have even guessed the resistance we would come up against in the museums? It never occurred to me that the museum personnel wouldn't allow us to carry a chair into their holy halls. If they didn't stop us at the entrance, they were sure to get us in the exhibition.

"Wait a moment, young lady! Where are you going?" a guard would inevitably ask.

"Where everyone else is going. To the exhibition."

"But not with that, you're not," he would say, pointing in the general direction of the chairs.

"They're seating accommodations," I would reply.

"Check them in the coatroom," came the clipped answer. "It's not permitted to take foreign objects into the museum."

"Foreign objects?"

Hannes usually capitulated under pressure. Although he was slightly amused by my antics, he was not overcome by the same impulse as I to needle the Germans' love of duty and their fear of — God help them! — disregarding rules and regulations. I, however, turning to the guard, would continue in my defense.

"It's only a chair," I'd say. "What's foreign about that? In fact, it's made in Germany."

"It could break something."

"But my camera could break something too," I'd argue. "We're allowed to take a camera inside. And besides, it's Japanese."

"Check it in the coatroom," he'd say, or, "Ask at the office."

Once, a highly creative guard actually said, "Do you have a handicap ID? If you have a handicap ID I can let you in with the chair."

I showed him my press card and he waved us in.

At any rate, we did manage to set up the Anywhere Chairs in the first museum we tried out, in front of the igloo prototype in the Völkerkunde Museum in Dahlem. It was the following Saturday. Hannes and I hadn't seen each other for three days, not since the Martin Gropius photo exhibition.

We sat side by side, giving our itchy feet a rest, drifting into unknown polar regions and listening to our hearts beat. After a few moments, Hannes spoke.

"Did you know that Eskimos often go crazy in the dead of winter? They lose touch with reality."

"Really?"

"Mostly women. They call it 'Arctic hysteria.' "

"Sounds pretty normal to me," I said. "The week before Christmas I lose touch with reality too. Don't you?"

"Not really," Hannes said, chuckling. "I'm not the hysterical type. I'm more the schizophrenic. Hey, these seats were a great idea." He swiveled around to me. "Do you know Alice Miller's book on schizophrenia and egotism, *The —*"

"*— The Drama of the Gifted Child.*"

"Right! One of my favorites!"

"Me too. I'm glad you like the seats."

"When I read it, I was sure she was writing about me."

"Really? I was sure she was writing about *me!*" I laughed. "So you think you're an egotist?"

"An egotist? I meant I was *gifted.* You too?"

"Both."

"You? An egotist?" he protested.

"But I am! And I'm not being coquette. You really should know this from the start."

"But *I'm* the egotist!"

"I wonder which of us is the bigger one?"

"It can't be all that bad," Hannes said, "especially if you say you know you're one. 'The worst egotists are those to whom it has never occurred that they are egotists.' Sigmund Freud. Alice Miller quotes him."

"How do you ever keep all that stuff in your head? A phenomenal gift. I adore people who can quote from memory. . . ."

"Anything else you adore that I should know about?" he asked flirtatiously.

"Well, I kind of get a kick out of schizophrenic egotists with a five o'clock shadow."

He kissed me. Softly. It was a solid beginning.

"And you?" I asked at the first opportune moment. "Anything special *you* like I should know?"

"Personally, since last Monday, I happen to have a soft spot for hysterical women with red lipstick. In fact, I think I'm in love with one."

I kissed him. Creatively. Our tongues introduced themselves to each other.

"As Bogart once said," Hannes murmured, " 'I think this is the beginning of a beautiful friendship.' "

That night we went home together. It was our third date.

The next three weeks are slightly fuzzy. Middles often are. I find it's usually beginnings and ends that stick out colossally, whereas middles get lost in the crunch.

I recall Hannes's apartment that smelled of cat and our catastrophic attempts to imitate the pictures in the *Kama Sutra*. I remember running up a bill for new lace undies and running out of my Scarlet Passion. Hannes ran around with a permanent two-day stubble which he learned to maintain for *my* sake (he never ceased to remind me), but soon came down with a bad case of bronchitis, contracted shortly after I got my first offer to host a TV talk show (later called *Breakfast at Becky's*) and he got three rejections of his novel. On the news we saw Hungary's borders open to the West.

I was dazzled — by current events, a summer bathed in golden light, Hannes's compatibility credentials. Maybe that's why I wasn't paying attention. Whatever the case, one soggy day early in the fourth week of our liaison, while a tidal wave of East Germans in ski jackets, scuffed running shoes, and stone-washed jeans MADE IN POLAND surged through Hungary seeking refuge in Austria, Hannes, for the first time since I'd known him, arrived clean-shaven for a date. I should have known as soon as I saw him that he was about to gnaw off a chunk of my heart. We were sitting ergonomically on our Anywhere Chairs in the hot tropics of the Alligator and Crocodile House in Berlin's fish museum, otherwise known as the aquarium. After sullenly watching the crocodiles snooze for a minute or two, Hannes told me in no uncertain terms that our honeymoon was over. To be exact, he said, *"Ich habe kein Herzklopfen mehr"* — he had lost the heartthrob, the palpitations, the pounding in his breast, the butterflies in his stomach.

It's one of those sentences you never forget, a sentence that leaves you floundering for words, gasping for breath.

"Ich habe kein Herzklopfen mehr," he said. "Do you have it?"

"No, Hannes," I replied rather dryly, already sensing sarcasm teasing my tongue, "No, Hannes, I didn't take your heartthrob."

"That's not exactly what I meant," he had the nerve, or rather the lack of humor, to say.

I turned away from him. In slow motion I watched an

alligator drag its heavy armor into the water and disappear. I would have liked to throw Hannes over the bridge into the swamps below. With that one sentence, he was out of my life anyway. Why not let those awesome carnivores feast on him? He was gone — just like the rest of them.

The rest of them. Them. I felt the wound tear open where all of those "thems" were stored, where all of the Konrads and Günthers and Alfreds and Nikolauses were kept at bay, held prisoner in the dark dungeon of my memory, all of those lousy bastards who over the years had taken potshots at my affections, who had smiled and caressed and whispered sweet everythings in my ear, only to suddenly pull out, stab, prick, jab, or perform whatever it was they do when they've had enough.

"I lost my heartthrob," redundant Hannes repeated.

"Are you sure?" I said. "Did you really look?"

He nodded.

"You shaved," I observed.

He nodded.

"Maybe you just misplaced the throb," I said. "Maybe you accidentally left it somewhere. Like where you slept last night."

My irony was clear. He could have denied it. He didn't.

So that was it. Another woman. And on top of it, one who liked a clean-shaven face. My wound oozed.

"When you eat filet mignon every night," Hannes said, "sooner or later you lose the taste for it."

Oh, he was a great one with words. "Is that *you* talking, or are you quoting someone here?" I asked.

Hannes shook his head. In all fairness, I should say that he looked pretty wretched.

"What would you rather I be, Hannes? Potato soup? Boiled turnips?"

A crocodile yawned broadly, moving ever so sluggishly and carelessly toward us. For many long seconds I watched its slow approach. Suddenly, with a great rush, it attacked, spreading its jaws and displaying dozens of razor-edged teeth. Its snout aimed and then clamped down around Hannes's shin. Thrashing about mightily, the giant crocodile yanked hard, biting, ripping, tearing off half of Hannes's long-boned leg.

"I'm going to the Baltic Sea this afternoon," Hannes said, rising and folding up his ergonomic, one-legged, height-adjustable, swivel-seat chair. "Perhaps I shall find my *Herzklopfen* there."

He tucked the chair under his arm.

What? He was going to leave *with* the chair? He was going to disappear out of my life with the Anywhere Chair, the chair that he never carried, never cared about, never fought for?

"Good luck," I said as he walked away.

And not once, not *once*, did we ever play Doppelkopf together.

Chapter Three

Sunday, October 25, 1992
Diet Week: 3
Day: 7
Weight Loss: 8 lbs.
Evening

"Does the mangold soup have any fat in it?" I asked.

Pierre, our waiter, looked puzzled. "No, I do not think so, *mademoiselle*," he answered tentatively.

"I mean, can you tell me what it's made of?"

"Of course I can tell you what it's made of. It's made of *mangold*."

Heike was waiting patiently for me to decide. She had already placed an order for lobster parfait as a starter, and then roast suckling pig sprinkled with parsley, adorned with raisins, smothered with glazed onions, complemented by Brussels sprouts doused in hollandaise sauce and a potato gratin *á la dauphinoise*. "And for dessert I'll probably have the *marquise au chocolat* with vanilla almond ice cream," she had concluded, closing her menu contentedly and reaching for her aperitif.

Oh, to be a size five/six petite.

"Are you aware of how many calories you're consuming there?" I told her. "Roast suckling pig! That alone has at least two thousand. That's enough to feed the whole French cavalry!"

"Stop exaggerating," Heike chided.

"Who's exaggerating? I'm just trying to lose some weight, that's all."

For three weeks I'd been watching my fat intake, had been sneering at sautéing and frying, glorifying poaching and steaming and grilling. I'd learned to nosh on nonfat yogurt, to drink my tea without sugar and eat my tuna dry on a plate as cats are wont to do. And I had become accustomed to waiters and waitresses who rolled their eyes at my special requests.

I will not let Pierre intimidate me, I thought to myself.

"What I mean, Pierre," I continued as sweetly as I could, "is, besides water, does the mangold soup come with anything extra *in* or *on* it? You know, cheese or —"

Pierre rolled his eyes, just as I knew he would. "Oh, *that's* what you mean! *Mais non, mademoiselle!* There's no cheese on it, it is topped only with *crème fraîche*. And croutons."

"You see!" I cried triumphantly. "I just knew it! *Crème fraîche* and croutons! Well then, no thanks, Pierre. I'd rather have a mixed green salad, please, no dressing, just a drizzle of olive oil. Better yet, give me the oil on the side. And I'll have the *coq au vin* without the skin. And without the *vin* too. The vegetables I prefer steamed, not sautéed. Thank you."

Pierre and Heike looked at me as if I had just ordered a king-size portion of boiled nuts and bolts.

"All right," I conceded, "put the *vin* back into the *coq*, but please, no skin."

"And to drink, *mademoiselle?*" Pierre queried.

"Mineral water, please, low sodium," I replied curtly. "With a slice of lemon."

Oh, the pain of it, the sheer pain of dining out when you're trying to lose an honest pound.

"You're taking this far too seriously," Heike said once Pierre was gone.

"That's easy for you to say. You never had to lose an ounce in your life."

"Weight reduction solely through dieting is temporary. You must increase your energy output accordingly." It was so early in the evening, yet her voice already had its pedantic edge. And mine, a brittle undertone. "But you look fine," she continued on a wiser note. "I can tell you've already lost considerably. Just go easy on yourself."

"If you think *I've* lost weight, you should see how many pounds my apartment has shed."

"Your apartment? Don't be silly."

"No, really! Yesterday alone it lost at least fifty kilos. All I had to do was get rid of some ring binders with old manuscripts and my accumulated bank statements from 1972 through 1984. You can't imagine the pleasure and satisfaction of watching my apartment lose its bulk. And the stuff I find — amazing. I found two gigantic red and yellow pompoms that — ouch!" As I raised my arms to shake my imaginary pompoms, pain shot through my back. "Oh, God," I moaned, "my back is killing me from all that stooping. And on top of it, I fell off a chair. Did I tell you about the chair?"

"What chair?"

"Remember Hannes?"

"Which Hannes?"

"The tall one with the toothpaste on his glasses."

"The computer musician?"

"No, that was Konrad. And he was shortish and wore contacts. No, Hannes was the writer."

"I can't keep them all straight. And?"

"And what?"

"And — what about Hannes?"

Heike Lindner was a straightforward, pragmatic, no-nonsense type with a style of speaking as lean and sinewy as her figure. When we lived together twenty years ago in our Neukölln *Wohngemeinschaft*, I used to call her Heike the Sensible One. With the exception of Jürgen, my ex, and Ruth Trautenau who also lived with us, Heike played the most significant role in improving my German language skills during my earliest days in Berlin. She took great pains teaching me only the most sensible and practical of phrases, things like *Wo sind die Toiletten, bitte?* In fact, a lot of what I know today is of her doing — though I never quite picked up her trim, precise way with words.

For the past several years Heike had been running her own translation and foreign-language editing bureau with five full-time and at least twenty part-time, freelance employees. Her work, most of which was bossing other people around and translating how-to manuals or academic hogwash, had added to her cut-and-dry, know-it-all air. I knew this for a fact because I had worked for her myself on occasion. But my last translation, concluded two weeks earlier, an advertising pamphlet for a designer coffee machine, was going to be the last. Heike had had the audacity to change my text without conferring with me first. And she'd done it in faulty English too! Why do they think they can get away with this —"they" being Germans who, simply because they spent a year in a high school somewhere in the middle of a wheat field in Minnesota, think they can write flawless coffee machine instructions in English.

"So what about Hannes?" Heike asked again.

"Hannes?"

"The chair."

"Oh! Well, while I was throwing out stuff a few weeks ago, I found this fold-up chair I had bought for Hannes and me to take on museum trips. And when I tried it out playing skat with the professor and Martin, it collapsed. . . ." My voice tapered off for a moment. "But I wanted to tell you something else. . . . Oh, right! The amazing things you find when you really begin to pull up the dross and the dregs. While I was cleaning the bathroom and throwing out all these old expired medicines, I found this." I pointed to my lips. "Scarlet Passion. I bought it a few years ago and forgot about it. But the best thing I found was some hair dye, a whole kit with gloves and a bowl and a plastic smock to keep you clean."

Heike chuckled softly. "Remember what a mess we used to make with the henna?"

"Who's we? Just you and Ruth. And anyway, this isn't henna. It's this new, natural, plant-based stuff that Ruth gave me before she moved to Gomera. 'Touch up your hair,' she told me. Her parting words. So I decided to do it tomorrow."

"Tomorrow? I like the gray."

"It's getting out of hand. When I saw my mother in June she was shocked to see all the gray. It made *her* feel old. She's coming for Christmas, so I decided to dye it. It'll be her Christmas gift. It'll make her feel ten years younger."

Heike giggled. "That's a new one."

"But I wanted to tell you something else —"

"The pompoms?"

"Right! I found these two old pompoms from junior high school in a carton of memorabilia. And this whole story came back to me. I *have* to tell you!"

At a table a few feet away, a roast suckling pig sprinkled with parsley, adorned with raisins, smothered with glazed onions, complemented by Brussels sprouts doused in hollandaise sauce and a potato gratin *á la dauphinoise* was being served.

Its aroma wafted our way, and I was conscious of my taste buds tingling to life. For a moment I felt weak, faint, so terribly, terribly hungry.

"I'm starved," I said impatiently, my eyes darting around the restaurant, looking for Pierre.

Heike let out an exasperated sigh. "Take it easy. You're not the only person in the restaurant, Becky."

"At least they should bring the bread. They would never stand for this shit in America."

"So are you enjoying cleaning?" asked Heike. She said it the way other people ask you if you're enjoying your meal. It was a typical question from a diehard cleanoholic.

"Enjoying *cleaning?* Who's even talking about *cleaning?* I'm the filthiest slob I know. You know that. The next time you come visit, I'll show you all the dust balls, the spiderwebs, the crumbs under the carpet, and the wads of hair stuffing up the drain in my bathtub. I'm saving it all to show you. I'm waging war against hidden *clutter*, Heike. That's all."

"Is that *all* you've been doing these past few weeks? Counting calories and categorizing your chaos?"

Heike's subtext stood out boldly. What she was really saying was, if all I was doing was reducing my junk, why couldn't I help her out with her tedious translations?

"Of course I've been doing more than that," I said evasively. "For instance, last week I did an interview with Umberto Bernini, the actor. It'll be on soon."

"And?"

"And what?"

"And what about him?"

"Nothing. Although I'm sure you'd like him. He was made for you. He loves gossip."

Heike, as tough and stubborn as she often was, had her

soft side. She was a rumormonger. Translating those treacherous scientific texts and computer handbooks day in and day out drove her to spend her leisure time reading the yellow press. She was my number-one gossip source. And sometimes, of course, I gave her dirt.

"Bernini told me that when he was a kid he was a thief," I said. I began imitating Bernini in a fake Italian accent. " 'When I had been a boy, I'm small, frail like dwarf. But I'm a good thief because I look pure and I'm speedy.' I asked him if I had to edit that out and he said, 'No, I proud of it. Gossip and metaphysics are the two things I like most!' Great interview."

Heike and I laughed at my Bernini imitation. It thawed the chill between us for the time being, but unfortunately it attracted the attention of the couple at the roast suckling pig table. Uh-oh, the woman recognized me. Don't ask me what it is, but I always know when it happens. The air starts to buzz.

"And?" Heike said.

"And what?"

"And what happened after?"

"After what?"

"After the interview."

"You mean, did I go back to his hotel with him?"

"Did you?" she said, her eyes widening.

"He told me he had a girlfriend. So I *in*discreetly asked him if he believed in being faithful."

"Is this on film?"

"You bet! So I asked him if he was faithful, and you know what he said?"

"What?"

"He said, 'What means that — faithful?' "

Heike and I were pretty near hysterical now. My stomach was so empty from dieting, just a few sips of my aperitif had already gone straight to the giggly side of my brain. The roast suckling pig lady smiled at me.

"I bet she'll come over," I said to Heike, lowering my voice. "She'll come over and say to me, 'Are you that lady from television?'"

"And?"

"And I'll say to her —"

"No, I mean *him!* And what did you say to him?"

"To who?"

"To Bernini!"

"About what?"

"About being faithful!"

"Oh, right. Nothing really. I told him what faithful meant, and he said, 'I no like betrayal,' so we went for dinner with the crew and that was it."

"You see, that's what bothers me," Heike said.

"What?" I said, confused.

"I'm talking about Bernini and you're talking about yourself. Frankly, I don't care whether that lady recognizes you or not. Free yourself of your narcissistic dictums."

"My 'narcissistic dictums'? I can't even pronounce it, let alone free myself of it. . . . What's the problem now, Heike?" I sighed.

"The problem is, you think you're a star."

"And *your* problem is, you don't realize that I am." My voice was getting louder.

"Oh, Becky, you think everything you do or say or write is a gift to mankind. I correct a few sentences in your translation and you hit the ceiling. You're self-centered and self-obsessed and you constantly need to be reassured of your own specialness. Stop talking about yourself and start listening to other people."

"Hold on a second! First of all, you sound like one of your

manuals. Secondly, it's my job to listen to other people, and I do it well. And thirdly, what's wrong with hitting the ceiling when some amateur comes along and 'corrects' my text?"

Heike blanched.

"You *are* an amateur when it comes to English," I said. "It's plain simple German arrogance for you to think you can correct my English."

"So now it's the Germans."

"I've been living here for twenty years. I think I know what I'm talking about."

"At least you're being forthright. You're usually too opportunistic to tell the truth."

"What you call opportunistic, I call nice." Heike snorted but I persisted, infuriated. "Why do you always have to be so goddamn tough and critical? I have never ever heard a German say he was sorry. It's as if those words don't exist in the German language. Why are you so stubborn? What's wrong with making a mistake and admitting it, for Christ's sake!"

Pierre appeared suddenly at our table with Heike's wine, my water, rolls, and butter. I grabbed a dry roll and twisted off a piece. I looked over again at the roast suckling pig table. The woman was eyeing me. At the latest, I reckoned, she'd be over at our table within four minutes. She had that look about her.

"So what else is new?" Heike asked with a tinge of facetiousness.

Was this her way of offering me a peace treaty? Let her squirm in her seat. I deliberately took my time chewing the roll, crunch by crunch.

" 'Bingo Berlin' has been accepted by *Mademoiselle*," I finally said. "Marsha's girlfriend Susan Josephs called about it yesterday."

"Hey, that's terrific." Heike seemed surprised. I didn't blame her. I'd been surprised too.

"She said it was just the right mix of funny and senti-mental, and that Berlin was a print-worthy, compelling, and exciting city."

"That's great. Really."

Yes, it *was* great. Just the thought of it made my stom-ach all warm and gooey and jolly. My only problem now was following up this success with another story. If the next piece wasn't a winner — forget it. "You're only as good as your next project," my producer Karla Menzel was always telling me.

The thought of Karla Menzel turned the gooey warmth in my stomach to slop. On Friday, while she was off some-where in Cologne at a media conference, she'd had Gisela, her secretary, call me to make an appointment with her for early Monday — tomorrow.

"What's it about?" I had asked Gisela.

"I don't know, but it sounded urgent."

"Please have her call me."

But Karla Menzel hadn't called. It could only mean trouble. In fact, I had fretted over it ever since. I hate not knowing. And Karla was so erratic and moody, you *never* knew what was poking around in her mind. One day she says I'm the greatest living interviewer this side of the Atlantic, and the next day she gets all huffy-puffy about my accent, my questions, the way I tilt my head too much to the left when I'm thinking on camera.

"You're worried about the inclination of my head, Karla?" I once asked her indignantly. "I'm concentrating on doing a good job, and you're worried about a forty-five-degree angle?"

"The ratings, Becky. I'm worried about the ratings. They're too low."

"I can't help it if you have me slotted on the artsy third channel. Even my Rochester Malone had low ratings. And everyone agreed it was terrific. And besides, on that interview I kept my head at a steady ninety degrees."

Indeed, everyone really *had* agreed that my interview with the Irish muscle-man megastar Malone was terrific, everyone except for me. I loathed it. In fact, it was in the middle of that interview that I suddenly realized what was wrong with *Breakfast at Becky's*, and me, and journalism per se.

I was one of Rochester Malone's last stops on the whirlwind German promotion tour for his action-adventure-comedy *McLimbo*. For the first few minutes of our interview he had been going on and on about his millions and his fancy cars, his Hollywood villas, about the swimming pools and all his successes. He was in a good mood — probably because he was finally talking to someone in real English — and began to unwind. He got all teary-eyed about his bad-boy Boston childhood and his mother's Irish stew, but mostly about the horrors of his second divorce.

It was a solid interview, cozy and revealing. And suddenly it struck me that I wanted to *talk* to Malone, not just ask but really *talk* to him, empathize with him. I felt this brimming urge to tell him about Konrad, the computer musician who had recently dropped me, and Hannes, the writer who had walked out on me in the middle of the Berlin Aquarium. I thought it would be congenial exchanging stories with him, the way strangers do when they encounter each other in a café on a lazy Sunday morning and within an hour or two are old buddies. I didn't have a villa, but I could have told Malone what it was like living with four Germans in a run-down walk up in Berlin in the 1970s, or what fun it is playing skat every Monday. There were so many tales I might have told. But I couldn't, of course. It wasn't my job. I was a journalist, an interviewer, *not* a storyteller. I had been taught that other people's stories are more interesting than mine, their villas and divorces and swimming pools more important to the world than my apartment, boyfriends, or pompoms. I had been taught that using the word "I" was egocentric.

The evening after the Rochester Malone interview I went home, sat down at my desk, and finally began work on "Bingo Berlin."

"That's really terrific news about *Mademoiselle*," Heike went on.

"They want me to find a good illustrator for the story," I said, banning Karla Menzel and Rochester Malone from my thoughts. "Modern. Witty. Brilliant. Fast. And cheap, they say. Do you know any?"

Heike replied after a moment's thought. "How about Benno Fabian? He did some very solid sketches for this book we worked on a little while back. A tall, skinny guy. A little shy, but with depth. The elegant, gentlemanly type. His lips are a little thin, but he's got nice, broadish shoulders and —"

"Heike, I'm looking for an illustrator, not a model."

We had almost forgotten our skirmish.

"Benno Fabian?" I wondered. "Is that Frido Fabian's brother? I interviewed Frido a few years ago, when his record *Happy Fruit* came out. I was wild about him."

"Benno designed the jacket. And if you're still wild about Frido, he's available. I read that his third wife just separated from him."

"I think I'll wait until their divorce is final, if you don't mind."

"Talking about men," Heike went on, "have you heard from your bunny?"

"My bunny? What bunny? 'Lousy bastard' bunny? I don't talk about him."

"Screw the moron."

"I found a pair of his stupid angora longjohns and made

dust rags out of them. I got rid of all those awful ring binders in the sliding drawers under my bed and then cleaned them out with the angora rags."

"Good for you."

"Although frankly, dusting with his longjohns didn't give me that much satisfaction. Somehow it didn't seem all that important anymore. I got a far greater kick out of finally getting rid of the binders."

"About your apartment," said Heike, "I recently translated something where someone was quoted as saying that people who are always trying to put order into their lives have an anal fixation. They were kept in dirty diapers too long when they were babies."

I giggled.

"No, listen," Heike insisted. "I'm telling you this for your own good. There's this whole school of thought that says that disorder indicates fertility of the mind, whereas neatness is an indication that a person is afraid of her own mind and is reflecting in her outward space an inward need for control. What do you think of that?"

"Can we change the subject?"

"But let me tell you, I really have to hand it to you. I respect your discipline. How do you do it?"

"Set a goal," I answered, flattered. "And no matter —" Uh-oh, the roast suckling pig lady was making motions to rise. "Heike," I whispered. "She's coming over. She's going to stop at the table, and say, 'Aren't you that lady from television?' "

"And you'll say?" Heike whispered back.

"I'll say, 'Yeah, I do that porno show on cable.' "

The woman, in her late forties, dressed to the hilt in a bright yellow Chanel-type suit with shiny gold buttons and black trim exposing rows of gold chains overlaying her ruffled white silk blouse, walked up to our table. A diffident smile played across her face.

"Excuse me," she said.

"Yes?" I replied, ever so graciously.

"Would you be so kind as to tell me the time?" she asked.

"Eight forty-five," said Heike promptly.

The lady smiled again and then walked toward the rest room.

"So I was asking you how you manage all that discipline," Heike said, not without some triumph in her voice.

"Set a goal," I humbly replied. "You must stick to your guns. No matter what happens, you must never let anything seduce you from your chosen path. Nothing!"

Pierre suddenly appeared at the table.

"*Mademoiselle,*" he murmured in my direction. "The chef is sorry to say we're out of the *coq,* with or without *vin.* Would you like to see the menu?"

"Oh no!" I exclaimed. "How disappointing. What could I possibly eat now?"

Heike and Pierre looked at me expectantly.

"Okay, I said, "I'll take the roast suckling pig. But please, you really must go easy on the parsley!"

I loosened my belt one notch.

"Barry asked me a few weeks ago what my IQ was," I said to Heike. "So I told him it's 148."

"Two cups of coffee, please," Heike managed to call out to Pierre as he dashed by. She lit up a cigarette.

The roast suckling pig had been quite amazing. My stomach was in a sated stupor, my lips were sore from rubbing all the grease off them with my thick linen napkin, my head felt heavy with satisfaction. And of course I felt pangs of guilt for not only *eating* a pig but *being* one too.

"Your IQ is 148?" Heike asked skeptically.

"No. Or rather, I have no idea what it is. Our scores were kept under lock and key. Once, though, when I was thirteen, I remember sneaking up to my teacher's desk while she was in the back of the room watering the plants. I was pretending to sharpen my pencil over her wastebasket while I scanned a list of numbers in a book she had left open on her desk. Next to my name I saw the number one-three-two —"

Heike made a who-are-you-trying-to-kid face.

"Okay," I said. "It might have been one-two-three because even then I was myopic. And when you come down to it, it may not even have been a list of our IQ scores. It could have been a list of just about anything."

"Becky, why are you telling me this?"

"It's the mental prep."

She nodded reluctantly.

"In any case," I went on, "I bent down to get a better look when Miss Cohen, my teacher, asked me from the back of the room what I was doing at her desk. Without batting an eye, I answered, 'Oh, nothing, Miss Cohen. I was just sharpening my pencil and some of the shavings fell on your desk, so I wiped them off so you wouldn't get smudged.' She smiled, thanked me for my consideration, and I went smugly back to my seat having then and there decided that henceforth my IQ was going to be at least 123, and maybe 132."

"So why go around saying it's 148?"

"Why *not?* At any rate, I felt very smart, not so much because of my newly acquired intelligence, but because I'd proven again how easy it is to be a fibber."

Heike's eyes narrowed.

"What I'm trying to say," I went on, "is that I tell lies."

"Oh?" she exclaimed softly, letting the revelation sink in for a moment. "You tend to exaggerate, okay. But there's a big difference between lying and exaggerating."

"Let it suffice to say that it has always been a problem for me keeping what *is* separated from what *could* be, what *really* happened from what *might* have happened."

"You're trying to say that you *could* have been sharpening your pencil, so why not say you were, or since you're not retarded, your IQ *could* be 148, so that's why you say that it is?"

"Exactly."

Heike the Sensible One, you see, was pretty smart herself. Her IQ is at least 120, I'm sure.

"But even more important, Heike, is that sometimes I *feel* like a 148-IQ brain. When I'm with Barry, for instance. He makes me feel so smart. Or another example of what I mean. Remember how I'm always saying that we were sitting in front of an igloo when Hannes, the writer with the toothpaste, told me he was in love with me?"

"At the Museum of Ethnology, if I remember correctly."

"It's not true."

"Really? He never said he was in love with you?"

"Of course he did! But it wasn't in front of an igloo. It was in front of a South Sea *korombu,* a cult house from northern New Guinea —"

"Becky, may I please ask you again, why are you telling me this? Not that I don't find it interesting. I just want to know its relevance."

"Heike, I'm going to tell you the pompom story. It's about something that happened to me when I was thirteen years old. And since deep down somewhere in my shameless heart I'm an honest gal, I wanted to let you know that even if I'm not qualified to give you a truthful account of those events, I promise to try my best to let you understand what those events at least felt like to me."

Heike raised an eyebrow. "And you remember what it *felt* like?"

"Yes, I think so. I still keep in touch with my thirteen-year-old self."

"Oh, please!"

"I'm serious!" I protested. "It's very healthy practice for adults to stay in contact with their younger selves."

"And how do we do this?" She was humoring me.

"Just let them in when they knock. My thirteen-year-old self wakes me up in the middle of the night sometimes, and if I let her, she'll remind me of what it was like being her: what it was like falling in love for the first time, for instance, or being embarrassed to death by her parents, or wanting something so bad she'd even grow up to get it. She's pretty okay, that thirteen-year-old kid, much sweeter, for instance, than my seventeen-year-old self. And my twenty-five-year-old self. Remember her? Remember how jealous she was, and dependent and thoughtless? She still scares the shit out of me."

Heike was eyeing me in sheer disbelief.

"In any case," I continued, "my thirteen-year-old self and I compared notes the other day, and I realized that we have much more in common than just a flat chest."

"Was she a liar too?"

"She had her moments."

Pierre was back at our table with coffee and Heike's *marquise au chocolat* decorated with three lustrous orbs of vanilla almond ice cream. "Dessert," he said. And then, whipping out a pretty, *petite cuillière*, he added, "For you, *mademoiselle*, if it would please you to have a taste." He carefully placed the spoon beside my coffee.

"Why, thank you, Pierre," I replied daintily, "but I'm

afraid I won't be partaking of dessert. I'm full as a stuffed pig."

Pierre withdrew.

I looked down at Heike's dessert plate. It was rather pleasing to the eye. "I've never tasted a perfect *marquise au chocolat*," I said, reaching for my spoon. I discreetly scooped up some chocolate and gingerly nipped off the tip of one of the soft white creamy mounds.

"At any rate, Heike," I said, raising the spoon to my lips, "my present self would like so very, very much to tell you the truth, the whole truth, and nothing but. Yet already she's rearranging reality, redecorating her memory. For example, she just decided to begin her story with the words 'one fine day.' She's terrible. Incorrigible. She knows perfectly well that when the story began it was really cold, cloudy, and drizzly!"

I opened my mouth and closed it upon the *marquise*.

One Fine Day, or How I Learned to Walk Straight (Early 1960s)

One fine day, back in the early sixties, all the way back in New York City, in the days when television was black and white and things always went better with Coke, my best friend Marsha Lipschitz and I are walking down our red and gold tree-lined street. It's a brilliant and crisp autumn afternoon. Royal blue sky, puffy white clouds, bright, stark sunlight.

The street is in Far Rockaway. If you happen to look at a map of New York you'll see that Far Rockaway is situated on pretty much the southeasternmost tip of the borough of Queens, right at the Atlantic coast, and at the most important border in the whole world: the border that separates New

York City from Long Island and therefore from the rest of the universe.

The beach is just a fifteen-minute walk from our street, which runs near the El. Right above us the A-train rushes to and from Manhattan via East New York in Brooklyn, which is where my family and I used to live. At our corner, standing in front of the Sugar Bowl, the neighborhood candy store, if you try very hard, and if a train isn't passing by at that very moment, you might possibly hear monster seagulls screeching at baby whales, or tidal waves rolling in from Europe crashing on the jetties. And when you take in a deep breath you can almost smell the ocean, the tar, the seaweed, the popcorn, the cotton candy, the boardwalk, and — iieegghh! — the decaying, gooey guts of a jellyfish washed up on shore.

Marsha and I have decided to spend our Sunday afternoon in the playground up the block. Marsha, a chubby, cherubic child with long, dirty blond hair, light brown eyes, a mouth full of silver braces, and a heart dipped in gold, is licking a vanilla ice cream cone. I'm wearing my kinky dark hair pulled back in a ponytail for want of knowing what else to do with it. I used to be an attractive kid, but now my hips are growing faster than my breasts, pimples are sprouting on my forehead, and my nose is getting a good bit too pudgy for my liking.

"It's in the family," says Grandma Rosie with her Yiddish-Russian accent. "It's a beautiful nose. Magnificent." I wish I could believe her. "*Oy vay iz mir!* What's wrong with having a nose a person can find, I ask you?! Look, *bubeleh*, you don't like it? You want a new one? So ask your cheap father to go and buy you a new one for the Sweet Sixteen."

Grandma — what does she know?

But now, walking next to Marsha, I'm not thinking of nose jobs. I'm concentrating on blowing huge pink bubbles with my chewing gum, and I'm listening to the Chiffons singing "One Fine Day" on my transistor radio.

So there we are bopping to the music, kicking and crushing and scrunching the fallen autumn leaves, Marsha in her white Keds sneakers and me in my — oh God, what *are* those terrible contraptions attached to my feet? They are the ugliest, most disgusting, heaviest pair of olive green orthopedic shoes a tenderhearted thirteen-year-old can imagine. Try as I might to conceal it, it's plain to see that I am pigeon-toed.

Pigeon-toed. Uugghh. It's a word with devastating connotations, a word that even today sends shivers up my spine. Well, perhaps I'm exaggerating. Being pigeon-toed is certainly not the worst thing that can befall a child. But still. How would *you* like to have some chiropodist threaten you with leg braces if you don't walk straight, or some pediatrician tell you to pick up a ping pong ball with your toes for fifteen minutes every day when all you really want to do is stretch out on your bed and read the latest *Intimate Confessions* love comic? How would *you* like to have all the kids on the block laugh at you when you run? Or wear olive green orthopedic shoes to the upcoming Thanksgiving Day dance when all the other girls will be wearing fancy pumps with high heels?

But now, on this brilliant autumn afternoon, walking across a glorious sea of red and golden leaves, my heart is bursting with happiness. I'm in love. For the very first time. Okay, two weeks ago I had a crush on my biology teacher, Mr. Holt, but that doesn't count. Now I'm *really* in love, in love with Mitch Lieberman, with tall, lanky, blue-eyed, nimble, charming Mitch Lieberman, the captain of the school's top-notch basketball team.

"You think Mitch'll be in the park? Yes or no?" I hear my little self say to my companion.

Marsha, a sober, taciturn, down-to-earth type, reflects before she answers. "I dunno," she finally replies.

"Well, he usually is on the weekend!"

"So then he'll be there!" But after a moment's pause she adds, "But it's kinda cool outside."

"Oh, but they even play outside when it's ten degrees below zero. Don't you think he has the most stunning nose? Oh God, Marsha, did I tell you that he said hello to me in the cafeteria on Friday and I almost spilled all my pea soup?"

"You told me at least a hundred times, for God's sake! But actually, you're right. His nose really is nice."

Mitch *is* in the park on this glorious autumn day, playing basketball with the boys. Marsha and I walk over to the cyclone fence and join our girlfriends watching the game: Judy O'Reilly, sporting a beehive with a yellow polka-dotted bow on top, knock-kneed Ellen Schultz, skinny Carol Sucarro, Lisa the Lady in her dainty black patent-leather maryjanes, and the twins Sandy and Sue Silver in their sailorette getup.

The basketball bangs on the fence, Mitch looks toward us, sees me, and waves. And my heart skips a beat.

"Well, at least he knows who you are. Maybe you do have a chance," Marsha whispers in my ear.

That's nothing compared to what happens during the break. Mitch could come over to any of the girls standing at the fence. But what does he do? He comes to *me*, to little pigeon-toed me.

"Hi. Do you have any more bubble gum?" he asks.

"Sure, here," I say, pulling a piece out of the pocket of my red-striped pedal pushers.

And what does Mitch do? He grabs my hand, drags me a few feet away, and starts dribbling the basketball with me. You may think it's nothing, but hey, the only boy that ever wanted to dribble with me was my older brother Davey and that's because no one else was around. And here I am, dribbling with the captain of the basketball team!

With beginner's luck I manage to steal the ball from Mitch, but then he grabs me from behind and the ball rolls away. But instead of going after the ball, Mitch leans back against the fence, tightens his grip around me, and pulls me back against him.

And there we stand and stand and stand. Me, Mitch, and the fence. What more can I say?

This is not the first time a boy has touched me. The year before I'd been invited to many a party, had been in many a dark basement rec room dancing with someone or other. But, aahh, this is seventh heaven: Mitch leaning against the fence, my back leaning against him, his arms wound around me. This is the first time anyone has ever touched me like that. And no one will ever touch me quite that way again.

"HEY, EVERYBODY! GET A LOAD OF THE KID WITH THE FEET!"

I'm jolted out of my blissful oblivion by the bellowing voice of Fat-Face Frankie Moronelli, the crude and hopelessly overweight school terrorizer.

"Hey, everybody, look at the feet!" Frankie's voice is so loud, its echo bounces off the wall of the handball court. And then straight at me he blubbers out, "Hey, you! Yeah, you! I'm talking to you, pigeon-toed. Pigeon-toed! Pigeon-toed!"

The other boys join in. My face turns red and my eyes tear up with shame. Why are they torturing me like this? What did I ever do to Frankie to deserve this treatment? And where's Mitch? Why doesn't he save me? But his arms aren't around me anymore. He's standing a few feet away, watching silently from the sidelines. I'll have to fend for myself.

"Oh, just shut up, Fatso," I hear myself shouting in Fat-

Face Frankie Moronelli's bloated face. "Fatso" is to Frankie what "pigeon-toed" is to me. Enraged, he grabs out for my barely existent breasts.

"Are you talking to me? Who's Fatso?" he says with a threatening tremor, clapping his pudgy paws to my chest. "Hey! You think you're so smart, pigeon-toed? Don't you? Huh? So come on, let's do 'it.' You wanna do 'it'? It'll only take two minutes. Just two minutes!"

I am completely and utterly shocked. Do "it"? And in two minutes? I give Fat-Face Frankie Moronelli a shove that sends him spinning, and Marsha and I dash away for dear life.

We take refuge in our secret hiding place, our favorite spot overlooking Far Rockaway from my apartment house roof.

"Isn't Frankie just disgusting?" I say, lighting up a cigarette I have stolen from my father, taking in a deep drag. My eyes grow dark and earnest. "Marsha, how long do you think it *really* takes to do 'it'?"

"How should I know? Do I look that type?" she replies, adjusting one of the rubber bands on her braces. Then she gathers her thoughts and adds, "But I think it takes my parents a little longer."

"Yeah?! How much longer?"

"Gee, I dunno. They keep a Frank Sinatra record on all the time so I can't hear."

I let out a discouraged sigh.

"But the record's on for a pretty long time," Marsha adds.

I turn the transistor on to my favorite rock 'n' roll station, listen to the Shirelles singing "Will You Still Love Me Tomorrow?" and fret about "it."

"No!" I suddenly exclaim with the authority of a scientist who has just made the discovery of her life. "No, it most definitely takes longer than two minutes. Look, Marsha, these songs on the radio are proof. I can't believe that all these songs would be written and sung about something that only takes two minutes. It just doesn't make sense!"

"Listen," Marsha interrupts. "If you're into worrying, why not just worry about why Mitch didn't defend you or anything."

"Oh, come on, Marsha. Why should he get in trouble with Fat-Face Frankie too?"

"Because I don't like him. That's why! Look, Judy told me in the park that he's been going with Glenda Lapidus for at least two weeks. She even has his ID. As your best friend I thought I should tell you. I'm real sorry."

"GLENDA LAPIDUS? That conceited bitch?!?" I cry out indignantly. Who could ever compete with rich, exotic Glenda Lapidus, Southern belle from Tallahassee — and a cheerleader, too. The cheerleaders are the prettiest, most graceful, most popular and most admired girls at the whole school. And one thing is sure: none of them are pigeon-toed.

"Forget him," Marsha says.

"I won't. I can't. I'll fight for him."

"Fight for him? Listen, what's your IQ anyway?"

"My IQ? Uuuhh — 148. Why?"

"Because for a girl with an IQ of 148 you're pretty stupid, that's why!"

Downcast by Mitch's supposed liaison with Glenda, I spend the rest of the afternoon sulking at home. My older brother Davey, a shy and withdrawn boy, is out of town learning to become a forward and outgoing man on a weekend camping trip. My sister Joycey, just a year and a half younger than me but ten times sweeter, begs me to help her with her math homework, but I refuse. She's bad at math and is bound to fail, but what do I care?

And there's Mom, in her *shmatte*, cleaning the apartment.

Meticulously she dusts the bookcase, taking out each and every Harold Robbins and James Michener, whisking them ever so lightly with her feather duster. She's just turned forty-two so her hair is probably gray, but you can't tell because she dyes it cherry blond. Well, she's a working woman, an executive secretary, so she *has* to look good. She even wears contact lenses!

Dear Mom, wasting her Sundays with dusting, vacuuming, washing the laundry, sweeping, ironing, polishing the furniture, and screaming at Joycey and me to get off our *tochis* and give her a hand. "For crying out loud!" Poor Mom, she tries her best and gets so little in return.

Uh-oh, there's Dad, sprawled across the couch. His cranberry bathrobe is half open so if you look the wrong way you can see his long white boxer shorts underneath. He's smoking a cigarette, following a football game on television, reading the sports section of the *New York Times* all at the same time *and* yelling at my mother, "Gloria, stop dusting the TV for God's sake while I'm watching!"

Dad's a gifted salesman. He can sell anything from ladies' garments and encyclopedias to sewing machines and life insurance. *If* he has a job. When he does, he's generous and funny. But when he doesn't, which is more often the case than not, uh-oh, just watch that blood pressure rise. Right now, sprawled across the couch, he's forty-three and out of work.

"What are you sulking about?" he asks me a few minutes later over dinner.

"She wouldn't help me with my math homework," Joycey butts in.

My mother looks at me with concern. "Princess, is there something wrong?"

"Oh, Mommy," I blurt out. "Oh, Mommy, can't I get high

heels? All the girls will be wearing them to the Thanksgiving Day dance."

The A-train races past our window, drowning out our voices.

"How many times do we have to say no?" shouts my father.

"What?" I shout back. "I can't hear! I can't hear!"

"Don't be so smart, you know you heard me," my father growls, raising his arm.

I duck just in the nick of time.

"Sam!" my mother exclaims. "Oh, my God!"

"The next time you talk back to me, I'll knock you in two!" my father threatens me.

"Don't scream at her!" my mother screeches at my father. And then to herself, or perhaps to her own private savior, she implores, "Peace, all I want is peace. Give me peace."

"Quit the crap, Gloria," my father shouts. "You sound like your sister Ethel."

"What's Ethel got to do with this?"

"She's the biggest phony actress on television. 'Peace. Give me peace!'" He's imitating my mother.

"My ears. You're killing my ears," Joycey squeaks.

"Honeybunch," my mother says to me in a somewhat softer tone. "Dr. Friedman said you can't wear heels until your arches strengthen. You know that."

"He also said she'd grow out of it!" My father bangs his fist on the table so hard a lamb chop jumps off his plate and falls onto the floor. Peppy, our maniac miniature salt-and-pepper schnauzer, pounces on it. "What's taking so long? What does it take to walk straight? Why can't my daughter walk straight? Do you know how much money we're dishing out to that foot doctor?"

"Oh Sam, how could you be so cruel?" my mother cries

out, beating her breast. "It's not her fault. If you finally got a decent job maybe we could send her to that physical therapist in Cedarhurst and buy her a new pair of orthopedic shoes. And we could move into an apartment where the A-train doesn't always come crashing through the kitchen window."

"I DON'T WANT ORTHOPEDIC SHOES!" I yell at the top of my lungs. "I want high heels! High heels!"

Peppy barks hysterically. Joycey chokes on a lamb chop. I run into the bathroom, lock myself in, and cry my eyes out.

Later, I go up to the roof and smoke a couple of cigarettes.

The next day at school, thank goodness, things take a turn for the better. In gym class I manage to steal the basketball away from my archenemy Glenda Lapidus and score the winning point for my team. Her face is livid!

On top of that — and now, finally, I'm getting to the heart of my tale — our gym teacher, Mrs. Lu Woo-Chang, announces that there will be tryouts for the cheerleading squad because one of the girls has switched schools. A new cheerleader? Omigod. If only —

"I think I'm gonna audition for the cheerleaders," I reveal to Marsha after class in the girls' locker room. "That way I'll get to see Mitch all the time and have more of a chance of winning him back."

"First of all, you can't win him back, because you never had him in the first place," Marsha says while fastening her stockings to her garter belt. "Second, be sensible. You have the spunk to be a cheerleader, but not the feet. They'd all laugh at you. And third, could you please help clip my stockings in the back?"

Suddenly, conceited Glenda Lapidus appears, all preppy

and perfect, her Tallahassee pageboy haircut glistening, every
hair perfectly in place.

"Just in case you're thinking of trying out," she sneers
at me, "don't. We won't accept any pigeon-toes on the cheerleading squad." She turns to Marsha. "And *you'd* have to lose
at least five hundred pounds before we took you on!" she says
before disappearing out the door.

Marsha is enraged. "Just who the hell does she think she
is anyway?" And then right then and there my life changes, utterly and completely. "Go for it!" Marsha cries out. "Go, go, go
for it! We're gonna make a cheerleader out of you, pigeon-toed
or not. We'll show 'em!"

My days are now entirely consumed by memorizing and
rehearsing the complicated jumps, splits, and footwork. I use
two of my mother's feather dusters as makeshift pompoms to
practice the hand movements. Whether I'm up on the roof
with Marsha, down in the subway with my mother, babysitting, visiting Dr. Friedman, walking Peppy, or in my room,
everywhere I am I practice. *When you're up, you're up. When
you're down, you're down. But no sweat, boys, you're the best
in town! Yay, team!*

I drive everyone around me crazy when out of the blue I
burst out with my favorite cheer. *Gimme a T. (T.) Gimme an
O. (O.) Gimme a P (P.) Gimme an S. (S.) What's that spell?
(Tops!) What's that spell? (TOPS!) Come on, boys, you're the
cream of the crop! Yay, team! Go-o-o-o for it!*

Life is quite exhausting — so exhausting, in fact, I more
or less forget about Mitch. That is, until the morning of the
auditions. To Glenda's horror Mitch wishes me good luck on the
school bus. But then to *my* horror, Fat-Face Frankie Moronelli
trips me on my way off the bus and I scrape my knee.

"Pretend it never happened," Marsha advises me.

"But it hurts like hell," I whine.

"Mind over matter" is her wise reply. "Do you want to be a cheerleader or not?"

"Of course I do."

"Then you fight for your right to the last."

I have stiff competition that afternoon. There are twenty-five other girls all fighting to the last for their right to be a cheerleader too. I'm a bit nervous and the bandage on my knee itches, but Marsha's out there rooting for me, so things could be worse.

I give it my best, what more can I say?

"You were fine, just fine," Marsha assures me. "They'd be crazy not to take you." And she's right, they *would* be crazy, and lucky for me, they're not. I'm chosen as the new cheerleader!

"Vely good, vely good," Mrs. Woo-Chang compliments me in her accented English. "You must implove your footwork, but your enthusiasm and your eneggy make up for it more than enough. Vely good work. Vely good."

"Good work, my foot. And who cares about enthusiasm and energy?" Marsha scoffs later that day. "That's just half the battle. Now look, the first game of the season is next week. We have to make your uniform, buy you two of the biggest, fattest, plushest red and yellow pompoms we can find, get rid of those disgusting pimples on your forehead, and iron your frizzy hair straight. We gotta *be* perfect and *look* perfect. Just think of Glenda and Fat-Face Frankie out there. They want you to be a flop. We cannot give them that satisfaction, so —"

"All right already," I break in, utterly surprised by Marsha's newfound verbal energy. "Where do we start?"

"With Dr. Friedman's toe exercises. Practice fifteen minutes with the ping-pong ball every night before you go to sleep."

I spend the next week preparing for my premiere, getting ready for the day I'll show Glenda and Fat-Face Frankie, all of Benjamin Cardozo Junior High School, all of Far Rockaway, all of New York City, for all I care all of the entire galaxy, how gracefully and beautifully I can run and jump, how energetically and enthusiastically I can shout the cheers. In brief, I'm mobilizing my powers for the first basketball game of the season, for the day on which Mitch Lieberman, that prince of a boy, will fall in love with me forever and drop that snippy Glenda like a hot potato. I have a goal in life.

The day of the game arrives, the truly most important day of my life. I wake up knowing that something awe-inspiring will happen to me and me alone. And it does.

In the stairwell on the way to math class I spot Mitch. Butterflies begin flitting around in my stomach, a whole batch of them, and I remember how one fine day, barely two weeks ago, he wound his arms around me and held me close.

"I haven't seen you around lately," he says, shifting his feet back and forth.

"Oh well, I've been real busy," I say.

"But I guess I'll see you later at the game," he says.

"Sure, I'll be rooting for you." And then, shifting my feet back and forth, I add, "Nervous?"

"No no, the team from Belle Harbor is a cinch."

"Oh," I say, lost in the deep blue of his eyes.

"Yeah, well."

"Yeah, well," I say, wondering if he wears long white boxer shorts like my father.

"You know," he says, kind of matter-of-factly, "maybe we can go for an ice cream soda after the game."

An ice cream soda with Mitch? My first real date ever! And with the *captain* of the basketball team! Oh, I just *knew* that this was going to be the most important day of my life. How will I ever be able to keep still until 4 P.M.?

School is non-stop torture. I can't concentrate on anything. All through social studies and English I look at my watch and dream of Mitch wrapping his arms around me again. Lunchtime comes, and I still have another three hours to go. Biology slowly grinds to a close, and somehow I manage to play my cello in music class without Mr. Tagliaferro noticing that I'm not working on the new Bach piece but on the melody to "Be My Baby" by the Ronettes. The bell rings and there's just one more class to go — French with Mademoiselle Rabinowitz.

Mademoiselle Rabinowitz reprimands me for not paying attention. I try my best to conjugate the verbs, but all I can do is picture myself as the most perfect cheerleader on the court or dream of Mitch and my chocolate ice cream soda with whipped cream and a maraschino cherry on top.

"*Je t'aime,*" I whisper. "*Je t'aime, Mitch.*"

I look at my watch. There's just one half hour left before the game, and I can't contain my excitement. I'm about to go to the girls' room for the tenth time that day, when suddenly the intercom system comes on and we hear a sobbing voice. Someone is crying over the loudspeaker. Who ever could it be?

"Hey, what do you know? Get a load of that. It's the principal. Mr. Dooley," blasts out Frankie Moronelli with a wild smirk plastered across his face.

The principal of our junior high school *crying?* What ever could have happened? Soon enough his sobs ebb and in a solemn voice, deep and heavy, in a voice that sends ominous shivers up my spine, he says, "Children, I have an important announcement to make. The basketball game scheduled for this afternoon has been canceled."

I can't believe my ears. My heart stops in midbeat.

"What?" I cry out. "CANCELED?"

Everyone starts to whisper among themselves.

"Ssshhh," scolds Mademoiselle Rabinowitz. *"Silence, mes enfants. Silence!* Oh keep still, for Christ's sake! Shut up!"

"The basketball game has been canceled," continues the scratchy, intercomed voice of Mr. Dooley. "Everything has been canceled. I'm sorry to say that the President of the United States of America, Mr. John F. Kennedy, has been shot in Dallas, Texas. We fear he's been wounded fatally. School buses will be waiting outside as usual. All classes are dismissed."

The loudspeaker dies out and the room is completely still. It's so still you really *could* hear a feather drop.

"No!" I cry out, jumping up from my seat. "No, it can't be true! It's unfair! It's unfair! It's not true!"

"Please control yourself," Mademoiselle Rabinowitz says to me. "Calm down. *Everybody's* upset about the President."

"The President?" I hear tumbling out of my mouth.

There I am, the prettiest little cheerleader you ever could see, with my two yellow and red pompoms, my short red skirt, my white sweatshirt with the big C sewn across its middle, my perfect, straightened, ironed-out ponytail and pimpleless face. And all I can think is, Damn it, damn it, why did the President have to go and get himself shot *today?* Like, why not *tomorrow?*

And then suddenly I find myself racing through the hall, looking for Mitch. I find him, standing tall and ever so earnest, with a whole bunch of kids, including Glenda. I walk straight up to him.

"We can still go for an ice cream soda, can't we?" I say to him ever so quietly and discreetly.

"How can you think of ice cream at a time like this?" he answers in a shocked and far too loud voice. "Think about the kids, about John-John and little Caroline. I'm gonna go and watch it on TV."

"Well, I was too. We can watch it together at my house."

For a moment I detect an affirmative light in the deep blue of his eyes. But then Glenda, the stupid eavesdropper, butts in.

"Oh, come to *my* house, Mitch," she coos. "We have *color* television."

It's not a big decision for Mitch. How could he decline an offer like color TV? Off he goes with Glenda, leaving poor little me all alone.

I have never been so hurt, humiliated, and disappointed in my entire life.

"I've been competing with a color TV. Would you believe it? I've been competing with a lousy color television," I say to Marsha on the bus home.

Outside, groups of adults are huddled together on every street corner, shocked into neighborly friendliness by the events.

"I will never forget this date as long as I live," I announce with great solemnity. "Friday, November twenty-second, 1963."

"Forget him," Marsha says. "Forget the jerk." She pats me on my back and gives me the biggest silver-braced smile she can manage on this most fateful and darkest of days.

Forget him, Marsha has advised me; forget the jerk. And I *do* try to forget him. There is certainly enough going on in the world to distract me: Kennedy doubling up in pain in the backseat of a black convertible, all the blood and brain matter on Jackie's hot pink two-piece ensemble, Lee Harvey Oswald being led away in handcuffs, Jack Ruby's smirk. All of this should make me forget Mitch, but it doesn't quite do the job.

"Becky, you really have to stop moping around the house. Get out in the world and claim what's yours," Marsha lectures.

She whips out one of her marbled notebooks and opens it to a fresh page. "Let's make a list of your assets. You're energetic." She jots this down. "Enthusiastic. You're a cheerleader. Let's not forget you have an IQ of 148, a lucrative babysitting job, a nose a person can find. And you own the neatest pair of olive green orthopedic shoes this side of the Atlantic." Marsha rips out the page, folds it carefully in quarters and hands it to me. "I'd be proud of myself if I were you."

"Thanks, pal."

"Plus, if you opened your eyes you'd see how Melvin Minsky has been mooning over you for weeks."

"Melvin Minsky?" I gasp.

"The safety guard at the corner of Seagirt Avenue and —"

"You don't have to tell me who Melvin Minsky is," I break in. "He's the safety guard with the ears that stick out all the way from here to Missouri."

"Beggars can't be choosers."

"Thanks, but no thanks. Melvin could never take Mitch's place."

"Well, perk up already!" she says in exasperation. After one of her formidable pauses, she adds, "Listen, if you ask me, a little ego could help."

"I didn't ask. And anyway, what can my ego do for me?"

"Ask not what your ego can do for you, ask what you can do for your ego."

But what in the world could I do for me and my ego? I rack my brains over this question. And finally I actually do come up with an answer. Once I do, I wonder why I didn't think of it earlier. "Go, go, go for it," I cheer myself on.

A few days later, without my parents' permission, I take the A-train into Manhattan and with the money I've earned babysitting I buy me and my ego our very first pair of high heels. They're red and shiny and gorgeous and we are going to wear them to the Thanksgiving Day dance no matter what!

Of course I will have to keep the heels a secret from my parents. My original idea is to sneak them into the house when no one's looking and hide them in my closet. My closet has recently been proclaimed a tornado catastrophe zone, so it isn't likely my mother will be snooping around in it. And then on the day of the dance I'll smuggle the shoes out of the house and put them on when I'm standing in safe territory.

In theory this is a good idea, but as luck would have it, my mother sees me returning from my shopping spree.

"What'd you buy?" she asks inquisitively, her x-ray eyes piercing my shopping bag. I have no choice but to show her my purchase.

"How could you spend your money on something as useless as that?" she scolds. Then she looks up at me and peers deep into my soul. Who knows what it is she sees? Whatever it is, it prompts her to say with a sigh, "Okay, put them on and walk. Show Mommy how you walk."

I slip on my new shoes and, wobbling noticeably, I traipse up and down the living room floor.

"Samuel, Samuel," my mother cries out. "Come, hurry!"

My father rushes out of the bathroom, the toilet flushing behind him.

"What's the matter?" he shouts. "Did the A-train crash through the kitchen window or something?"

"Walk for Daddy," my mother commands. "Walk."

Once again I model my shoes.

"Do you see, Sam," my mother's excited voice rings out. "Do you see?"

"What am I, blind?" my father growls. And then, turning to me, he exclaims, "I'll be a son of a gun. You're walking

straight. My daughter's walking straight! Just like a little lady.
I knew you could if you just tried!"

"Sweetheart!" shouts my mother.

"Princess!" yells my father.

"My ears!" screeches Joycey.

Peppy chokes on his lamb-chop bone, Davey chuckles,
and I feel my face light up and turn into sunshine — pure,
unadulterated sunshine.

Chapter Four

Sunday, October 25, 1992
Diet Week: 3
Day: 7
Weight Loss: 8 lbs. (?)
A bit later that same evening

"So that's what happened one fine day when I was thirteen, more or less how I learned to walk straight."

The restaurant was emptying out in back and filling up in front around the bar. Heike and I had just paid the check.

"And?" Heike said, downing the last drop of her wine. "What happened with the shoes?"

"Which shoes?"

"Your high heels. The Thanksgiving Day dance."

"I vaguely recall catching the flu and not being able to go."

Pierre swept over to the table with our change. "A cognac, *mesdames?*"

We nodded and he swept off.

"So did you ever get to wear the heels?" Heike asked.

"Sure, but then they died on me at Melvin Minsky's bar mitzvah a few months later. We were dancing to *hava nagila* and I slipped, the heel broke off, and I sprained my ankle. After that I never wore high heels again."

Heike lit up a cigarette. "We were about to go to sleep when we heard about Kennedy," she mused. "It was on the radio. My mother was so shocked, she spilled a whole container of syrup on the kitchen table. Weeks later everything was still sticking to the tabletop. My parents were crazy about him. Me too. I didn't kiss my boyfriend for a whole month after he was killed."

I had heard her tell this story at least 11½ times, but I decided I'd humor her.

"I was in mourning until Christmas Eve," she went on. "And then finally I let Micha kiss me. Micha Schlembach." Heike took a long, contemplative drag on her cigarette. "I even saw him. I saw Kennedy at Rathaus Schöneberg."

"You *saw* Kennedy?"

I was really humoring her now.

"I can't quite say I *saw* him, because there were so many people there and I was standing pretty far away. But I *heard* him. And that was exciting. Everyone went wild. I remember being a little scared. I was only fifteen and the crowd was like a wild animal. I thought I'd be squashed to death."

"When you think about it now, it's hard to imagine that anyone could get so excited about a politician."

"He was a beacon of hope," Heike enthused, "even if it does sound corny. On the other side of the Wall, too. My parents and I went to East Berlin later that day. My uncle Eberhard and my aunt Brigitte lived there. We had paper flags from the parade and some newspaper and magazine clippings about Kennedy. We had even bought souvenir coins commemorating the visit. My mother sewed it all into the lining of her tote bag and I remember how scared we were that the border control people would find it."

Hey, this part of the story was new to me.

"But we passed through," Heike went on, "and when we

got there my aunt Brigitte cried over the gifts. And I remember my cousins Paul and Gudrun fighting over the American flags and the coins. My aunt and uncle had this *Westaltar* set up in their living room, and —"

"A *Westaltar?*"

"A shrine. The people in the East set up shrines with products from the West, with cigarette packs, coffee cans, and soap powder cartons, whisky and brandy bottles. Anything. Boxes of candy."

I was flabbergasted.

"It was all arranged perfectly on a mantle or on a hutch," Heike remembered. "The people from the East were almost as anal as you."

"Empty or full? Did they put all that stuff up full? With the candy still in the boxes? And the liquor in the bottles?"

Heike gave me a look of sheer disbelief. "Is that all you can think of? Of course they *ate* the candy first. They put *empty* boxes on the altar."

"Your cognac, *mesdames*," said Pierre, suddenly beside our table. He reverently placed the glasses in front of us. "Forty-five pure calories — compliments of the house," he added in his *accent français très coquet.*

No, I thought, I will not let him intimidate me.

"*Santé*," I toasted.

"At any rate," Heike went on, "my uncle Eberhard and aunt Brigitte hung one of the magazine pictures of Kennedy all the way up on top of the altar, like Jesus. So now, whenever I hear the name Kennedy, I always have this image of him hanging all the way up there on top of the altar."

We were silent for a moment.

Heike reached for her cognac and took another sip. "There's something I've been meaning to tell you." She inhaled deeply on her cigarette. "I'm sorry."

"You're sorry? For what?"

"I'm sorry about the coffee machine text. I was wrong."

The translation. I had completely forgotten about it. I leaned over the table and gave Heike a peck on the cheek. "I forgive you."

"But this doesn't erase the fact that you're still the biggest egomaniac I've ever met," she said.

"You should get out in the world more often. For instance, you've never met my aunt Ethel, the comedian."

"Tell me, did you really wear orthopedic shoes?"

"I did. And they were really olive green, which made color coordinating quite a problem. I remember wearing a lot of green-toned madras prints. I had a larger collection of madras dresses than Glenda Lapidus."

"And what ever happened to her?"

"Glenda Lapidus, the lass from Tallahassee, became a hippie freak. I moved away from Far Rockaway a year later, so I don't have this firsthand, but I was told that in high school Glenda became a pothead. She managed to get into a junior college, but then she dropped out, went to San Francisco, and was last seen late in 1969 taking a nap out on the street in Haight Ashbury."

"And Mitch?"

"Poetic license."

"Oh, Becky. You really are hopeless." Heike chuckled. "He never existed?"

"Of course he did! He most definitely did!" I protested. "It's just that his real name was Bruce Abramowitz and he wasn't a basketball player but on the soccer team, which was very unpopular at the time."

"And what happened to *him?*"

I shrugged. "No idea. For all I know he could be selling hot dogs on Red Square in Moscow. I forgot him, Heike. I simply forgot the jerk." My voice dropped to a hush. "But I'll tell you something. I never forgot the way he touched me that autumn afternoon in the park. Never. And no one has ever touched me quite that way since."

That hit a nerve. I felt it. "I see, I see," Heike said. "So *that's* what we're all looking for, isn't it?"

"Maybe," I replied after a second's thought. "Maybe that's what we *are* all looking for. The Bruces of our youth. The Original Urge." I contemplated this for a moment more. "And *your* present urge?"

"Norbert just gave me a set of keys to his apartment."

"Keys to his apartment? Oh, so we're talking serious here. Too bad, though. Barry was just asking about you."

"Barry? Too cute. And too young. I need an edge."

"I just need," I said with a sigh.

"Hey!" Heike exclaimed. "What ever happened with the blind date?" The gossiper in her had suddenly come to life.

Obligingly I proceeded to fill her in on what had happened after I agreed to give Professor Bloch's proposed match a try. A few days later I had answered the phone and found myself talking to a Dr. Egon Dingeldein. His name was so remarkably dreadful that I decided anything after that could only be an improvement. And it was. He had a charming voice, strong yet velvety, complemented by a slight Bavarian accent. I have a weakness for southern German accents. I was charmed. Barbie's dream date, I thought. I'm in love.

And then we met. At the Prager-Bar.

And he was pretty perfect. His voice was even better in person; his accent rolled smoothly off his lips. He had the best smile. Sweet dimples. The right height. Mid-forties. His hair was graying handsomely with twinkly highlights. He was wearing a fine-looking pair of loafers, nice woolen slacks, stylish suspenders, a flattering shirt. His hands were well groomed.

We ordered drinks, engaged in small talk. Our cocktails came. Mine was garnished with a fat red cherry pierced by a toothpick. I picked it up to pop it into my mouth.

"I think I should tell you something," Egon said. "I usually make it a point only to date women twenty years younger than me."

My hand froze in midair.

"At *least* twenty years younger than me," he stressed.

"Well, then," I said, looking at my cherry on the toothpick, "would you like me to pretend this is a lollipop?" He didn't get the joke. "Why younger women?" I asked, curious.

"They think I'm brilliant. Everything I say amazes them."

"I find it pretty amazing too, what you're saying."

He looked at me blankly.

"Well, *are* you brilliant?" I asked.

"I'm depressed. I'm getting divorced."

"I see."

We were silent a few moments.

"Are you upset, or what?" he asked.

"I suppose I'm what."

He didn't get that either. As I told Heike the whole story, all she could do was shake her head sadly.

"We spent the rest of the evening talking about his job in cancer research," I went on. "No wonder the guy's depressed. And then during dessert, after a half bottle of wine, he announced that I had cured him."

"You're kidding. Jesus. Men."

"And then this guy came in selling flowers, and I thought, God, please don't let Egon buy me a rose. So what happens? He goes and buys me the whole damn bunch. Thirty roses! He was so happy. He thought it was such a generous gesture. And it was — I mean he'd told me how much that divorce of his was costing. But it meant nothing to me."

"And when did all this happen?"

"Last week. Last Tuesday. And I haven't heard from him since. The professor thinks I shouldn't give up on him. He says Egon's only going through a phase. But I think I'll pass on this one."

"Don't worry, darling," Heike said, patting my hand. "We'll find someone to service you soon."

I laughed. Sometimes Heike the Sensible One really did have a great way with words.

"As soon as my apartment and I go off our diet," I told her. "I'll let you know, okay? I haven't given up looking. Believe me, you never know what can happen one fine day!"

I had a bad night. A *particularly* bad night. For one, my back hurt. For two, the roast suckling pig was playing hopscotch in my stomach. And thirdly, when I got home I had several disturbing calls waiting for me on my answering machine.

The first of my messages was from Susan Josephs at *Mademoiselle*, a leftover from Friday I had decided not to erase. I listened to her uplifting comments about "Bingo Berlin" and let my stomach get all warm and gooey and jolly again.

"Hel-lo, Beck-y," began the next call. "This is your mo-ther speak-ing." My mother spoke to my machine as if she were communicating with a deaf person, putting equal emphasis on each syllable. "Are you home? It's me Beck-y, Mom-my. Pick up the phone! I know you're there. Hel-lo? What's that click-ing?" For about a half second she waited for me to pick up the phone, but then bolted straight into her agenda: should she bring me fresh-cooked *kasha varnishkas* when she comes for Christmas, or would I rather she schlep one of her homemade fruitcakes? "I know you want both, honey bunch," she enunciated into the phone, "but it's too much to car-ry on and of course I can't put food in my suitcase. Your old Mom's not rea-dy to kick the buck-et but I am sev-en-ty one and have to trav-el light." I shuddered at the thought of her forthcoming ten-day visit. I already envisioned her swinging open all my kitchen cupboards, scouting for cockroaches.

Any residue of warmth, gooeyness, and jollity that may have been left floating around in my stomach was flushed away by the next message. It was Felix, the lousy bastard — the first sign of his existence since the Venice non-affair. "Hello, Becky. It's me," he said in that upbeat voice of his. "You don't have to pick up. This way you can't hang up on me. Ha-ha-ha." Terrific sense of humor, that guy. "We kind of lost touch with each other and I was wondering how you're doing. I thought we could meet for a chat. I'd like to explain things to you." Right, Felix. Exactly what I need. Let's get together and you explain to me, please, what the word *space* means, as in "Becky, I need some space." The nerve of that guy!

My girlfriend Marsha Lipschitz, these days a successful film publicist, was the next caller. "Guess what?!" she exclaimed all the way from Manhattan's Upper East Side. "I may be visiting you soon. Finally, after all these years! It seems that the Lance Lester movie I'm publicizing is going to be invited to the Berlin Film Festival in February. But don't worry. I don't plan on staying with you. The thought of climbing up five flights of steps every day is unbearable! Oodles of hugs and kisses, sweetie. Don't call back. I'm flying down to Florida to visit my mother. I'll call back soon."

The next call was Marsha again. "I told you I'd call back

soon." Giggle, giggle. "I forgot to tell you something. I have a
date next week with the dentist I told you about when you were
here. Remember? The one my mother tried to fix me up with
over Passover. Cross your fingers!"

After Marsha's, there were two more calls. Egon, timidly
asking me out to the movies whenever I could find the time,
and Karla Menzel, my producer. My stomach died on me when
I heard her voice.

"You wanted me to call," she began. "What had to be said
that couldn't wait for our meeting tomorrow? I have better
things to do than chase after you. Tomorrow, 10:30." From the
way she sounded, our meeting could only mean trouble. What
disaster was in store for me?

A vision of Karla Menzel rose in front of me, her glow-
ing blond hair meticulously swept back in stylish 1930s curls,
her thin limbs wrapped in a designer robe, something black
and sleek and devastatingly expensive, her every movement
calculated and exact. She tiptoed when she walked, carefully placing one foot in front of the other, every step of
the way in control. An exquisite dragon with not a creative
bone in her body, she fed on other people's ideas, draining
them of their inspiration. And what a moody bitch she was.
For the past ten years I'd watched her discard writers and
directors and editors and camera operators with the cold,
petulant disregard young girls sometimes show for an old
doll, throwing it cruelly into a carton in the back of the
closet or a dark corner in the attic, banishing it from their
lives forever. She treated the romantic interests in her life
no differently. Her men came and went, and if they stayed
they always gave her something in return: a job, money for
a film, part ownership of a luxury apartment for next to
nothing.

I distrusted Karla Menzel. I disliked her tactics, was wary

of her whims, and loathed her perfume. It made me queasy.
But there was no getting around it: she and I were a team. We
needed each other. I needed a producer and she an artist. "You
don't need her," Professor Bloch once said to me. "You can go
out on your own now." Maybe I could. But I wasn't so sure I
wanted to. And until I knew what I wanted to do, it was best
to stay put.

In any case, I had a bad night.

After an hour of tossing and turning, I summed up my
options. I could 1) remain in bed torturing myself, counting
sheep or roast suckling pigs, searching my soul for the origins
of my insomnia, waiting for sleep to finally overcome me; 2)
finish off the bottle of raspberry schnapps I still had left over
from Felix, hoping I would eventually pass out; 3) boil up some
water and brew a cup of chamomile tea, letting the herbs nurse
me naturally into snooze mode; 4) take two of those over-the-
counter sleeping pills Marsha gave me during my last trip to
New York, accomplishing the above chemically; or 5) sit down
at my desk, and start transcribing the tapes from my trip to
the States in May and June.

I opted for a combination of 2, 3, and 5.

I never used to have trouble falling asleep. I could conk
out anywhere: in a car in transit through East Germany to
Helmstedt, at a table in a crowded, smoky bar, on the beach
in the sun, at my typewriter, in the A-train. But for the past
year, especially since my enlightenment during the Rochester Malone interview, I'd been plagued by irregular sleeping
habits.

"It's nerves," said Heike the Sensible One.

"Nah," said Barry. "It's hormones. You're not getting
enough sex, sex, sex."

"You need a new mattress," said Martin. "Be nice to your
back."

"You need exercise," said Professor Bloch. "Be nice to your heart."

"It's Germany," said my mother. "You're homesick. Be nice to me and come home."

"Homesick?" said Marsha. "You're just sick. Period. Find a psychiatrist."

Personally, I thought they were *all* right. I was a mess, a nervous wreck, the neurotic sum of all my fears. I was afraid of failing; I was afraid of succeeding. I was afraid of not being taken seriously; I was afraid of being taken too seriously. I was afraid of losing my health. I was afraid of losing my mind. I was afraid of losing the lease on my apartment. The only thing I wasn't afraid of losing was a pound or two and there I was botching it all up by gorging on roast pig!

I sneezed. The dust in my apartment was monumental. My clear-the-clutter binge had given the scuzz cells in my apartment more breathing space, new life, new strength and stamina, and they got a kick out of attacking my nose.

The apartment was cold; the heat had been off since I left the house at seven. I shuffled into the kitchen, put up some water, and poured myself a quick shot of schnapps.

"Achoo," I sneezed.

Actually it was five achoos. I always sneeze five times in a row, something that never fails to make my friends crack up.

Once, years ago, on my live radio show, I sneezed, and a few days later I received fan mail from East Berlin. Fifteen kids had joined in what they called a "citizens' initiative" and signed an appeal demanding that I sneeze again on my show. This was during the days of the Wall. It was quite daring of them and I felt very flattered. Then, just a few days ago, while I was in the midst of writing all this down, a fellow came by

to put up new venetian blinds. We got to talking and he recognized my voice from radio and mentioned that he had been
in that "citizens' committee." He also told me that a few years
after the Great Sneeze, while in the East German *Volksarmee*,
he was on duty one night and was caught by a superior listening
to the radio without authorization. To be precise, he was caught
listening to *West* radio. To be even more precise, he was caught
listening to *me*. As a result of this heinous crime he was put into
military prison for three days. "And that's no bowl of cherries,"
he told me. I gave him a twenty-dollar tip.

Now I turned the thermostat up and went to the hall closet
for a sweater. As I opened it, my father's gray pin-striped suit
jacket jumped out at me. I had forgotten to take it to the tailor's.
I had found it a few days before in the carton with the pompoms and the rest of the memorabilia I had shipped to Berlin
in June. It was the only thing of my father's that I managed to
rescue from my mother.

It was quite a treasure. It was a treat just running my
fingers across the soft, fine cashmere. Custom-made and lined
with pastel gray silk, it bore a label on the inner breast pocket
that read McByrne's of Beverly Hills.

I pulled the jacket off its hanger and slipped into it. It was
far too large across the shoulders and chest, too tight across
my hips, with sleeves too long and too wide. But my tailor was
a genius. When he got finished with this, no one would ever
know it had once belonged to Mr. Samuel Nathan Bernstein,
the Swindler.

The kettle whistled. As I prepared my sleepy-time tea, I
made a mental note to go to the tailor's the next day. I grabbed
the raspberry schnapps and headed for my desk.

The Swindler
(December 1980)

"Isn't it beautiful?" my father said.

Indeed it was. Two Hundred South Bellamy Drive was a magnificent structure. Its twin white towers soared skyward above the otherwise imposing ranch-style stucco villas of the area, making them look strangely stunted. This elegant edifice seemed to have dropped from the sky onto the outer fringe of lovely, demure Beverly Hills, bullying the neighborhood into surrendering an entire county block for it to spread out its two twenty-story-high wings.

"Isn't it beautiful?" repeated my father, Samuel Nathan Bernstein. "To think that we live here! I love it. I love California. It's like being on vacation every day of the year. That cold of yours will be gone by morning."

Just the mention of the word *cold* brought on another sneezing and coughing attack. The flight from New York, where I had spent ten days after arriving from Berlin, had been quite an ordeal. My head felt like a slab of concrete, my throat like sandpaper, my chest was like a sack of gravel.

The light turned green and the Silver Shark, my father's brand-new fresh-from-the-factory powder gray 1980 Cadillac sedan, glided across the street.

"What weather!" he exulted. "Just last week your mother threw out all our old winter clothes. Who needs them? Those blustery New York winter days are history. Still, I wish she hadn't thrown out my black overcoat with the epaulets. That was dumb of her. You never know."

As we passed the building's front entrance, an old lady in a sundress and a veiled straw hat was pushing a shopping cart full of grocery bags up the red-carpeted incline. A little white poodle pitter-pattered beside her. The dog barked at a black doorman in livery standing under the striped canopy.

"That's Huey," my father reported. "The doorman, that is. The poodle's Pepita."

The Silver Shark slowed down. "Ralph's Supermarket is just down the block, right next to your mother's hairdresser. Your mother saw Jane Fonda there the other night at the frozen foods. Then when she went back to her cart, she realized someone had stolen her purse. That was very stupid of her. You gotta watch out around here."

"Dad," I said as we made a sharp right, "don't you have any other adjectives for Mom except dumb and stupid?"

"Hey, can't you take a joke? Here's the garage."

He reached up to the sun visor and pushed a button on a little box that looked vaguely like a television remote. "Open sesame!" he said with exaggerated bravura. The garage gate lifted and we descended into the dark underbelly of 200 South Bellamy. Then he pressed another button and the gate lowered behind us. "A genie, it's called. Great invention. Whoever patented it must be a millionaire by now. Have a look." He leaned over and pried the remote off the sun visor, gasping from the exertion.

"Hey, take it easy," I said. "How's your heart?" He'd had three bypasses.

Steering the car carefully through the garage aisles, he said, "Hey, did I tell you that Davey'll be here with Sheila on Sunday? And Joycey'll be here in a half hour or so —"

"Dad, what does the doctor say?" I blew my nose.

"My pressure's normal." A pause. "With medication." Another pause. "But it's not bad for a sixty-year-old. It went up the day that charlatan Reagan won, but now it's back down again. I can safely say that at the moment my heart's doing better than your nose."

I sneezed.

"So what do you think of the place?" my father asked.

As garages went, it was quite attractive. Its collection of Lincoln Continentals, Rolls-Royces, Ferraris, Porsches, BMWs and Jaguars made my father's Cadillac look modest by comparison.

"I did good, didn't I?" he said, sliding smoothly into his reserved parking space, his face beaming. "Tell your father how proud you are."

"The building's very nice, Dad."

"Is that all you can say? Give me a kiss and say it like you really mean it."

"I'm tired, Daddy. I'm jet-lagged. I'm sick. Gimme a break."

"What are you so touchy about? Is it so hard to tell your father you're proud of him? Look, I don't want any bad moods in my house. Don't let your mother see that mug of yours. She's a nervous wreck as it is."

On the way up from the garage we paid a call on Huey. The lobby was one-hundred-percent state-of-the-art schlock: marble floors, velvet wallpaper, plastic rain-forest flora, overstuffed couch landscapes, signs pointing toward the fitness room, the sauna, the swimming pool, the roof garden, the sun terrace.

"Hey, Major, how ya doin'?" Huey greeted my father.

Major? Since when was my father a major? He left the air force a first lieutenant.

"I'm doing just fine, Huey. My little girl's in from Germany. From Berlin." My father put his arm around me possessively. I hated it when he did that.

"How ya doin', Miss Bernstein," Huey said politely.

"Here, Huey," my father said, pulling a twenty-dollar bill out of his wallet and tucking it ostentatiously in the doorman's breast pocket. "Take good care of my daughter while she's here."

"You bet, Major," Huey grinned, picking up my suitcase and pressing the elevator button.

"What's this 'major' stuff?" I asked once the elevator doors had closed. "Since when are you a major?"

"That's what they call me around here."

"You told them you were a major?"

"A little fib can't hurt."

"Why so modest? Why not a colonel? Or a general? Doesn't a general command more respect than a major?"

"Don't be such a smart aleck. Is that all we're going to be doing the next ten days — fighting?" He was shifting into his feisty mode. "And when you call me at the office, don't use my name. Just ask for the Major. The boys call me Major. Or Benjamin Franklin."

"Benjamin Franklin?!"

"Don't make those big eyes at me! It's my name for the customers. They get a kick out of it. It's a name they can't forget."

"God forbid they should have to remember you're a Bernstein instead of a Benjamin."

"An all-American name can't hurt in my business."

"What, Bernstein's not American enough for you?"

"Don't be such a sourpuss."

At fifty-eight, when most men his age were acquiescing to their aches and pains and pension plans and retiring to a one-bedroom condo in Florida, Samuel Nathan Bernstein had still been dreaming big dreams. Flouting the gods, my mother's fears, his cholesterol levels, long-overdue debts and bounced checks, my father decided to make one last go for it. He gathered up his life's savings (the returns from a big win at Aqueduct the week before) and bought some sunglasses, a pair of bermuda shorts, and two one-way tickets to LAX.

"Telephone sales — that's the future," he told me ecstatically when he called me in Berlin shortly after his arrival in Los Angeles in 1977. "Selling stationery en bloc on the phone. To companies, schools, corporations. Let me tell you, it beats selling rubber raincoats in Newfoundland, right?"

"Well, I guess," I said evenly.

" 'You guess'? Boy, does it take a lot to please you! In just a few hours I take in thousands of dollars of orders! It's great! I'm home by one in the afternoon and I spend the rest of the day out at the swimming pool, or reading. And if I decide to play hooky, I got twenty other guys working the phone lines for me."

What? Samuel Nathan Bernstein, the perennial loser, the job-to-job, door-to-door con artist, this one and only father of mine was a *boss?* And not only a boss, the *president* of a company?

"Becky, you still on the phone? The connection with Berlin is awful."

"Yes, Dad."

"Tell me how proud you are of me."

"Dad, do companies really buy stationery and things sight unseen?"

"There are suckers out there, baby. They buy anything. Besides, everyone knows what a legal pad and a number-two pencil look like, right?"

"But to buy in *bulk*, sight unseen?"

"If the customer's hemming and hawing or isn't ordering enough, I give them some bait. Maybe I offer them their own personal portable TV or a cassette recorder."

"So you make them into criminals too! You bribe them."

"There's nothing criminal about an incentive."

"And where do you get these incentives?"

A pause.

"Dad?"

"Overstock."

"What does that mean, 'overstock'?"

My mother suddenly piped up on the other extension. "Let's change the subject. Come on, Sam, this is an expensive phone call. Becky, how's the weather over there?"

"It's so cold, the wolves have left Czechoslovakia and crossed the border into Germany. What does 'overstock' mean? Hot goods?"

"What are you, the FBI? Why should I tell you the tricks of my trade?" my father snapped back. "You're my *daughter*."

And therewith the subject was dropped, blotted out of existence. It dived headfirst off the face of the earth.

"I did good, didn't I?" my father said into the phone.

"My God! You look awful!" my mother exclaimed, hugging me. "What did they serve on the flight, pneumonia?"

She, though, looked terrific, bubbly and smily, a little chubbier than when I had last seen her, her hair redder than ever, curlier, and stiffer than cardboard. Her hairdresser must have been doubling as a sculptor to get it all chiseled into place like that.

She took a few steps back to study me, then shook her head. "Good thing I have some chicken soup on the stove. Okay, so you'll have a quick dinner, take a decongestant, a warm bath, and go straight to bed."

"Thanks, Mom," I said dryly. Here I was, less than a minute in her presence, and she was already mapping out my schedule.

"But first, Gloria, we take her on a tour of the apartment,"
my father put in.

Drenched in golden late-afternoon California sunshine,
their new three-bedroom apartment overlooking the city was
more spacious and more sumptuous than any home my parents
had ever known.

"Look at this," my mother said proudly, leading me into
the kitchen, "one of those new microwaves."

"Gloria," my father needled her, "I bought it a year ago,
and you still don't know how it works."

My mother's mouth twitched. "Leave me alone, Sam! I
haven't had the chance to read all the instructions yet."

"What a waste of money! What a waste!" he repeated,
shaking his head.

Jesus, who was *he*, crabbing around like that? *He* was the
one who threw the money out the window. There was a time
when he had gambled away every last cent at every damn race-
track up and down the northeastern seaboard, when he had
run up so many debts and had so few reserves that he went
and hocked our stupid *toaster* to pay for breakfast. Maybe
that's why my mother was so leery of tackling the microwave.
She probably thought it would end up like its predecessor in a
pawnshop.

"So show me the rest of the joint," I said, opting to evade
trouble.

I was duly guided through two bathrooms, a family room,
two bedrooms, and then the master bedroom done up
Japanese-style with fake ginkgo floral arrangements and a
silk screen with Mount Fuji-ish motifs. On my mother's night
table was a Barbara Cartland novel and a Weegee book I
had sent her for her last birthday with photographs of New
York from the 1930s and 1940s. On my father's night table
were the three "bibles" he always kept at his bedside: Dale

Carnegie's *How to Win Friends and Influence People*, star attorney Louis Nizer's autobiography *My Life in Court*, and the
1958 bestseller *Only in America* by Jewish humorist Harry
Golden.

"Wait till you see the closet," my father said. "It's bigger
than our whole bedroom in Forest Hills."

He wasn't exaggerating. It was a walk-in closet of at least
a hundred square feet. Quite a luxury for the son and daughter
of immigrants, for two people who had spent so many years
living from hand to mouth.

"And here are my shirts," my father said, pointing to a
shelf in the closet where a jolly array of Chinese-laundered
shirts lay neatly folded. "Look at those colors! The blues and
the greens. Aren't they beautiful? Feel the silk."

"My fingers are dirty," I said, twisting a tissue in my hand.
"I'd just get them full of germs and snot."

"Do you have to be so graphic?" my mother said, making
a face.

"What do you think of this?" my father said excitedly.
He pulled a gray pin-striped suit jacket from one of the
upper racks. "I'm going to wear it to our party tomorrow
night."

"Party?"

"I'm throwing a party for some friends. I'll brief you
later. So what do you think?" He slipped into the jacket. "It's
custom-made. I got it at McByrne's of Beverly Hills. Cost me a
fortune, but it's worth every penny. Feel the cashmere. Isn't it
beautiful?"

I started to reach out, but my mom jerked my hand away.
"No you don't! Wash your hands first, Becky. They're full of
you-know-what."

Something glittery on the jacket's breast pocket caught my
eye. "What's that?" I asked, pointing.

"Your Phi Beta Kappa pin."

"That's what I thought. You're wearing *my* pin?"

"So?"

"You go around wearing *my* pin? You go around letting people think you're in an honor society?"

"What's the matter? Is there a law against getting top grades in college?"

"Of course not. But they weren't *your* grades, Dad. They were *mine*."

"And you're my daughter. And I'm proud of you!"

I sighed, and just then the doorbell rang.

The chicken soup helped. The steam unstuffed my nose. I sneezed, my ears unplugged, I heard my father's voice.

"I don't want you and Joycey going to that Hungarian deli, that Szolnok's! The other day the shoddy Romanian restaurant around the corner from it was robbed. They locked all the customers and the personnel up in a freezer and ran off with the cashbox."

"Listen, Dad, why are you telling me this now? I'm eating, for God's sake. And I have a cold." I sneezed.

"Daddy's telling you this because" — my mother interrupted herself to reach into the pocket of her smock, pull out a Kleenex, and thrust it at me — "Daddy's telling you this, sweetheart, because he wants you to know that you have to be careful around here."

"Do you know how many people were murdered last week in Los Angeles?" my father continued.

"I know, I know! It was the first thing you told me on the way home from the airport."

"And listen," said my mother, "just last week in the supermarket at the frozen foods —"

"Your purse was stolen! Everything including your driver's license, credit cards, and sunglasses. So I know!"

"And don't you forget it!" said my father. "Promise me you won't go out alone at night."

"I promise."

"And promise me you'll hide your money in your bra when you go out."

"I can't promise you that."

"Why not?"

"I don't wear a bra."

"Are you telling me they don't wear bras in Germany? And they don't shave their legs either. Right? Do me a favor, Becky," he said, slapping a twenty-dollar bill down on the table. "Buy yourself a bra. And while you're at it, get a razor and some shaving cream."

Joycey squeezed my thigh under the table. "You don't know how happy I am to see you, sister-belle," she whispered in my ear.

I knew.

"Becky," began my mother, "did I tell you that your sister-in-law has a new —"

"My sister-in-law?"

"What, is Sheila not your sister-in-law?"

"Oh, Sheila. Well sure, but —"

"You don't like the word sister-in-law?" my father butted in.

"What makes you think that? I just think of Sheila as Sheila and not —"

"Don't people get married in Germany?" my father went on. "Do they all live like you?"

This territory was too dangerous to tread.

"So, Mom, what about my sister-in-law?" I asked.

"Forget it," she said.

I sneezed, and then coughed. My father slurped a spoonful of his soup, and then gagged. "The soup is cold!" he growled. My stomach somersaulted. Joycey froze in her seat. "The soup is cold, Gloria!"

"It was hot when I brought it to the table," came my mother's reply. "You haven't stopped talking long enough to eat."

He held up the bowl. "Heat it up!"

"Dad," I interceded as good-humoredly as I could, "don't you know how the microwave works? Why don't you just go and heat the soup up yourself? Or haven't you read the instructions yet?"

Samuel Nathan Bernstein stood up, made a beeline for the sink, and poured my mother's broth down the kitchen drain. "Where's the meat loaf?" he asked gruffly.

My mother rose to serve the rest of dinner.

"Isn't that awful about John Lennon?" Joycey said. "I felt so bad."

"Me too," I agreed. "Imagine being gunned down by someone who wants your autograph. I was deejaying the day we found out. I changed my whole radio program and played Beatles songs for two hours straight."

"You, a disk jockey," said my father with a smirk. "As if you knew anything about rock music. You know books and you know *Annie Get Your Gun*. You can't fool me."

He was not too far off target. I loved musicals. And literature. Rock 'n' roll was not a passion, just something I sometimes liked. But never would I admit that to him.

"My radio work pays the rent more than sufficiently," I replied.

"You're not a disk jockey. You're a fake."

"Me, a fake? Oh please, give me a break! Who am I talking to here? Sam Bernstein? Or Major Ben Franklin?"

"Well, if you ask me," he said, ignoring my comment, "you would have been better off becoming a lawyer. You're smart enough. You still can."

"Or at least you could marry one," added my mother.

"I'm fairly happy with Jürgen, thank you. Even if he is only an architect."

"Well, if you change your mind, this town's full of lawyers," said Joycey. "Lawyers and realtors."

"They're all crooks," said my father.

"Right, Dad!" I shot back. "They're all crooks, and you want me to be one, too. And anyway, who's the crook around here? What about all of you over at Beverly Hills Paper and Pen?"

"Larry's not a crook!" came Joycey's protest. Larry Scadutto, my sister's boyfriend, was one of my father's better salesmen. And the only honest one. Maybe.

"But his family's Mafia. His uncle's been in jail for over ten years!" said my father.

"Larry's uncle's really Mafia?" I asked.

"Joey Coca Cola," said my father with reverent awe in his voice.

How enamored my father was of all the Joey Coca Colas of the world, of all the con artists, petty thieves, and grand impostors he had known or hoped one day to meet. When he was growing up in the twenties and thirties, most boys his age dreamt of becoming Coolidge, Hoover, or Roosevelt. But not my Dad. His heroes were Dutch Schultz, Al Capone, Meyer Lansky, Lucky Luciano.

"He's not his *uncle*," Joycey said. "Joey Coca Cola is Larry's *cousin* twice removed. You can't really call that family."

"It's family. And it's the Mob," my father said, putting an end to the subject, period.

We turned our attention to our meat loaf, mashed potatoes, and green beans.

"Talking about lawyers," said my father, "there's something I want you to know about tomorrow night, Becky." Uh-oh, it was the 'briefing.' "The party's gonna be a small gathering — the four of us and Larry, my partner Ernie . . . and three other guys and their wives. Some rich friends of mine."

"Rich friends? From where?" I asked. "The Phi Beta Kappa Beach and Cabana Club?"

"Don't be such a smart aleck!"

"Okay, so some people are coming. I'll say hello. What's the big deal?"

"No big deal. I just want you to know that your mother and I are thinking of buying a horse and they may be selling it to us."

I was shocked. "A horse? A racehorse? You're thinking of buying a horse?!"

"It's a good investment!"

"A good investment? Health insurance is a good investment. A pension plan is a good investment. Dad, you're sixty years old. What do you want with a horse?!"

"Look, I don't need you to tell me what to do!" He was really getting angry now. "I just want you to know that my business with those three men is very delicate. I want you to know that they trust me. And I want you to know that they think I'm an attorney. I'm telling you this so you don't go and blabber something stupid. I don't want to lose their good-will."

"They think you're an attorney?!?" My voice had risen a few decibels. "How do you do this? How do you pull off this shit? Where do you get all your information? From Louis Nizer?"

"I told you, Sam, she'd never go along with this!" My mother was pretty upset.

"Just count me out!" I screamed at him. "I'm supposed to lie for you? I'm supposed to tell people you're a lawyer? My God, are you drawing up contracts with them as if you really *were* a lawyer?"

"Of course not. But I could have been a great lawyer!"

"But you're *not*, Dad!" I got up.

If I was a kid and my father hadn't already had three heart bypasses, I'm sure he would have smacked me. Instead, he just jumped up from the table so abruptly his chair fell over backwards.

"Ooohhh!" my mother screeched. "Ooohhh, he's breaking the furniture. Omigod, he's breaking the furniture."

"I'll break your *head*, Gloria, if you don't shut up!" It actually sounded like he meant it.

"Calm down, Mom," Joycey begged.

"Where are you going?" my father barked at me gruffly. I was near to tears.

"I'm out of here," I said. I grabbed my cigarettes.

"Where are you going?" I heard my mother shout after me.

"To Szolnok's!" I shouted back, slamming the door.

It was pleasant up in the roof garden of 200 South Bellamy. It was nicer than Szolnok's, that was sure. The sun had already gone down, but the winter sky was still streaked with wisps of oranges and pinks and reds. Nighttime Los Angeles was spread out before me: thousands of miniature houses twinkling far below in a sea of glittering, jittery lights. There was a soft breeze, and you could hear the water lapping against the sides of the rooftop swimming pool. Plop-plop-kerplop. I smelled chlorine. And jasmine. It was surprising to catch a whiff of jasmine at Christmas.

I lit another cigarette and inhaled long and deep, coughing.

Why did I always forget how ugly it was being home? When I hadn't seen my parents for any length of time, I often envisioned us being friends. I saw my mother and me going off together, shopping contentedly for a whole day, perhaps taking in a matinee; later, my father and I would sit around smoking cigarillos, warmly and intelligently exchanging our views on the merits of Mario Puzo's *The Godfather.*

No way. No way was reality anything like that. No matter how much I willed it, it wasn't meant to be. But why, I wondered, was I fighting it? Why couldn't I just accept it, laugh at them and go on with my life, a little the wiser for it? Why did I always come back hoping we'd be different?

The moon came up. I sighed, leaning on the ledge of 200 South Bellamy Drive.

"It's chilly outside. Take this."

I whipped around, startled by the sudden nearness of the voice. My father was holding out his gray pin-striped suit jacket. Damn it!

I turned back away from him, toward the moon, toward downtown L.A., toward the world.

My father took a step forward and gently placed the jacket over my shoulders. I refused to move, wince, flex a muscle, breathe.

He took another step forward and leaned against the railing beside me. "I figured you'd be up here," he said.

Silence.

"I remember how you always used to hide up on the roof in Far Rockaway when you wanted to get away."

More silence.

"Remember?" he said.

I did, but I said nothing.

"Remember the time the super caught you and your girl-friend Marsha smoking up there?" I wasn't looking at him, but I knew he was smiling. "Remember how he went up there with his hunting rifle because he thought you were robbers?"

Oh, how could I forget?

My father was laughing now. "He should have been sent to jail, chasing after two twelve-year-olds like that with a loaded rifle and a German shepherd!"

"But instead of getting *his* ass, Dad, you got mine!"

"Oh, the young lady has finally found her voice?"

"Instead of reporting *him* to the police, you smacked *me* around."

"Come on! You shouldn't have been up on the roof smoking at your age. You could have gotten killed up there."

I looked down over Los Angeles. The sky was black now, the stars were out. Somewhere not far below us I heard "Jingle Bells" on a radio. I took a drag on my cigarette.

"But then right in the middle of hitting me, you stopped," I said.

"I did?"

"Yeah. You kept on asking me where I got the cigarettes. So finally I said, 'From you. I took them out of your pocket.' And when I said that, you suddenly stopped hitting me and started to laugh."

"Yeah, I remember that now." There was a note of wonder in his voice. I believe he did remember.

"I guess you realized how hypocritical you were," I said.

"I remember now. I remember thinking how smart it was of you to give me that answer. Not just because you showed me I was a hypocrite. But because you one-upped me at my own game."

"I did?"

"The cigarettes weren't mine. The super showed me yours.

They were menthol. I never smoked menthol. I smoked plain Tareytons until I quit and switched to pipes."

"Right. I remember that now. I forgot."

"You got me at my own game. And then I bawled like a baby."

"You cried? No, you didn't. You were laughing. You were laughing so hard your eyes teared up."

"I was *crying*. It hit me that you might turn out like me."

"God forbid."

"So I bawled. I thought you'd end up a wise-guy gun moll or something."

"Right! Phi Beta Kappa scholar runs amuck."

"And then I hugged you. Remember? I hugged you so hard, Mommy thought your lungs would collapse."

Silence.

"You don't remember, Becky?"

"Maybe. I dunno. No. I don't." But I did.

My chest hurt. It was raw. I evaded my father's gaze, taking a last drag on my cigarette. I coughed — a raspy, miserable cough.

"But you didn't turn out like me," my father said. "Although when I think about it, I *should* have beaten you to a pulp." He wagged his finger at me. "If I had beaten you to a pulp, maybe you wouldn't be smoking today."

"Maybe." I chuckled softly. "But then maybe I would never have —"

"Never have what?"

"Forget it."

"What?"

"Nothing."

"Come on."

"I said 'nothing'!"

I took in a deep breath. The jasmine stung my nose. It was lovely.

"Listen," I said, "I'm tired. I'm jet-lagged. I've got a cold. I'm going down."

"Go on. I'll come in a few minutes," he said softly, looking out over twinkling, moonlit Los Angeles. And then, gently shaking his head back and forth, he said one last time in sheer wonderment, "Look, Becky, look. Isn't it beautiful?"

"Yes, Dad, it is," I whispered.

I turned away from my father and started walking toward the exit, snuggling into the soft cashmere of the gray pin-striped suit jacket. My head was clear now, but my chest still hurt. I really shouldn't be smoking, I thought. What a lousy habit. Maybe he's right. If he had beaten me to a pulp, maybe I wouldn't be smoking today. But then maybe, I thought again with astonishment, but then maybe I would never have loved him either.

I opened the door to the roof garden of 200 South Bellamy Drive.

"Night, Major," I said softly, but loud enough for him to hear.

Chapter Five

Monday, October 26, 1992
Diet Week: 4
Day: 1
Weight Loss: 6 lbs. (help!)
Very early morning

After five hours the roast suckling pig seemed to have finally receded into my digestive past. My head, on the other hand, felt cranky and unfocused. It desperately needed sleep, although for the last five minutes it had begun to feel light and silly from alcohol.

The desk clock blinked 2:31 A.M. I took a long gulp of the chamomile tea. And then another tiny sip of the raspberry schnapps. I had to be careful with the schnapps. It contained dangerous calories that could sneak up on you in the middle of the night.

An image of my bathroom scale flashed in front of me. I shuddered at the memory of standing on it a half hour before. Cruel, but true: I had gained two entire pounds. How could one roast suckling pig and three spoonfuls of *marquise au chocolat* wreak so much havoc?

I shook my head and reached for my Dictaphone. I

began transcribing a conversation with my brother-in-law,
Larry Scadutto, during a car ride last summer.

> ME: Sunday, June 29, 1992, 7 A.M. Larry's driving me to the airport.
> We're at a gas station near Mission Viejo. Larry, you were just
> saying something about my mother.
>
> LARRY: I was saying your mother always buckled under your father.
> It was his fault.

I locked the pause button, scribbled the sentences down, re-
leased the button again. The minicassette tape jerked forward.

> LARRY: The ridiculous things he did. He spent $45,000
>   to buy a racehorse. Who in their fucking right
>   mind does that?
>
> BACKGROUND VOICE: Bring me two packs of sugarless Dentyne!
>
> GAS ATTENDANT: That'll be $10.00.
>
> LARRY: Here you go.
>
> GAS ATTENDANT: Have a nice day.
>
> LARRY: You bet.

I transcribed it all — word for word.

I yawned. Or was it a belch? Or had I possibly cried out
for help? If I had cried out, maybe I could still hear the tailend
of my echo. I froze for a moment and listened. Nothing — just
my apartment breathing, the #101 bus passing by five flights
below, the wild beat of my heart. And in the bedroom, CNN
was having a hell of a time: *Governor Bill Clinton of Arkansas,*

hot on the presidential campaign trail, took time off for a nice cold beer. . . .

A pang of anxiety shot through my stomach. I *had* to sleep. There was no way I could get through the next day on no sleep, especially if I started it out drunk. I pushed the schnapps away, plopped the Dictaphone down on my desk, and grabbed my appointment calendar. Before meeting Heike for dinner I had jotted down my to-do list for the next day:

1. plants
2. eyebrows
3. Menzel — 10:30 A.M.
4. fruits
5. bed?
6. hair
7. Professor > skat?
8. ring binders: 1985–1987
9. Bernini press release

I took a deep breath. I'd survive. My appointment with Karla would be a nerve-racker, but otherwise it looked like an easy day. Who needed a brain to water plants, buy cantaloupes and cucumbers, pluck eyebrows, telephone Martin about delivering a new bed, unclutter three years' worth of binders with old radio manuscripts, or play skat? Granted, if I couldn't sleep, I might be too tired to write a decent blurb for my Bernini interview. Would I be too distracted to dye my hair? But if I did get some sleep, maybe I could take another look at "Bingo Berlin" and shorten it a bit. Which reminded me —

I picked up my pen and wrote down:

    10. call *Benno Fabian* / Illustrations
and then added:
    11. Tailor — Dad's suit jacket
to the list.

I looked again at the clock — 2:42 A.M.

I took a gulp of my sleepy-time tea and then a sip of my schnapps. I picked up my Dictaphone. It wasn't as nice as the one I'd had with me in New York — the one that disappeared from my pocketbook on a shopping trip to Macy's. This one was a cheap replacement I'd bought after my arrival in Orange County. I tapped the forward button. The California highway came into view.

> ME: We've paid for the gas and Larry is steering his fire red Chevy Camaro sportscar out of the gas station onto El Toro Boulevard. Where are we going, Larry?
>
> LARRY: A few blocks down on the right we'll get the bagels, although the coffee's not so great.

I liked Larry Scadutto's New Jersey accent. My brother-in-law reminded me of the Italian boys I used to go to school with, Fat-Face Frankie Moronelli, Joey Depinna, and Jack Bianculli.

> LARRY: They don't have the fresh-roasted gourmet coffee there, you know, the vanilla nut and the Kona Blend, the kind your sister likes. But the bagels are good. The best in Orange County. (Pause)
>
> ME: (to the Dictaphone): We're looking out the window at what must be a typical southern California summer morning. The streets are completely empty of humans but packed with a never-ending procession of well-kept, squeaky-clean, middle-income cars. The sky is a dirty gray, heavy with a blanket of

smog which looks to me like it won't burn off for hours. We see a doughnut shop . . . a hamburger takeout . . . the entrance to a minimall . . . two used car lots, and on the right a cleaners, a medical building, and a drive-up bank. Now, Larry, you were saying —

LARRY: I was?

ME: You were saying my mother always buckled under my father.

LARRY: Yeah. You know, Becky, your mother's a pretty tough lady. How the hell could she let him convince her to do that? A racehorse. So stupid.

ME: Who was stupid? Him or her?

LARRY: Both! Him. You know, maybe I'm blowing my own horn here, maybe I have too much ego, but when Joycey and I were getting started and were going to get married, your father should have taken the opportunity to get me involved in his business. Instead, he got this ex-con criminal Ernie to run the joint for him and then run it into the ground. He should have thrown the bum out on his ass.

ME: So you think it was Ernie who messed everything up?

LARRY: He stole from your father!

At this point, I remembered, Larry had gotten a little hot under the collar. He realized it himself and started fumbling with the knot of his tie. It was a nice tie. In fact, my brother-in-law was quite attractive, especially all dressed up for work in a navy blue linen suit, light blue shirt, maroon tie. He headed a sales brigade for professional video equipment in Long Beach.

LARRY (somewhat quieter): An ex-con. The guy was an ex-con.

ME: Why do you think my father did that?

LARRY: Listen, the Major got lazy and let Ernie run the business for him. He stopped checking the books. So Ernie went and sold the orders to other people. He ran him into the ground. He took the money and ran.

ME: But why? *Why* did my father get lazy? Because of his health? Because he —

LARRY: There's the bagel place.

ME: Good. I'm starved.

According to the desk clock it was now 2:53. I locked the pause button on my recorder and took a sip of tea. A bagel. Oh, what I would do for a fresh poppyseed or garlic bagel. But there was none to be found in all of Berlin. No *kasha varnishkas* either, no *kugel*, no fresh *challah*, no borscht with sour cream, no blintzes. No *babka* cake. If ever I decide to give up on the arts, I will open a bagel bakery. Becky's Bagels, I'll call it. Or a fast-food Jewish-American restaurant called Kasha Kitchen. I love alliteration.

A fire engine screeched by, making enough racket to wake up half of Wilmersdorf. I went and pulled open the door to the balcony, letting the cold, damp air rush in and tickle my nose. It smelled like autumn outside. Like wet earth, fallen leaves, and the first day of school. It was exhilarating, a change of seasons. If only I didn't have to exhilarate all alone. If only I didn't have to crunch the crisp leaves under my feet by myself. Would I ever find someone to love and care for and share with me the sudden happiness of crunching autumn leaves?

I stepped onto the balcony and leaned out into the night. The wind crawled up the sleeves of my black silk robe and a chill rose to the nape of my neck. In the apartment across the street someone was looking at slides. Another insomniac? The curtains were open and I could see colorful images flashing on and off a naked wall. A bride and groom. A buffet. Endless smiling faces seated around endless rows of tables.

And what would he be like, and look like, this person I'd crunch leaves with? Would I know it was him if he came and knocked on my door? If he whispered "I love you, I love you," would I hear him? If he *screamed* "I love you, I love you," would I hear him?

I went back to my desk and my Dictaphone.

LARRY: Your father got lazy, Becky. (Slurp of coffee) He got lazy. (Mouth full of bagel) He left L.A., went to Vegas, bought a beautiful condo, decided to enjoy life. And that's where he went wrong. When you have a partner, you can never relax. Because you never know what's going on.

ME: Unless you really trust your partner.

LARRY (shouting): There was no reason why the Major should have trusted Ernie. No credibility. No reputation! (Chokes on the bagel, has a coughing fit, takes a slug of coffee) How's that garlic bagel?

ME: Fine. You know, I wasn't around. But if you knew all this, why didn't you or Joycey say something?

LARRY: What are you going to say to the guy? Tell him he's a jerk? And then all of a sudden it was over anyway. He went bankrupt, his arteries clogged, his kidneys failed. He was dying. What should I have said? It wasn't my place to say anything. And anything I may have said may have made your father feel that I was just trying to worm my way in, feed off of him and his business, like I was looking for an easy ride.

I paused for a moment, remembering. We'd been getting close to L.A.; I could still see Larry maneuvering the red Chevy sports car into the exit lane, the sign directing us toward Los Angeles on the right.

LARRY: But I would never have moved to Las Vegas. I would have bought a house in Del Mar, some place down in north San Diego County, down by the ocean, a nice clean area, something for your mother. Las Vegas! Jesus Christ!

ME: It surprised me too. I thought they loved California.

LARRY: Your father got the Bug. That's what it was. They used to drive there every weekend from L.A. to gamble. (Steps on the gas) Okay, we're on Highway 5 now. We take this all the way to the airport.

That was when I began to notice the fog.

ME (nervous): Look how foggy it is. God, I hope it's not like this at the airport. If the plane's late, I'll miss my connection to Berlin when I get to New York.

LARRY: You're such a worrywart. What time's your flight?

ME: 9:30.

LARRY: I think it'll be okay. It'll probably burn off by then. The sun's out.

ME: Where? Where do you see the sun?

LARRY: Believe me, it's there.

ME: The Bug. You were talking about the Bug.

LARRY: It's okay if you gamble once in a while, but when you live in Vegas and have those bad habits, forget it. And that's another thing. He and Ernie, they just gambled away a lot of money. On the weekends, when Joycey and I went to visit your parents, it would be nothing for them to go through a couple of thousand dollars each, placing hundred-dollar bets on three or four games at a time. That's sick!

I shut off the Dictaphone. 3:09 A.M. My eyelids felt heavy. Where was I when all this was happening to my parents?

When I visited them in Las Vegas with Jürgen in 1983 everything seemed fine. We had a splendid big-spender dinner at
Caesar's Palace. My father had just acquired his second Cadillac, the one I christened the Blue Whale. But in March 1985
when Heike and I and our old *Wohngemeinschaft* roommate
Ruth visited them, they were already selling the condo. So it
must have been 1984. They lost it all in 1984. I recall finding out about it in little snippets. Davey was angry at my father for asking him again for money. Sheila, my sister-in-law,
was angry at Davey for giving him some — the money *she*
wanted for a new dining-room set. Joycey called Ernie a free-
loader. My mother's letters to me got scarcer and scarcer. Sheila
mentioned that the $45,000 horse had broken his leg in his
first race.

"*What* happened to the horse?" I asked Sheila on the
telephone, shocked.

"Ask Davey," she said.

"What *happened* to the horse?" I asked Davey.

"Ask Mom," he said.

"What happened to the *horse?*" I asked my mother.

"Ask your father," she said.

"*For Christ's sake, what happened to the horse?*" I asked
my father.

"Ask Sheila," he said. "She seems to be telling the whole
world anyway."

But somehow I wasn't really listening.

They lost it all in 1984. They had it good for about six
years, and then *wham bang* the bubble burst. That was the
year Jürgen and I split up. Maybe that's why I wasn't paying
attention. I was in mourning. And fucking my brains out with
anyone who made the mistake of even glancing at me. I was
reinventing myself, orbiting away from radio to television. I
despised 1984.

I took a sip of the schnapps. It burned my tongue, then my throat, finally coating my stomach with another thin layer of liquid heat. I was getting noticeably drowsy.

In 1984 Jürgen and I were living alone in the Neukölln apartment.

"I must tell you something," Jürgen said to me one hot summer night as he turned out the light over the bed.

For thirteen years I'd been living in fear of those words. Someday, I knew, they'd come. And I knew I would never be the one to say them. I'm far too sentimental a girl to ever say goodbye.

"I must tell you something," Jürgen said.

And I knew it was over.

Oh, we'd both cheated. It was the era. It lent itself to flirtations and one-week flings. But neither Jürgen nor I had ever felt the urge to *tell* each other anything. Our affairs were far too unimportant and unthreatening for that.

But this, this was a threat.

No, it was more than a threat. This was *it*. This was the neutron bomb.

"I must tell you something," Jürgen said.

"Who is it?" I replied, opting for a candid blow. I dug my forehead into the pillow, hoping to fend off the growing maelstrom of emotion, but further down, in my chest, I already felt a gaping hole.

"Who is it?" I said again.

"Libgart."

"Oh, how could you. How could you?"

"I'm sorry," he said, his voice thick with contrition.

"How could you? Oh God, Jürgen," I said with all the disgust I could muster. "She has such terrible teeth!"

Jürgen turned the light on. "What did you say?" The contrition in his voice was gone.

I raised my eyes. He was looking at me as if I had gone insane.

"What did you say?" he repeated.

"I said, 'How could you? She has such terrible teeth.' " And she did. Libgart, a mathematics teacher from Minden and a friend of Ruth's, had the crookedest set of teeth I'd ever seen.

"Is that all you can say?" came his clipped reply.

"What do you mean, is that all I can say? You want me to congratulate you? Give you a medal?"

"You don't have to get so upset about this."

"About what? Her teeth or that you're nudging them?"

"For your information," he said, "she's decided to go to an orthodontist."

"Ha!" I cried out. "What people will do for love."

Jürgen jerked around, switched the light off, pulled the covers over his head, and turned his back to me. "We'll talk about it in the morning," he mumbled.

"What will we talk about in the morning? Do you need my advice or something? Would you like me to recommend a good orthodontist?"

He whipped around. "You think you're being funny, but I think you have a sick sense of humor. Are you aware that you're talking about someone I care about?"

I jumped out of bed. "Someone you *care* about?!" I screamed. "Well, excuse me for thinking you may have cared about how *I* felt." I grabbed a blanket and my pillow.

"Becky, it's not the end of the world."

"I'm not stupid. I know that. It's only the end of *us*."

I stormed out of the bedroom and into the living room, throwing my bedding down on our new Italian-design pull-out sofa. One of Jürgen's classy Scottish tweed blazers was hanging on a chair. Ever since he began earning money, he started

wearing those conservative saccos. I threw it down and
stamped on it. One of his smart paisley scarves slid elegantly
to the floor and I stamped on it too.

I marched into Jürgen's study and flicked on the lights.
The walls were freshly painted in eggshell white. The parquet
floors, recently sanded and varnished, gleamed in the bright
glow of the indirect halogen lighting. The furniture was stylishly new-wave, industrial metallic gray, austere and clean-
lined. Architectural plans for the roof garden of a squatters'
house in Kreuzberg were clipped to a rack hanging on the wall
near the balcony. On his desk were calculations for the reno-
vation of a dilapidated building near the Wall, right across
from Checkpoint Charlie. It was owned by the city and under landmark protection, being one of Berlin's oldest houses.
Jürgen planned to start work on it next year, and when it was
finished, he and his partner Ulf hoped to open up a café-bar
on the ground floor.

I spun away from Jürgen's desk and lunged for his "finished projects" cabinet. Crazy woman that I was, I pulled
out one of the two-and-a-half-ton ring binders, raised it over
my head, and heaved it down on the parquet. It landed on its
spine with a loud thump, bounced up, and fell back again,
bursting open and strewing its contents onto the floor. I kicked
the papers and they slid across the parquet in wild disarray. I
grabbed a second binder and threw it down too. And then another. After murdering the fifth binder, I returned to the living
room, collapsed on the Italian pull-out and slept fitfully until
the next morning.

Indeed 1984 was a terrible year for all the Bernsteins.

I flipped on my Dictaphone and returned to the summer of 1992 and the increasingly heavy traffic on Highway 5 as Larry's red Chevy got closer and closer to Los
Angeles.

LARRY: When you have money like that, it's important to invest it in things you can't get hurt with, because you're not going to make that kind of money year in and year out forever. Your father thought it was going to keep going nonstop. But it's just not that way. (Pauses to sip coffee) He had the time to piss away $45,000 on a racehorse, but not to take the same amount and put it in a mutual fund, in some kind of shelter so that later it would be there earning interest for him! And it's your mother who got stuck holding the bag. Your father dies and she gets stuck holding the bag. Let's face it, Becky. Your mother's gonna be 72 years old. She should be working six days a week in a hotel candy store to pay the rent?

ME (finishing bagel): She told me the other day that the Pink Palace was only giving her a 2% raise, but everyone else gets something like 4%.

LARRY: Jesus, they're real skunks over there. Your mother's not the outgoing type and that's what they like to see in the hotels, someone who can shmooze people into spending money. In the competitive world of Las Vegas it only makes sense that they want a younger, sexier kind of employee. In the back of their minds, they're hoping that if they only give her a 2% raise, she'll quit. And then they wouldn't have to pay any unemployment benefits.

ME: She's not the quitting type. But it's so cruddy. So demeaning.

I was starting to nod out. Well, it *was* 3:21 A.M.

LARRY (turning off at airport exit): We told your mother she could live here with us. But she doesn't want to come here. Your mother's a pretty stubborn lady. She — Hey, look! I think it's strawberry season.

ME: Yeah? Where?

LARRY: Over there. Just a couple of weeks ago I watched them cutting celery. Ever see celery?

The tape was over. I turned off the Dictaphone and put it down on the desk.

Celery. Didn't the hair coloring kit that Ruth gave me have celery in it?

I went to the bathroom cabinet for the botanical hair dye instructions and trudged off to bed with them. The clock blinked 3:27.

Are you tired of your limp, lifeless hair? Do you long for the silky, natural texture and the bright highlights of your youth? Whatever your reasons for being dissatisfied with your present hair color, you'll have every reason to try the new look of GENESIS.

"Let me give you one last tip," Ruth had said to me before she left Berlin for Gomera to open up a feminist beauty farm. "Fix up your hair. Touch it up. Don't they do anything for you at that TV station? It looks like that field of dried-out sorghum grain we saw in the middle of the prairie in Texas. Remember? It was grayish and dusty, and there were those old Mexican women selling lukewarm lemonade in the sun?"

"Melvin Minsky, my first boyfriend," I answered, "once told me that my hair looked like the burning bush in *The Ten Commandments* — *after* God set fire to it."

"Genesis is the name of this new product line. All natural substances, no peroxide, no nonoxynol-9, just lavender, avocado, peach, geranium, henna, basil, peppermint," she went on, handing me the kit.

And rhubarb. Not celery, but *rhubarb* was in it.

Step One: Wash hair thoroughly with enclosed scalp-stimulating shampoo of avocado and peppermint. Step Two: Rinse hair carefully of all residual shampoo. Step Three: Carefully mix, heat, and then apply the hot rhubarb rejuvenating treatment. This is a thick, sand-like substance created espe-

cially by GENESIS *to strip the gray from your hair follicles,*
allowing them to take on the natural nuances of your new hair
color. Step Four: Leave on ten minutes, then —

Oh boy. I lay down on the bed and pulled the cover over
my head. This was going to be quite a procedure. Where
in the world did Ruth ever find the time and patience to
do this? And the havoc it caused! For a moment I saw the
muddy, gooey mess she used to make in our bathroom. For
days afterward we would find drops of henna sprinkled on
our toothbrushes, decorating the wastebasket, mushrooming
on top of a powder puff. I wouldn't be able to handle that
here.

I pulled myself out of bed, stumbled through the dark into
the living room and then into my office, and finally over to my
desk. I tore open my diary and wrote:

12. Beauty parlor appointment

I got to Media Menzel at 10:30 on the dot. Don't ask me
how.

"And?" I asked Gisela, Karla Menzel's secretary, gesturing
toward Karla's door. "What kind of mood is she in?"

Located in a well-kept turn-of-the-century building on
a side street off the Kurfürstendamm, Media Menzel, though
expensively and modernly decorated, still showed traces of an
earlier era. The door to Karla's inner office domain was one
of them. Upholstered on both sides in black leather like a
tufted sofa in a Victorian men's club, the door was acoustically
impenetrable. It was very intimidating.

"Can't tell," Gisela answered. "She's either euphoric or on
the warpath. Sorry."

My stomach cringed. If Gisela was unsure about Karla's
mood, then something was definitely awry.

"Take a seat, Becky," Gisela said sweetly.

"What does she want? Is she ready to ditch me or something? Or maybe there's something wrong with the Bernini interview? Did anyone complain? Did she say anything?"

Gisela looked concerned. "I have no idea, Becky. Really, I don't. But I don't think you should be worried. Where's your self-confidence today?" She glanced at her watch. "She shouldn't be long. Patrick's in there with her now. How's your apartment doing?"

Patrick Sauermann, a twenty-eight-year-old dynamo, was Karla's latest acquisition. Newly set up at Media Menzel as head of development, he was also doing his stint as Karla's love interest. He was rather too eager for my taste and was not high on my list. And though I wouldn't have called him dull, he had that blank collegiate jock look I've never found appealing in men. And he had no manners. When I went to say goodbye to him after a recent dinner party, he stuck his tongue in my mouth. I was about to give him a peck on the cheek, but he aimed for my lips instead and then attacked. Karla was sitting on a sofa a few feet away. I was so shocked, I almost bit off his tongue.

I sighed and slid down into one of the Thonet chairs across from Gisela. "My apartment's doing just fine," I said. "It lost about a hundred pounds over the weekend."

"And you?" she asked.

"Maybe a pound and a half."

"I mean, how are you *feeling?*"

"Oh," I said, shaking my head at my own dull-wittedness, "I could have had another hour or two of sleep. But I'll —"

"Is Becky here yet?" Karla's voice boomed out over the intercom. Both Gisela and I jumped.

"Yes, she is," Gisela buzzed back.

"Send her in."

This was not euphoria. It sounded like warpath to me. I stood up to face my destiny.

"I think it'll work," Karla said. "An American discovers East Germany. A little like Rod Taylor in *The Time Machine* when he lands among the Morlocks. A stranger in a strange land. An outsider looking in. What do you think?"

I was dumbfounded. "Karla," I managed to say, "do I understand correctly? You've been asked to develop a series about East Germany after reunification —"

"For national television!" she interrupted, leaning toward me. I caught a whiff of her nauseatingly sweet perfume. It made me feel even fainter than I already felt.

"— for national television," I continued, "that presents the state of Brandenburg, that is to say the epitome of the East, to a large audience in an informative but entertaining manner."

Karla nodded. Her perfect, springy blond curls glittered.

"You've been asked," I went on like a long quotation, "to develop a unique and witty television program, mixing documentary observation with feature film elements, sitcom with cabaret, sketches with authentic interviews. And you want me to host it?"

"Correct. But you will not just host it. You'll also write it."

"And in every program, I pack my bags and hop on the commuter train to Brandenburg?"

"Or a bus or a trolley."

"Or walk," Patrick added.

"Or roller-blade," I wisecracked.

"Great idea!" He grabbed his notepad. "You'll roller-blade there! Very visual."

"So," I continued, abstaining from rolling my eyes,

"you're talking about something like, uh — I don't know — *Becky Goes Brandenburg?*"

"Hey, that's a great title!" said Patrick, slapping his hands down on his designer jeans. "I knew it was up your alley. Great title. *Becky Goes Brandenburg — An American Discovers the East*. Fantastic. Tongue in cheek, self-ironic, charming." He looked at Karla for encouragement, but she remained impassive. "It'll be a bit of this and a bit of that," he went on with gusto. "VIPs and vagabonds. Politicians and peddlers."

Where did Karla ever find this clown?

"Patrick," I said, "Karla. Don't you think *Becky Goes Hollywood* would be more up my alley? I'm very flattered that you're asking me, but let's face it, I don't know anything about the East. All I know about the state of Brandenburg is that Berlin is situated in the middle of it, and if I tried hard, I might be able to hum a few bars from the *Brandenburg Concertos*. That's it."

I was more than a little skeptical. Journalistically I was thoroughly unqualified for the job. National television was certainly nothing to sneeze at, but —

"But that's it, Becky!" Patrick was very excited. "*Nobody* in the West knows anything about Brandenburg. But you, a foreigner, are less biased than a West German would be. You'll see it with the eyes of a newcomer. That's the twist that our competition hasn't come up with yet. And that's why we want you. This'll put Brandenburg back on the map — and you in *Who's Who*."

"Don't you think I should at least know *something* about the subject of the show I'm hosting?" I went on.

"You've never been to Potsdam, Brandenburg's capital?" Karla's perfectly eye-shadowed eyes narrowed.

"Once."

"What do you remember?" She smiled encouragingly.

"I remember going on a tour of the palace, Sans Souci. We all had to take our shoes off so we wouldn't mess up the floors. They gave us these gigantic fuzzy woolen slippers. I swam in them, and they were so slippery, I fell and had a black-and-blue mark for days."

"Great story! Fantastic!" said Patrick. "We'll put that in. Very visual." His pen was at work.

"Start reading up on Brandenburg," Karla said. "Read Theodor Fontane, a few tourist guides, local Brandenburg news in the paper. Talk to people."

"Don't worry," Patrick added. "There's only four things you have to know about Brandenburg to understand it: the people are poor, it's mostly woodland, it's built on sand, it survives on brown coal. That's it."

"Sorry, Patrick. That's not enough information for me to base a whole television series on," I said dryly.

"We're only developing a pilot now, Becky," Karla said. Despite her momentary charm, I detected a tinge of impatience in her voice. It was clear to me that she wanted this project badly.

"The theme for the pilot is 'Men,' " Karla continued. "What kind of men live in Brandenburg? Who are they? What do they think, feel, want? Are they different from men in the West?" She smiled again with her perfect red lips. She had very straight teeth. "The pilot's forty-five minutes, each segment after that thirty. If we get the project, I promise you your own makeup girl. On location. We'll have to do something about your hair anyway."

"Men? Forty-five minutes on *men?*"

"Yes! That's up your alley, isn't it? You go to Brandenburg looking for men."

"Me, look for a man in Brandenburg?"

Karla laughed. She had a curiously natural laugh, something that often endeared her to me for odd split seconds.

"I would never go to *Brandenburg* to look for a man," I went on. "I need glamour, power, wealth. I need a *millionaire*, Karla, not a coal miner. Where would I ever find a millionaire in Brandenburg? I'd never —" I stopped in midsentence. The idea of searching for a millionaire in Germany's poorest province suddenly struck me as a rather intriguing concept. "A millionaire in Brandenburg," I repeated slowly, savoring the words.

"That's it!" Patrick cried out.

"Yes, maybe," I said, the idea beginning to blossom in my brain. "What if I go to Brandenburg with the inane goal of looking for a millionaire?"

"Where would you look?" Patrick asked, reaching out again for his pad and pen.

Thoughts raced through my head. "Well, in the movie *How to Marry a Millionaire* Betty Grable meets one in a fur store."

"Super!" Patrick exclaimed, jotting it down. "We'll shoot you in a Potsdam fur shop."

"But instead of bumping into a millionaire in the fur shop, I meet up with a member of a fruit farm brigade looking for a fun fur for his mother."

"We're moving in the right direction," Karla said briskly. "It could be funny. As long as the fruit farm brigadier is interesting." She stood up from the conference table. "Fine, Becky. You and Patrick set up some meetings."

"Wait a second. I haven't agreed to this. What's the time frame, for instance?" I asked.

"We begin tomorrow." Karla sat down at her desk and started signing some letters.

"Tomorrow? *What* do we begin tomorrow?"

"Research and brainstorming," Karla replied without

looking up from her desk. "And we'll start location scouting next week, before it gets too cold and gray. Our outline has to be in by mid November."

"This is really short notice, Karla." I could feel my chest muscles tighten up on me.

"Becky, you're a pro. You could interview a coal miner today if you wanted to."

"That's not the point."

"I'm going to be up front with you." Karla put her pen aside for a moment. Her voice rose in intensity. "I'm vying with two other firms to get this project. It means a lot to me. So much, in fact, I'm putting my own money into it. And that's because I believe in you and I believe in Patrick and I believe in the idea. We're talking national television. It's the chance of a lifetime. *Breakfast at Becky's* is not doing great in the ratings. Remember, you're only as good as —"

"—as your next project."

Karla smiled. "And you'll never have to worry about your next paycheck. Have you thought of that?"

I sighed.

"Becky, you'll have so many offers after this, maybe you *will* end up going to Hollywood."

I sighed again.

"So what do you say? Will you give it a try?"

I was aware of my precarious position. If I declined, wouldn't Karla make my professional life hell?

"Give me a day or two to think about it," I replied. "It's so sudden. I'm not very well versed on the subject. And I have other commitments. What about *Breakfast at Becky's*, for instance?"

"If you don't want to be hassled by a new guest, we'll air a backup interview."

"And I'm right in the midst of straightening out my apartment."

Karla's eyes narrowed noticeably. "Your apartment? You're straightening out your apartment? I'm offering you the chance of a lifetime and you're worried about doing the laundry?"

She made me sound like an imbecile. Maybe I was.

"And I'm writing. I told you about 'Bingo Berlin.' A big project like this would take me away from my writing —"

"But you'll be writing the series. You'll win a prize for it! You'll be just fine." This was Patrick from the peanut gallery.

"I don't like writing in German."

"But your German's terrific. It's better than most Germans'. You must have been very disciplined to learn the language so perfectly. How long have you —"

"I don't speak perfectly, Patrick." Oh, boy, he was really putting it on thick. "For instance, I still can't even pronounce the second word I ever learned in German."

He looked puzzled. "The second word?"

"*Stores*," I said, pronouncing it incorrectly, I was sure. "Huh?"

"What on earth are you talking about?" Karla asked.

"The curtains. The white, see-through curtains."

"Oh, *Stores!*" they both exclaimed. To me, it sounded just the same when they said it. But I'd never met a German who understood me when *I* said it.

"You see! I told you I can't pronounce it."

Karla laughed — that wonderful laugh of hers. Oh, it was so difficult to dislike her when she did that. She got up from her desk and walked toward me. "And what's the *first* word you ever learned?"

"*Mäuschen*," I replied. Little mouse. I couldn't even hear the word without remembering —

"*Mäuschen?* Great story!" Patrick said. "We'll put it in *Becky Goes Brandenburg.*"

"So what do you say?" Karla asked.

She was standing so close to me, I could have sworn *I* was wearing that awful perfume of hers. What was the name of it? Something Japanese, I thought.

"Well?" she said.

"I said give me a day or two to think about it."

"Fine, fine." She raised her arms in feigned resignation. What a *macher.*

I took a sip of my coffee. National television. It was so tempting.

"Your German's fine," Patrick said encouragingly. "How long have —"

"Do you really promise me my own makeup girl?" I asked Karla.

She nodded.

"On location?"

"Of course."

"You'll be fine," Patrick went on. "Your German's terrific. How long have you actually been here?"

"Twenty years," I answered. "I came to Berlin exactly twenty years ago."

An Education in Neukölln, or My Life Before the German Dative (1972)

Mäuschen. It was the first German word I ever learned. No, wait a second, that's not quite true. Technically speaking, the first word I ever learned to say in German was *Wohngemeinschaft*, the special "lachsery duplechs for many people"

Jürgen told me about in the sculpture garden of the MOMA. But that's not right either: the *very* first thing I ever learned in German was *auf Wiedersehen*. I picked it up in my teens along with all the lyrics to the song "Edelweiss" while listening to the soundtrack to *The Sound of Music*.

Nonetheless, I still think fondly of *Mäuschen* as being my first German word. Jürgen said it to me one evening a few days after we had met. We were sitting, or rather reclining, on a bench in Central Park, in the midst of a hot kissing session. It suddenly struck me that maybe we were courting trouble and might soon be attacked by some wandering muggers.

"*Mäuschen*, do not worry, yes?" he said to me with his clear blue eyes, that amazing grin of his, and the blatant naïveté that only a stranger to New York could possess. "*Mäuschen*, do not worry. Here we are under a light and there is Fifth Avenue and the hotels and so forth. I can even hear the taxi whistle of the doorman of the Plaza Hotel."

"I'd feel a lot safer *in* the hotel," I answered. "And, may I ask, what precisely does *Mäuschen* mean?"

"It means a little mouse," he explained matter-of-factly.

Although I was mildly shocked at being likened to a rodent, I did persuade him to find a safer (though not more comfortable) bench, where we continued to deepen our relationship.

The following day I went to Woolworth's and bought him a bright yellow pencil sharpener shaped like a mouse with a long red tail. In magic marker I wrote 'Your Moyshen' on the back of it and then signed it. He used it for years.

The second word I ever learned in German was *Stores*. I picked it up the very day I first set foot in Berlin-Neukölln. It was a glorious wintry morning. I can still remember the sunny, resplendent sky, the icy-dry air that stung my cheeks, singed my lungs, and brought tears to my eyes. I was young. I was impressionable. I was very cold.

And I was limping down the street.

My ankle had just barely escaped a break. Somehow, while walking from Jürgen's car to his apartment, unaccustomed to cobblestones, I had gotten the heel of my boot stuck in a crack. It now hung by just one nail like a milk tooth about to fall out.

It wasn't the first catastrophe of the day. The first catastrophe was Jürgen's herpes. A festering cluster of sores covering no less than one-third of his beautiful bottom lip had greeted me upon my arrival at Tempelhof Airport. He blamed it on the sudden change of weather. Yes, it *was* arctic in Berlin. The one thing I knew about Berlin before I got there was that on the map it was situated between the fifty-second and fifty-third parallels. That was the same latitude as icebound Newfoundland, where my father was once sent into exile to sell rubber raincoats. Now that was really pushing it when it came to the chill factor.

Despite the herpes, Jürgen and I kissed at the airport gate, but it was painful for him, and I must admit the taste of his medicated lip ointment was a bit unromantic. It remains one of my earliest sensory memories of Berlin.

What a sight we must have been: me hobbling down the cobblestone street with my loose right heel and my left shoulder drooping under the weight of my backpack. And there was Jürgen, his mouth covered by simplex-one parasites, striding beside me, carrying or rather *dragging* my two colossal suitcases.

The street — Kleine Oderstraße — was just one block long, dark, narrow, and lined on both sides with high, scrawny, leafless trees and crumbling gray turn-of-the-century buildings. Its sidewalk was dotted with tiny piles of frozen dog droppings. To my immediate left I noticed a row of windows in a ground-floor apartment, all dressed in flowing white semiopaque curtains.

I tottered along looking at the identically adorned windows of what must have been a very uniformly decorated apartment: one room, two, three. And then another. And another. The apartment was monstrous.

"My God," I exclaimed, stopping a moment. "How big are the apartments here anyway?"

"Which apartments are you meaning?" Jürgen asked.

"This one, for instance. Look at all the windows it has." I counted all the windows, retracing my steps. There were nine. "It goes on forever!"

"But that is more than one apartment. That is many apartments."

"But how can that be? Look, they all have the same curtains."

It took Jürgen a moment to grasp what I was getting at. But finally he did. "Aahh," he said. "The curtains."

"Yes," I said, "the curtains."

"Everyone in Berlin has them. They are *Stores.*"

"Everyone in Berlin has them? They are *Stirs?*"

"No, no. *Stores.*" He enunciated precisely.

"*Sters.*"

"*Stores.*"

"*St —*" It was exasperating. "Jürgen, do you mean to tell me that everyone in Berlin has the same white net curtains?" Was it really possible that everyone in Berlin had the same white, sheer, gauzy, gossamer, semitransparent curtains?

"No, of course not," Jürgen answered. "Sometimes they are beige."

I was shocked.

"But why *every* window?" I asked in amazement. "There

are other ways to ensure privacy. What about a little ingenuity, originality, creativity? Don't Germans believe in individual, personal taste?"

Jürgen pondered this a moment. And then another moment. After what seemed like at least half an eternity he said, "Once I have seen yellow *Stores.*"

I looked up and down Kleine Oderstraße. I went to the curb and stretched out my neck. I peered to the right of me. Behind me. To the left. And he was right. Every window far and wide was decorated with more or less identical white sheer curtains. *Every* window.

But then out of the corner of my eye I detected a naked pane, a black void, a drapeless vacuum. And then a second and a third next to it.

"Look, Jürgen!" I cried out. "Not everyone has them. Over there on the second floor. At the corner above that cigarette sign. Look, those windows don't have *Stores!*"

"You are right," he said, grinning. "That is *our* apartment! Our *Wohngemeinschaft.*"

"*Na endlich!*" said Ruth when we came through the door with my luggage. She was wearing an aluminum foil helmet on her head. "*Der Brenner ist kaputt. Kaum warst du weg, ist er kaputtgegangen. Natürlich gerade, als ich duschen wollte.*" And then turning to me she said, as if in afterthought, "Nice to meet you."

She spoke an avalanche of German. Jürgen translated while Ruth gave me a quick welcome hug. It seemed the hot water heater had given out right in the middle of Ruth's shower. I smelled something odd emanating from the helmet. It was, I was soon to learn, the sticky, muddy henna Ruth slopped on every few weeks to cover her premature gray.

Jürgen led the way into the kitchen at the back of the apartment.

"Be carefully where you are walking," Ruth warned me. "I have just only moved in."

It was a long trek down two corridors, which were cluttered with moving crates and cartons. I almost tripped over a cactus plant.

"Oh, I love the boots!" Ruth exclaimed. She pointed to the heels. "How is that named in English?"

"Heel."

"Yes. What for interesting heels. I saw a pair boots like that at Karstadt, over on Hermannplatz."

"I got them at Macy's, over on Herald Square."

Ruth was a shopper. I knew it instinctively. We would be friends.

We found Heike and Erhard, my other two new roommates, in the kitchen. They were crouched over a black, potbellied, stovelike contraption with a thick pipe that went straight up three feet and then at a right angle into the wall. It was something I believe I saw once in a movie about hillbillies.

"We are the only ones in the house with central heating," Jürgen explained. "If something goes *kaputt* we ourselves must repair it."

"And pay for it, too," Erhard added.

Central heating? Was this thing called "central heating" because it was centrally located in the middle of the kitchen, or because the dentist who had lived in the apartment before us had simply christened it that? He had stuck a tank in the basement, filled it with oil, put in some pipes, and then installed a pump to get the oil up to the second-floor kitchen where the potbellied heater boiled the water for the apartment's radiators.

"We paid the guy who lived here before five thousand marks for this piece of shit!" Erhard commented, shaking his head. "I'd be happier with a coal-burning tile stove."

Jürgen, obviously the apartment's handyman, set to work on the heater, turning switches, pushing buttons, twisting knobs. I sat down at the breakfast table.

Just one quick glance was enough to tell me two things: one, the kitchen was the apartment's family room; and two, the furnishing had not been the work of a professional interior decorator. Here were no clever themes or carefully contemplated *Better Homes and Gardens* color compatibility schemes. The yellow walls were faded and cracked and pockmarked. They were lined with wooden fruit crates painted in lively hues of red and blue and filled with the necessities of modern kitchen life: cookbooks, teas, spices, a pair of socks, dishes, noodles, plants, a curler with a clip, dried beans, a Frisbee. The windows were large, *Stores*-less and see-through-able, but the royal blue paint on the window frames was a peeling mess. A massive brown drop-leaf table that had an uncanny resemblance to a coffin stood in the center of the room. It was set for breakfast: chipped cups, a large loaf of unsliced black bread (*black* bread?), liverwurst (for *breakfast?*), a jar of honey that looked as hard as a rock, and what I presumed to be cheese — a flat, oozing, chalky white disk. Sections of a newspaper were strewn on two padded red leatherette benches that looked as if they had come straight out of a booth in a 1950s greasy-spoon diner. The linoleum was a dull olive green. I noticed a fridge without a freezer, and a sink without an automatic dishwasher. High above the sink was a plywood shelf supporting an ancient black-and-white television set. It was on. An elderly, unassuming, white-haired man with glasses was leading a round-table discussion with five grave men in serious suits.

"The *Internationaler Frühschoppen*," Erhard said. "The International Early Morning Drink." He giggled.

The international early morning drink?

"Small talk," Heike said. "For journalists. Like *Meet the Press*."

Heike had obviously been to America if she knew *Meet the Press*.

"How's your German?" she asked, pointing to the television.

"Brilliant. I can pronounce the word *Mäuschen* and I know what *Stores* are." I held out my hand.

"You know what *what* are?"

"Never mind."

"Well," she said encouragingly, shaking my hand. "I'm Heike Lindner, Edina High School, Edina, Minnesota, Class of 1966." Heike's handshake was as robust and healthy as the almost perfect American English she had learned as an exchange student. She was to begin her studies as a translator the following year, but was working for the moment as a foreign correspondence clerk to get job experience. She was my self-appointed German teacher. "We begin our studies tomorrow," she said, adding, "Your hand is like ice." What could I say? I was young. I was impressionable. I was cold.

"The International Early Morning Drink with Werner Höfer," Erhard repeated, again giggling. He was getting a kick out of his translation. He pointed his butter knife at the television set. "Four journalists from six countries." He burst out in laughter.

Four journalists from *six* countries?

"I read somewhere that Höfer is building a luxury vacation house on Sylt," Heike said to her roommates. "It's a gift from his wife's best friend. She's giving him millions to —"

"Heike, is this really important?" Erhard interrupted, stopping her in midsentence. "She likes all that gossip," he said to me. Pointing to the television with his knife, he went on, "Today they discuss about China. The People's Republic is now in the UNO instead of Taiwan. It is a big step for the International Workers' Revolution. Do you know it?"

"Yes, I have heard about it," I replied.

"Aah! So you are knowing about the International Worker's Revolution?"

"No, I meant the People's Republic. I have heard of the People's Republic."

Erhard frowned, scratching his goatee. "We must raise your political consciousness, as they say in your country, no?"

"Raise your ass and give me the paper. You're sitting on it." Ruth snatched the newspaper and sat down at the table with a cup of coffee.

"Wait a minute. I have to check the lottery results." Erhard grabbed the paper back.

"He plays the lottery every weekend," Heike said, winking at me.

"In late capitalist society," Erhard began in his defense, "the lottery is the only way to get rich without dirtying your hands."

Ruth snorted.

Erhard ignored her, pulling two lottery tickets out of his back pocket.

"I think I've got it," my Jürgen said, wiping his black, oily hands on a dish towel. "Cross your fingers." He clicked on a switch.

The potbellied stove began to shake. Then, from deep within it, a faint rumble could be heard. After a moment the shakes turned into rattles, the rumbles into thunder. And then the rattles became convulsions and the thunder a volcanic explosion.

Whoops and shouts, general rejoicing and backslapping.

"I get the shower first!" Ruth called out.

Heike placed a cup in front of me. "Some coffee?"

"What?"

The racket from the boiler was deafening.

"HAVE SOME COFFEE."

"THANKS."

"Don't worry," Jürgen said, sliding into the seat next to me and raising his voice a few decibels. "It is this loud only for a few minutes. When it reaches the right temperature it stops." He took a sip of his coffee. "For about five minutes it stops, and then it starts over again. You get used to it."

I took a sip of my coffee. It was *very* strong. I made a face.

"You will get used to the coffee too," Ruth said.

"Shit," Erhard muttered, crumpling his lottery tickets.

Heike rolled her eyes. "And *him*. You'll get used to him too. You'll get used to everything. Everything except maybe the German dative."

There was no doubt in my mind that I'd get accustomed to the German dative as well. Why not? I may have grown up in New York, but look out, you great, wide, wild world, now I was ready to be all grown-up in Neukölln. I'd learn German, get a job, and raise my political consciousness so high I'd soon be *floating* to all the protest marches!

Jürgen was terrific with his hands. Screwdrivers, hammers, and jimmies came to life under his steady, capable grip. He was more than well equipped to tutor me and the others in the wonders and quirks of the heating system in our new apartment. He was studying architecture, but before moving to Berlin from Germany's provincial northern lowlands in the mid-1960s, he had worked as an apprentice to a house painter. He was a proud member of the dying species of *Handwerker*, an artisan, although that word hardly does justice to the reverence Germans feel toward anyone privileged enough to carry the title *Handwerker*. It was an occupation, a calling, that had long since lost all significance in America.

Jürgen taught me how to get rid of holes in walls and rust in shower stalls, how to whitewash a room, mix paint and water, hang wallpaper without pasting myself to a wall, and, when we were sanding down and shellacking the parquet, how to style our daily newspaper, the *Frankfurter Rundschau*, into a protective cap, making sure, of course, that the green stripe from the title page was centered in front.

The two hundred square feet of space that Jürgen and I shared in our Kleine Oderstraße *Wohngemeinschaft* had once been a dentist's examining room. An art-deco sign on the door, BEHANDLUNGSRAUM, and an old leather reclining dentist's chair now rotting on the balcony were proof of the room's professional past. But these days, decorated in stylish junk-yard chic with furniture found on various Berlin street corners during the city's carefully orchestrated clean-out-your-cellar month in 1972, it became a lovers' den and a hub of creative energy.

We may have been living in what most people would consider cramped quarters, but to Jürgen, the youngest child in an East Prussian farm family of eight children, three of whom had been his roommates in a tiny attic dormer, it was like a convention hall. And for me, thoroughly unaccustomed to thirteen-foot ceilings with decorative floral ornaments or to rich and

succulent oakwood parquet floors, it was like residing in one
of Ludwig the Second's ballrooms.

Our balcony was an extra attraction. Besides serving as a
sundeck and a garden for parsley, basil, and chives, it was our
own little weather station, featuring a built-in wind-direction
detecting system. When we stretched ourselves out on the dentist's chair and caught a whiff of chocolate in the air, we knew
the wind was coming from the candy factory far to the east of
us, at the border with East Berlin near Treptow. The headachy,
stuffy smell of hops flew our way from the brewery just a few
blocks to the southeast. From the west the breeze blew in the
promise of green beans or cabbage from the public cafeteria
in the Neukölln town hall. The acrid smell of burning brown
coal in winter was often overpowered by the odor from the fish
packaging center right behind us to the north.

How wonderful it was — especially on warm summer
days when the wind was still and we were wafted peacefully
to sleep on the perfume of the linden trees that lined the
street.

There I was, breathing the famed *Berliner Luft*, the city's
famed "fragrant" air, living in a grown-up world with grown-
up people who knew how to renovate their own apartments,
repair fickle oil pumps, and grow fresh parsley. Here were
earnest members of society. They were nothing like the New
York theater students I knew who smoked grass on the weekends until their brains went haywire, cooked frozen TV dinners when they were hungry, and thought they were the
epitome of intellectualism when they stayed up late debating
what movie was going to win the Oscar for best film. Jürgen
& Co. were different. Hey, they discussed Marx and Freud of
their own volition. Even better: they *read* Marx and Freud
of their own volition. It was romantic. It was Europe. It was
Neukölln. And there I was, gravitating somewhere between

the fifty-second and fifty-third parallels, right in the center of a city where even in midwinter people took cold showers in the morning. And at night they slept with the windows open.

I was young. I was impressionable. I was cold.

"*Ich bin kalt, ich bin kalt,*" I complained to Jürgen when I crawled into bed at night and my naked body hit the icy sheets.

"*Mäuschen,* mir *ist kalt,*" Jürgen said, correcting me. "In German you must not say 'I am cold' but '*to me* is cold.' It's the dative. You must learn soon the dative."

And then he'd put his arms around me, hold me close, and ever so gently begin to warm me up.

As I say, Jürgen was terrific with his hands.

I was young. I was impressionable. I was in love.

"*Wo ist der Spüllappen, bitte?*" Heike said to me.

"Heike, can I ask you —" Heike gave me the evil eye.

"*Wo ist der Spüllappen, bitte?*"

I resigned myself to my fate. She wanted me to say, "Where is the dishrag, please?" For this I was putting my mouth and tongue through phonetic torture? But who was I to protest? I was young, I was impressionable. I repeated the sentence. Slower than she had said it, but correctly.

"*Gut!*"

"Thanks," I said, beaming. "Good" was about the best you could ever get out of Heike. She was very stingy with her accolades.

Heike and I were doing kitchen duty and practicing German. She was cleaning, or rather *sterilizing*, the garbage pail. I was in the midst of washing the dishes. Erhard, who was responsible for the week's food shopping, was sitting at the table drinking tea, nibbling on some bread and sausage, and calculating our household costs.

"Hey guys," he mumbled under his breath. "I've got bad news. It's only Thursday and the till is almost empty."

"I've got it!" Ruth suddenly exclaimed. "What would you two say to *Kiwischnee mit frischer Minze?* How would you say in English — Kiwi Mint Soufflé? Becky, what do you think?"

"Mmmhhh, delicious," I replied.

Ruth was rummaging through a cookbook. She had just discovered the wonders of the kiwi fruit and was looking for a dessert recipe for our Sunday meal. It was her turn to cook this week and she took it very seriously.

Jürgen was somewhere in the apartment, vacuuming. I had vacuum duty last week. It was the easiest job. Cooking was for me the most arduous, a real chore, as the only things my mother had ever taught me in the kitchen were how to defrost the peas and carrots and how to exterminate cockroaches.

"Heike," I said, "can I ask you —"

"*Wo ist das Scheuermittel, bitte?*" Heike continued. Where is the scouring powder, please? Now we were really getting down to the nitty-gritty.

"*Wo ist das* — what was the word again?"

"*Scheuermittel!*"

Oh God, I'd never learn German! "*Wo ist das* Scheuermittel, *bitte?*" I repeated, imitating her exasperation.

Heike the Sensible One — that's what I called her in secret — was the ne plus ultra of the German *Hausfrau*. Apart from my mother, she must have been the most thorough cleaner I had ever met up with. She was the type that vacuumed under the carpets, wiped the refrigerator down with vinegar, and polished the silverware even though it wasn't silver. But she was also a persevering and patient German teacher, for which I was grateful, even if I did sometimes wonder at the importance of the vocabulary she chose for her linguistic examples.

"*Wo ist das* Kursbuch, *bitte?*" she said to me.

Ah, now we were getting down to weightier matters. The *Kursbuch* was an independent leftist quarterly, a must for would-be intellectuals like this bunch.

"*Wo ist das* Kursbuch, *bitte?*" I dutifully repeated after her. "Heike, I have to ask you something really impor —"

"Later, Becky. *Bitte.*" She paused for a moment and then carried on. "*Wo ist das* Kursbuch *29, bitte?*"

"*Wo ist das* Kursbuch *29, bitte?*"

"*Wo ist das* Kursbuch *29, 'Das Elend mit der Psyche,' bitte?*"

Oh no, help! "The Misery of the Soul." There was no way to escape German storm and stress. "*Wo ist das* Kurs —" I began.

"*Teil II!* Sorry, I forgot it had two parts."

"*Wo ist das* Kursbuch *29, 'Das Elend mit der Psyche' — Teil II, bitte?*"

"*Gut,*" Heike commented.

"*Gut?* Just 'good'? It was excellent!"

"It was good," she said dryly. "And now: *Wo sind die Toiletten, bitte?*"

"*Wo sind die Toi* — Oh, Heike. I can't. It sounds so awful. Do you really use the word *toilet?*"

"*Ja!* We really use the word *toilet. Toi-lette.* Feminine. *Die Toilette,* from the French — but let's get back to work. I've told you a hundred times."

"And I've tried to ask you a hundred times why I can't say 'bathroom' or 'restroom' or 'ladies lounge.' Or 'powder room.' Why not 'powder room'? *Wo ist der Puderraum, bitte?*"

"*Nein, nein, nein.*"

"Toilet? I *have* to use *toilet?*"

"*Ja, ja, ja!*"

"Okay, here goes. *Wo sind die*" — I grit my teeth — "*Toiletten?*"

"*Bitte!* You forgot to say *please! Wo sind die Toiletten,* BITTE! *Bitte* you must never forget. Especially when you're trying to get something out of someone."

Looking up from her cookbook, Ruth said, "Otherwise the Germans will find you impolite. They'll think you're not being *höflich.*"

"Not being *hoflich?*"

"*Höflich!*" all three of them cried back at me in unison.

I rolled my eyes in despair. Two dots at the top of an *o* were going to be my ruination.

"Anyway, I don't see why anyone would find *me* impolite," I replied. "*You* use the word *toilet.* Americans think *that's* impolite."

"WC," Erhard said, interrupting his calculations for a moment. "Just say WC." He pointed his knife at the budget book, shaking his head gravely. "Listen, we're all going to have to bite the bullet this week. Each of us has to cough up at least another seven marks and sixty-six."

"You're going to bankrupt me," Ruth replied dryly.

"So no more smoked ham and Italian salami," Erhard continued. "Only liverwurst and —"

"— *und Senatsreserven,*" said Heike.

Senatsreserven? What in the world were the senate's reserves?

"*Senatsreserven!*" said Ruth with a grimace. "Listen, I'll give you ten marks instead and you can throw in a few slices of ham for me, okay?"

I turned to Heike. "Heike, can I ask you —"

"*Wo sind die Senatsreserven, bitte?*" Heike said, gesturing to me to repeat after her.

Heike and Erhard were a good match. Her purism fit Erhard's fastidiousness. He had once been a trained precision toolmaker, but now he was studying sociology at the Free University and training himself in the tools of leftist scholarship. He was a nice enough guy, friendly, perhaps a bit too pedantic and exacting, with a pale, goateed face and a room full of hairy cactuses. And he had two bad habits.

"Wo sind die Senatsreserven, bitte?" Heike repeated.

"Wo sind die Senatsreserven, bitte?" I echoed, dunking the teapot into the dishwater. "By the way, Heike, I have this really important ques — Oh no! How disgusting!" Dozens of tea leaves were now floating in my beautiful lemon-scented dishwater. "Erhard," I said, "you forgot to throw out the tea leaves again." *That* was his first bad habit. He *never* emptied the teapot.

"There are more important things in life," he said, pointing the butter knife at me and then at a dark blue book with gold lettering lying on the kitchen table in front of him. That was the *other* bad habit: the way he would emphatically point the butter knife at us whenever he wanted to make a point. It was very irritating.

"Becky, Ruth?" he now asked, tapping the book again with the tip of the knife. "Have you read today's chapter, 'Exchange'?"

The book was volume 23 of Marx and Engel's complete works, volume 23 being only Book One of *Das Kapital*. The bookcase in his room was full of these blue, gold-trimmed volumes. And whenever he went to East Berlin, he'd bring back two or three more in the series.

Actually, I *had* looked at the 'Exchange' chapter, but had failed to appreciate its significance, even though I had read it in English. "For every owner of a commodity, every commodity owned by another person counts as a particular equivalent for his own commodity, and therefore, his own commodity counts as a general equivalent of all other commodities. . . ."

It wasn't so much that I didn't comprehend the meaning of the words. I did. More or less. What was really too much for me was why I was spending my time trying to understand it in the first place.

"*Ja*, Erhard! I read the chapter, and I'm going to take another look at it," I answered, fishing the tea leaves out of the water. "But first I have to prepare tomorrow's English lesson," I said.

I had been lucky and had found work teaching English twice a week at the Volkshochschule in Spandau. My only problem was that my German was far worse than my students' English. They were continually asking me questions I couldn't answer because I hadn't a clue as to what they were saying. When I heard, "*Entschuldigen Sie, bitte, ich habe eine Frage, und zwar —*" I would hasten to say, before they could finish their sentence, "This is an English class. Please pose your questions in English." But my students didn't seem to mind that my German was weak. On the last evening of the spring semester they even surprised me with a fat bouquet of roses and a German textbook which to this day still stands regally in my bookcase.

"Here's something," Ruth cried out. I had forgotten Ruth was even sitting at the table. "Kiwis in a ginger yogurt mousse. That even sounds better than the Kiwi Mint Soufflé. For either recipe, I need eight kiwi fruits, Erhard."

"Who says so?"

"Professor Bloch says." She held up the cookbook. I read *Intelligent Cooking: Desserts with IQ, by Professor Bloch*. "Get eight, Erhard."

"Please," I put in. "Ruth, you forgot to say *bitte. Das ist nicht höflich.*"

"*Höflich, du Klugscheißerchen,*" she replied.

Uh-oh, the two dots again!

"Ruth, kiwis are expensive," Erhard said tersely.

"What is a *Klugscheißerchen?*" I asked.

"It means 'smartass,' " Heike explained matter-of-factly. And then: "*Becky, wo sind die Senatsreserven, bitte?*" Heike was not one to be side-tracked.

"*Wo sind die —*"

"Ruth," Erhard went on, "why don't you make something with apples? They're cheaper."

"But Kiwi Snow tastes much better than applesauce. I'm sure. Minted Kiwi Snow. Mmmhhh," I said.

"What do *you* know?" Heike said, jabbing me good-naturedly in the ribs. "You're what we call an *Allesfresser!*"

That was a brand-new word for me. "An *Allesfresser?* What's an *Allesfresser?* "

"A *Klugscheißerchen* who eats everything, even *Senatsreserven,*" Ruth offered.

"And what are *Senats —*"

"Chris and Hannelore will be here at seven," Erhard said, opening up his gold-trimmed blue bible and beginning to read.

"Are they going to bring that awful noodle salad again?" Ruth asked.

Once a week, on Thursdays at seven, our *Wohngemeinschaft* congregated with some friends in Erhard's room for our dialectical materialism lessons. We read Karl Marx, discussed, complained, drank beer or Lambrusco, and nibbled on noodle salad we scooped out of a big orange plastic basin.

Erhard had the nicest room in the apartment, three hundred square feet with a large bay window. In its former life it had been the dentist's waiting room. But now the walls were covered with posters of young Trotsky, Che Guevara, and the Indian chief Sitting Bull. Sometimes, on rainy afternoons, shortly before a big anti-Vietnam demonstration, Erhard would invite me into his sanctuary and give me private lessons in political correctness. I could barely say *"Wo sind die Toiletten, bitte?"* but there I was, screaming at the top of my lungs slogans about Nixon the murderer: *"Nixon Mörder! Nixon Mörder!"* The umlaut in *Mörder* often gave me trouble, but other slogans like "Ho, ho, Ho Chi Minh, Ho, ho, Ho Chi Minh," once I got used to the rhythm of them, were easy, since the words were the same in English.

"Now say 'U, S, A, S, A, S, S.' Okay?" Erhard commanded one evening.

"Oo-es-ah-es-sah-es-es," I echoed. But something bewildered me. "But Erhard, what exactly is a Es-sah-es-es?"

"S, A, S, S!" he answered, annoyed. "Letters! S, A, S, S."

"Ach so!" I said, it slowly dawning on me. "The SA and the SS!"

"Right!"

"In other words, you want me to say that the USA . . . is comparable to . . . is like the SA and the SS?"

"Correct!"

A formidable pause.

"Erhard," I said. "I know I have a lot to learn in life, but somehow I don't really see the USA as embodying an equivalent to the SS. Do you know what I mean?"

Erhard shook his head and scratched his goatee. I was a hopeless case.

Dejected, I'd go to Ruth seeking consolation for my lack of political correctness. I'd find her in the dentist's lab, the smallest room in the apartment.

Ruth was going to night school. She had once been trained as a pharmacist's assistant but now had ambitions of becoming a biologist. She lived comfortably on a generous student grant for the children of the war-disabled. It seems that

her father, a simple East Prussian farmer, had lost his health
through a bad case of pneumonia contracted during the war.
The German veterans' agency thought he had contracted it
while in action. Ruth's relatives, though, knew better. Family
legend had it that Friedhelm had been recruited into the
Volkssturm, the home guard, but ran away the first chance
he got, taking the cashbox along with him. During this escape, while wading in the River Memel in hopes of covering his tracks, he accidentally dropped the cashbox into the
murky depths. Old Friedhelm dived into the freezing waters
and found it, but unfortunately surfaced with pneumonia. And
now, thirty years later, his daughter was still reaping the benefits of his daring — or foolhardiness, depending on one's point
of view.

Ruth had a lot of free time, so together we often set out
on extensive shopping expeditions. Her greatest passion was
scrounging through the thrift shops. At first I had a hard time
understanding her penchant for secondhand clothes and vin-
tage fashion, but when I began hitting Berlin's boutiques and
department stores in a serious way, I began to see her ra-
tionale. Fashion was simply not a top priority in the city. In
fact, I soon missed the extravagance of New York, its creative exoticism, the certain knowledge that on any street corner in Manhattan at any time in any season you'd have no
trouble bumping into anything from haute couture to off-
the-wall wackiness. But even during the summer, and especially on cold, charcoal gray winter days, Berlin's fashion
tended toward dark and dowdy understatement, straightforward solid colors, thick, bulky fabrics, functional, classic cuts.
It was well made, and expensive. And there was the crux of
the matter. Why spend a lot of money if you're only going
to end up looking like a chunky, fuddy-duddy grandma anyway? Ruth's solution was thrifty hand-me-downs. My

solution was to save my money and buy clothes during trips back home.

But here I was in Berlin. I had to shop for *something*.

I became enamored of the stationery sections in the city's department stores. I'd never seen the likes of them — such a wide selection of office supplies. I was especially fascinated by the black and white marbled ring binders in various sizes, some thin and some wide, tall and short, with two rings, four rings, some with a side grip, others with a spring clasp, and all with spine labels in every color of the rainbow. I ran my fingers over onionskin paper and linen paper and lightweight airmail paper, index cards in chartreuse, magenta, and azure blue, some with normal lines, others with a grid, and in solids too. I debated with myself: should I buy a straight-cut file pocket, an accordion file, or a simple folder in pink? And what a selection of plastic sheet protectors, clear or in various colors, with two open sides or three, some with zippers, or colored edges, with or without holes for binders! I read the words on the packages and practiced pronouncing them, letting the strange sounds roll off my tongue. I meandered down the aisles in constant amazement, oohing and aahing, touching and smelling. Here, I thought, is a nation thoroughly determined to document, organize, and file its life down to the very last tab.

Sometimes, instead of shopping, Ruth and I would take a brisk walk along the Landwehr Canal, just a few blocks to the north, where we would come to the Wall. I'd climb the rickety steps to the observation tower and peer into the East across the street. I noticed that they had *Stores* there too.

We'd have a coffee in a café on Paul-Lincke-Ufer and then cross the bridge to the other side, to Maybachufer and the outdoor market. And sometimes we'd just hang out in Ruth's dental lab.

I can still see her now, sitting crosslegged on the bed cro-
cheting. Or maybe she's filing her nails. Several weeks' worth
of *Spiegel* magazine are scattered about the satin linens. One
day Simone de Beauvoir's autobiography has center stage on
the night table, the next day it's *The Feminine Mystique* by
Betty Friedan. Leonard Cohen is singing in the background.
Or possibly it's James Taylor. Maybe John Lennon. For sure,
though, Ruth's head is covered with an aluminum foil helmet beneath which sticky, muddy henna is seeping into the
roots of her hair. In the middle of her conversation with me,
she suddenly jumps up and rushes into the bathroom to wash
out the henna. I can still see the red dots on the bathroom
walls where the shower curtain was ripped and the splotching
began.

Ruth was a grooming freak and the most feminine feminist I had ever come across. Her shelf in the bathroom did her
ex-drugstore days more than justice. It contained a fascinat-
ing array of mud packs, natural sponges, hairbrushes made
of wild boar bristles, herbal bath suds, more nailpolish than a
manicurist, and the widest assortment of medicated pads and
cushions for blisters and corns and bunions you'd see outside
of a podiatrist's office. Anything a slob like me could possibly
not need was there.

I learned a lot from Ruth, and not just how to cure Jürgen's
herpes, get rid of sweaty feet in sweltering heat, or moisturize
your hands with buttermilk and cream of wheat. Ruth was a
woman of great taste, with *savoir vivre* and a fine eye for the
good things in life. And she passed it on to me. She loved French
perfume, antique lace tablecloths, silk underwear, Goethe,
crispy Peking duck, museums. And Doppelkopf — I almost
forgot.

It was Ruth who taught me how to play Doppelkopf one
bleak, snowy Sunday. An eerie silence had descended over

Neukölln. It was so quiet outside, I could hear the footsteps of a passerby mailing a letter across the street, and Frau Hagelkamp, the janitor's wife, walking her dachshund near the police station, encouraging him with a "Come on, do it for Mommy." Otherwise there was nothing outside but the splatter of snow flurries against the window and a lonely #4 bus drifting by, its sounds muffled by a thick cushion of snow. Inside our house it was warm and safe and lazy. I loved the rhythmic slap-slap-slap of the playing cards on the tabletop. I felt a part of a larger something, a member of a community. I was a Doppelkopf player, and to this day I thank Ruth fervently for this gift.

"Heike," I said, "Can I please ask you some —"

The door swung open. It was Jürgen. "Hannelore's on the phone. She wants to know if we can play Doppelkopf tonight instead of reading from *Das Kapital*. What do you guys think?"

"Yeah!" the women in the room cried out.

"No," Erhard answered with authority. "*Kapital* at seven."

"Tell Hannelore she doesn't have to bring that awful noodle salad," Ruth said.

"Maybe I should eat something first," Jürgen remarked as he exited.

"Go easy on the ham." I called out after him. "Heike is threatening to buy *Senatsreserven*. What *is* that, anyway?"

"Chopped corned beef in a can," Heike answered. "Dog food for people."

"I'd really rather play Doppelkopf," Ruth said without glancing up from her cookbook.

"Me too," I agreed. The thought of delving again into that chapter on 'Exchange' was almost as unappetizing as *Senatsreserven*.

"We can't change that now," Erhard replied, pointing his knife at volume 23. "Maybe next week."

"*Wo sind die Doppelkopfkarten, bitte?*" Heike said to me.

"Oh, Heike, stop it already!" I said with mild exasperation. "Who cares where the Doppelkopf cards are!"

"Becky," she threatened me.

"*Wo sind die Doppelkopfkarten, bitte?*" I repeated, rolling my eyes. "Heike, for the past twenty minutes I've been trying to ask you something!"

"Then ask. Who's stopping you?"

"It concerns men. In the subway."

I taught English all the way out in Spandau, at the outer rim of the city's boondocks, right at the border with East Germany. The trip home at night was long and complicated, entailing a walk to the bus stop, a bus ride, a trek to the subway, a change of trains, another hike on foot. I had no real gripes with Berlin's public transportation. The buses and trains were efficient and comfortable. My problem had to do with the people I met along the way. More specifically, it had to do with the men. And even more specifically than that, with the lousy drunken bastards who wouldn't stop bothering me. A week didn't pass but some subway rider with a face the color of ashes and a mouth that smelled like them would saunter over to me on the platform, reach out for my hair, bend over me, and whisper lewdly in my ear, "Hey baby, what a head of hair! What a head of hair!"

Granted, my hair *was* somewhat exotic. It was long and dark and bushy. But, hey, it wasn't blue wool or copper wire, for Christ's sake! What gave them the *right?*

Now, I was from New York City. It's not that I was some naive babe from Edina, Minnesota. I knew big cities. And I knew from experience how crude things could get in the New

York subway. Once, on the way to dancing school, I almost
got squashed to death on the A-train when two obese men at
the Hoyt-Schermerhorn subway stop in Brooklyn got into a
fist fight and I, eight-year-old shrimp that I was, got caught
in between. When I was fifteen I remember sitting opposite a
woman who pulled out a hunting knife and started cleaning her
nails with it. And then *paring* them. I have stepped in a puddle
of piss at the Brighton Beach Avenue station, gotten my camel
hair coat sullied by an ejaculating pervert somewhere between
Delancey Street and West Fourth, and was even threatened by
a guy who told me that under his coat he had a gun aimed at
me. His eyes were popping out of their sockets and the nice
black fellow sitting next to me on the F-train tried to calm me
down. "Keep cool, sister," he whispered out of the side of his
mouth. "Just keep cool."

So, as I say, I sort of knew what subways were like. But
believe you me, one thing you didn't get on the New York
City subway was a continuous flow of drunks lumbering over
to you and pawing at your hair. The only thing drunks did
on the New York City subway was sleep. Sometimes they'd
totter around the middle levels, hiding in dark corners that
smelled of urine and sour vomit, and drink wine out of bottles
in brown paper bags. Every so often they were sighted *riding*
the subway, standing very still, holding on tight to the over-
head handrails, staring into space, hoping no one would notice
them.

But the subway drunks I encountered in Berlin weren't
scruffy Bowery bums in tattered coats, they were your everyday
Otto Meiers from next door. They were men like Herr Blaschek,
one of the tellers at my bank, dressed in cheap plaid suits from
the winter of 1959 with white button-down shirts and wide
polyester ties with some sort of vaguely floral design. Or they

were like those fellows at the police station when I went to register. It was bad enough that you had to inform the police where you were living, let alone being given the third degree by men with beer bellies in bulky brown corduroy pants, dull-patterned shirts, and beige scoop-neck polyester vests. But whether blue or white or no-collar, they were almost always carrying a cumbersome briefcase that surely contained a local tabloid, a thermos flask with leftover peppermint tea, and half a mettwurst sandwich that their wives had made for them that morning. It got so that if I just spotted one of those briefcases, I automatically kept my distance. It could only mean trouble.

Anyway, since I was new to the situation, I hadn't a clue how to deal with it tactfully. It happened once, it happened twice, it happened over and over again. I just didn't know how to get rid of these guys with their pudgy hands and dirty nails going for my kinky dark hair. I couldn't speak German, so what was I supposed to say to them? *"Wo sind die Toiletten, bitte?"*

"So what should I do?" I said to Heike, who was putting a fresh plastic bag into the garbage pail. "What should I say to these guys? How do I get rid of them?"

"Take a taxi home instead," said Jürgen, grinning, smearing schmalz on a slice of bread.

"Get your hair cut," Ruth added. "I know a good hair-dresser in Halensee who —"

"Forget it!" interrupted Erhard, pointing his butter knife at me. "Just yell at them. Why don't you yell 'Ho, ho, Ho Chi Minh'? That'll scare 'em. And you say it well, too!"

Obviously no one was taking me seriously, no one save Heike the Sensible One.

"Okay," said Heike, rinsing her hands. "I have it. Repeat after me. *Hau ab . . .*"

"*Hau ab . . .*" I began.

"Good. That means 'scram.' Now say *du alter Knacker.*"

"*Du alter Knacker.*"

"Good. That means 'you old creep.' Now all together: *Hau ab, du alter Knacker!*"

"*Hau ab, du alter Knacker*, bitte!" I shouted.

"Without *bitte!*" Heike reprimanded. "Never say *bitte* in this situation. It's a command, not a request. This is war!"

"*Hau ab, du alter Knacker!*" I repeated without the *bitte.*

"With feeling!" Heike exhorted.

"*Hau ab, du alter Knacker!*" I cried out with feeling.

My roommates cheered. Erhard, seized by a laughing fit, dropped his butter knife.

Heike repeated the sentence, over and over again, each time stressing a different word until I understood all the various shades of meaning.

"Bravo, Becky!" Ruth said. "If you can swear in a foreign language, it means you're beginning to understand the country and its people."

I smiled sheepishly, like a second-grader who had just been awarded a gold star for penmanship. With this one sentence, a door had suddenly and miraculously swung open. The German language, until that moment wrapped in a shroud of mystery, had finally been stripped naked. And I liked what I saw.

"*Mäuschen,*" said Jürgen, gathering me in his arms. "*Mein Mäuschen!*" He kissed me.

"Yuck," I said. "That lip ointment again!"

"Good, Becky," Heike said. But then on second thought she added, "No, I think it was excellent. Yes, I think so. Excellent."

I was bursting with pride.

I was young. I was impressionable. And I could speak German!

"Well then, Becky," Heike resumed crisply. "It seems the honeymoon's over. Tomorrow we begin on the German dative."

Chapter Six

Tuesday, November 10, 1992
Diet Week: 6
Day: 2
Weight Loss: 12 lbs. (go for it!!)

"Achoo," I sneezed, five times in a row.

More than two weeks had come and almost five pounds had gone since the roast suckling pig. I must admit I was looking pretty okay. For one thing, my jowls had disappeared. I didn't mention this before, but prior to my reduction program I had begun to notice in the immediate region of my lower cheeks the soft beginnings of a fleshiness that resembled my Grandma Rosie's jowls. That, thank God, was now a thing of the past — or possibly of the far future but, as I say, not of the present. My apartment and I (although at a far slower pace) were nearing our ideal weight. Indeed, after five weeks of rummaging, my living space had begun to look as I have always wanted it: large, easy, emptyish, and clutter-free. I found that with every dubious article that fell into the clutches of my decluttering fingers, all I had to do was ask myself, Does this (or will this ever) enrich my life? With every honest no, I came closer to my goal. For example, midway through Week Five I had finished with the kitchen, gotten rid of all the rusty potato peelers, the chipped china, the countless jars I had saved in case I ever made fresh strawberry preserves. I discovered Teflon pans without Teflon, pots without tops, and thyme from my trip to Greece ten years ago. Out they went. And then, finally, I began tackling my last big project.

"Aaachoo," I sneezed. I was crouched in my office in front of my record library, taking inventory. The dust on the records tickled my nose.

I hated my records. All 2,500 of them. And believe me, that is a lot of hate. The years in which I appreciated the records, my radio days, ended long ago. I wonder whether record companies are still so generous with their goods? There was a time when every major record company sent me every minor disc they ever produced. It was like Christmas every day, year round. But crouched there in front of my shelves and shelves and more shelves packed with records, I despised every last one of them.

Don't get me wrong. It wasn't the *music* that I hated. I'm not a heathen. I *enjoy* music. It was the bulky, ridiculously square-shaped, flimsy, space-consuming, unwieldy, dust-collecting *packaging* of the music that I despised. "Such dust collectors! Throw them out already!" my mother would have advised. True enough: I rarely listened to any of the damned things, having long since switched to the clean and elegant sound of CDs. At least I should get rid of the useless records, I thought as I crouched there flipping through them.

Ricky Dee's Happy Sax Party. Who the hell was Ricky Dee? Or *Spec and the Spiders.* What a god-awful name. And how about *Heavy Metal Hothouse?* I studied the cover. It portrayed a woman dressed in a bra and bikini panties chained to a bench in a steamy sauna. What ever possessed me to file this in my collection? It never ceased to amaze me how much garbage was produced, packaged, hyped, sold, and then forgotten in the rock business.

I tossed Ricky and Spec, the hothouse bondage scene and dozens of other discs across the room like paper airplanes, flying saucers, Frisbees. They landed in a giant heap of cardboard and vinyl. I terminated *Die Punkies* and *Mauerjungs* and *Sturm and the Drang*, but did put Nina Hagen back on the shelf, along with Frido Fabian's records. As Heike had told me during our roast suckling pig dinner, his cover art was designed by his younger brother Benno Fabian, and it was actually quite good. I was more than a little impressed and was keen on meeting this "tall, skinny, elegant, gentlemanly type." He seemed to be just what I needed — that is, for the illustrations for *Mademoiselle*'s publication of "Bingo Berlin." But his answering machine kept telling me he was on vacation.

As always, the thought of "Bingo Berlin" sent waves of warmth surging through my bloodstream. It might even be filmed. Karla Menzel had finally gotten around to reading it. She liked it, reluctant though she was to admit it. "Becky," she had said when she next saw me, "I'm so amazed. You really *can* write. I had no idea you had such narrative talent."

Thanks, Karla, you're a real pal, I just love how much faith you have in me.

"But we won't think about it now," she said imperiously. "First we get *Brandenburg* in the bag. If *Brandenburg*'s good, we start on *Bingo*." She made it sound like a threat. And what if *Becky Goes Brandenburg* really *wasn't* any good? The surging waves of warmth degenerated into anxiety pains, and off they went galloping through my veins, raising hell.

"A . . . aaa . . . choo!"

I pulled more records off the shelves and, one by one,

whisked them across the room and out of my life. I calculated that I would need until Saturday or Sunday to finish the
job, especially since I was going to Brandenburg on Thursday
and Friday. Patrick had interviews lined up with a count in
Rheinsberg and two flamboyant manager types near Potsdam.
Maybe it would be the breakthrough we needed. And maybe I'd
even find — you never know — someone interesting. I mean,
for myself.

"Aaa . . . CHOO!"

I blew my nose and looked at my watch. It was after five.
I'd work on the records for another hour before getting ready
for the Reinhard Beck opening Professor Bloch and I were
attending.

I was looking forward to my evening out. Not only was
the movie supposed to be funny — imagine! a German *comedy!* — but I hadn't been to a big splash in weeks. I needed
to get out and show my face, remind the world that I was still
around, even if I did spend most of my time thrashing around
in piles of junk, brainstorming with Patrick, sitting at my computer with "Bingo Berlin," concocting calorie-free meals, and
staring at the mirror not believing that that leaner-looking
person there was really *me*. Too bad, though, that I hadn't yet
gotten my hair colored. Pedro, my hairdresser, was out sick
with two broken toes he injured when he dropped a weight in
the gym on his foot. It would have been nice to go to the opening
after Pedro had hidden my gray.

In a moment of weakness the night before, I had lamented
the postponement of my appointment with Pedro to my weekly
skat partners.

"My lovely, you shall always be beautiful to me. With or
without the dye," dear Professor Bloch had said consolingly.
"Wear your best smile and that pretty off-the-shoulder black

dress you bought for your trip to Venice and the men will swarm around you like bees around honey."

"I asked you not to ever mention that lousy bastard again," I said.

"Who mentioned *what* lousy bastard?" the professor said with a wink.

"If you do happen to find someone who wants to swarm around you, doll-face, you can start nesting again this weekend," Martin put in. "Your new bed's due in the next shipments. We can bring it over after we close on Saturday."

"She doesn't want to nest," Professor Bloch said. "She broke poor Egon's heart."

"Professor, let's not go through that again." I spoke a bit more sharply than I should have. We had gone over this countless times over the past two weeks and my patience was wearing thin.

"Hey, hey, don't get nasty with me."

"He just wasn't right for me. And it's true, I'm not looking, Martin. My back, though, will be thankful for the new mattress."

"And the count, if he's a man of aesthetic sensibility, for the sleek and simple design."

"What count? What are you talking about?"

"I'm talking about that count in Rheinsberg you're meeting on Thursday. I'm a sociologist. I understand the magnetic attraction of high social position. And you're not immune, doll-face."

I had stuck my tongue out at Martin.

"A . . . aaa . . . CHOO," I now sneezed — five times in a row — and threw more records across the room.

Sneezing was a leftover from my adolescent bout with asthma. The illness had appeared quite suddenly one late

Sunday afternoon when I was twelve. My father was in the living room watching the races, and my mother was dusting the bookcase. Davey was in his room with his friend Bernie giggling over a *Playboy* they had snuck into the apartment. Joycey was playing with her new Barbie. I was at the kitchen table munching on Oreos and writing an essay for school about the origins and evolution of our solar system. I was in the midst of reading about the earth, amazed to discover that if a three-hundred-foot model of the sun were placed in Times Square, the orbit of the earth, drawn to the same scale, would pass right through Far Rockaway where I was sitting that very moment.

"Oh my God!" my mother suddenly cried out. "Volume 23 is missing. The encyclopedia is gone!"

The *Encyclopedia Britannica* was the only thing in our house of any value. My father, at the time a *Britannica* sales rep, had won a deluxe set for attaining the highest sales quotient in the borough of Queens.

"Mom, it's right here. I have it."

"Where? What — you're *reading* it?"

"That's what it's here for, isn't it?"

"Don't be fresh to your mother, young lady," my father admonished.

"Did you wash your hands first?" asked my mother. "I don't want you to smudge the pages."

"Mom!"

"They'll be collector's items someday! And when you're finished, make sure you shake out the cookie crumbs. I don't want those books attracting cockroaches."

"Gloria!" my father hollered. "Would you please lower your voice. I'm trying to follow the race."

Suddenly, I felt my chest go itchy. Within minutes I was gasping for breath, wheezing as though I were about to suffocate. My mother dragged me into the bathroom, shut the door, and turned the hot water on full force. The steam bath did its job and my attack passed.

But then the following Sunday it happened again. That time my mother was vacuuming in the living room and my father watching the fights. I was hanging out on my bed reading a *Seventeen* magazine when my mother called in to Joycey and me to straighten up our room. That's when the attack hit. It was the same ordeal all over again.

My parents were concerned, so my mother took me downtown to an allergy specialist, Dr. Greenbaum. He conducted a series of tests, pricking my skin with fifty different substances in fifty different places. According to him, if a hive developed, I was allergic to that substance.

When the torture was over, I had developed approximately 48⅓ hives. Among other things, I was allergic to golden hamsters, goose feathers, blooming trees, shaggy dogs, and assorted mushrooms and fungi. But my super-duper weakness, my Achilles' heel, my whopper of an allergy, was ordinary house dust.

My mother was shocked. "But, doctor," she objected, "how can that be? My home is spotless. There's not a speck of dust in the whole place!"

Dr. Greenbaum just shrugged his shoulders. And then, turning to me with an enormous needle in his hand, he said, "Young lady, this is going to be the first of approximately sixty allergy shots you'll be given over the next four years. You may not enjoy it, but when this therapy is over, you'll never wheeze again. In the meantime, stay away from dust." He was right. I did not enjoy it. But frankly, the shots didn't bother me all that much, for he had said the magic words *Stay away from dust*. Hidden within that sentence was the happy realization that I would never, ever, pick up a dust rag in my mother's house again.

Poor Mom. What with all her worries during the week —
getting to work on time, typing impeccable letters, keeping the
IRS away from her boss, keeping her boss away from the track,
getting the lamb chops on the table by 7:30, keeping the IRS
away from my father, keeping my father away from the track,
finding the time to manicure her nails — she really needed
some help on Sundays, the only day she had time to scrub
and scour and scourge. Early Sunday morning at the breakfast table she would assign her accomplices, Joycey and me,
our chores: dust the furniture, polish the furniture; sweep the
floors, wash the floors, wax the floors; wash the laundry, dry
the laundry, iron the laundry, fold the laundry; strip the beds,
make the beds; vacuum the drapes, vacuum the rugs, vacuum
the couch; unclog the toilet, clean the toilet, disinfect the toilet,
wipe dry the toilet; dust the blinds, polish the windows, scrub
the windowsills, water the plants, and don't forget the kitchen
fixtures!

Davey was occasionally asked to take the garbage to the
incinerator. My father was occasionally asked to get up from
the couch a second so we could puff up the pillows, please.

My mother hated anything that resembled dust or dirt. To
her, spilling a glass of milk was a federal offense, a stuffed-up
drain was a catastrophe, a cockroach on the kitchen counter
was cause for a nervous breakdown.

You didn't have to be a psychologist to see that asthma,
at least in part, was my way of getting back at my mother for
forcing me to become both witness and accomplice to her ma-
nia. My repressed anger must have found a way out through
my congested lungs. Maybe I really wanted to scream at her.
Or hit her. What I ended up doing, though, was straightening
up my room and going into the city for my allergy shots.

I was a good girl. But deep down in my slutty heart I
remained a closet slattern.

And who knows, maybe my mother too was a crypto-slob. Maybe somewhere in her home she was also rebelling against *her* mother. Perhaps locked in the bottom drawer of her vanity table, or in one of the hatboxes hidden behind the handbags on the top shelf of her closet, she too cultivated her own variety of chaos. But if she did, she never let us know it.

My mother lorded over our household. My father and, I fear, we children were mere props in her dollhouse. But it wasn't until years later, long after Davey and Joycey and I had become dictators in our own homes, that the extent of my mother's domestic tyranny fully dawned on me. It was the summer of 1990, just a few weeks after my father had died, and I was sitting in my parents' living room in Las Vegas with a camera in my hand.

To be exact, I was sitting on the left-hand side of the living room couch, in the very spot where my father's heart had stopped. He had died right there on the couch waiting for my mother to call. She was at work in the hotel candy store. She hadn't wanted to go in that day, but my father had persuaded her. She said she'd call him during her break.

Later, my mother found a mug in the sink, so she says he must have had some tea. And there were matzoh crumbs all over the coffee table and rug, so she thinks he had a little something to eat, too. And he must have tried to read a bit, because Isaac Bashevis Singer's *In My Father's Court* was lying open next to him on the sofa. But when my mother called during her break at two fifteen, my father didn't answer. He was a light sleeper. He would have heard the phone if he had been napping. She tried again. No answer.

She dashed out of the Pink Palace. She couldn't find a cab, so, forgetting for the moment that she was seventy years old, she ran all the way home, straight down the Strip, right through Harrah's parking lot, clear across the street and up the stairs.

She found my father sitting comfortably on the left-hand side of the couch with the brown princess phone right next to him on the end table.

CNN was on. And Dad was dead. He must have died watching the news and waiting for her to call. Maybe he had heard the phone ring. His left hand was *on* the phone. It was gripping it. It was postmortemly *stuck* to it.

And there I was, two weeks later.

I sank into the couch, snapping pictures, documenting the last images he had ever seen: the giant-screen Mitsubishi with its video beam scan, his pride and joy, although everyone agreed the picture quality was lousy; the elephants my mother collected, dozens of them, made of china and clay and plastic and wood, all of them filling the nooks and crannies of the hutch and the glass vitrine, styled into candleholders and lighters and catchalls; the empty wine rack; the orange armchair where my mother sat to knit because the light from the window came in from the left. Perhaps, just before he died, my father had looked at the armchair and thought of the itchy tags she sewed into the socks she knit for him. MADE ESPECIALLY FOR YOU BY GLORIA BERNSTEIN. Perhaps he was thinking that he loved her. Or maybe he had glanced to his far right where a blowup of my aunt Ethel from her 1961 sitcom *The Ethel Sylvester Show* was hanging. Maybe that's when his heart stood still, looking at that picture. He always was intimidated by Ethel.

I snapped picture after picture, recording the last things my father's eyes fell on before they closed forever.

And that's when it struck me. It suddenly occurred to me that only two weeks after his death there was nothing left in the apartment that reminded me of *him*. Had anything in this place *ever* been his? Surely there was something, something that was his and his alone, that embodied what he liked and loved and was. But what? And where? His pipes, for instance.

Where were his pipes? How I loved the smell of the moist to-bacco before it began to burn. And the pipes were so sleek, dashing and elegant, always leaning on an ashtray ready for a smoke. But now the ashtrays were empty.

And how about his toothbrush? Where was Daddy's tooth-brush? Or his shaving cream? Were they still in the bathroom cabinet? His Hush Puppies in the bedroom closet? His white boxer shorts in the dresser? And the ten-gallon cowboy hat he once bought on a trip to Texas? I opened up the closets. My father's suits were gone. His pants, shirts, ties. Everything was gone. Even the toothbrush.

"Mom," I cried out, "where are all Daddy's things? What'd you do with everything?"

"I got rid of it. I gave it all away. Friends. Family. The Salvation Army. I couldn't stand looking at it."

"But how could you part with everything? His pipes? What about his pipes?"

"They're dust collectors. What do I want with dust collectors?" she snapped at me in her grief. "And stop screeching. You sound like those women on Pitkin Avenue. The ones that used to sell live chickens."

Oh, she had kept some things, I was sure, hidden them in some secret compartment marked with my father's name. And in the end I did manage to salvage the gray pin-striped suit jacket, although without my Phi Beta Kappa pin on its lapel. The pin was gone forever. My father asked to be buried with it.

Poor Mom. I don't really blame her. Of course if I still had asthma, maybe I would. But I don't. And anyway, I now know that she couldn't help herself. It was in her genes. Neatnikism and compulsive cleaning are hereditary diseases transmitted through the female line in my family. My grandmother Rosie died of a heart attack waxing the kitchen floor. Her sister, my great-aunt Shura, broke her neck when she fell off a ladder while dusting the family heirloom, a six-tiered chandelier. And my aunt Ethel Sylvester, the *famous* Ethel Sylvester — God, she'd strangle me for divulging this — well, she almost threw me out of her apartment once for putting a wineglass down on her coffee table without a coaster.

Ethel's apartment, overlooking Central Park West, was a museum. It was so jam-packed with pop art *tchotchkies*, antique collectibles, memorabilia from her career, photographs, costumes, fans, paperweights, jewelry, and sundry objets d'art, a visitor was lucky if she could find a square inch of space to put a coaster down in the first place. Talk about clutter.

"Even Tennessee Williams, the lush, used a coaster in my house!" Ethel shouted at me. "Look, Becky, do me a favor. Go in the kitchen and drink your wine over the sink, okay? I just know you're going to spill it all over that book Andy Warhol gave me. It's a collector's item, for Christ's sake!"

Collector's items, be they Warhol prints, six-tiered chandeliers or deluxe encyclopedias, were high on the list on my mother's side of the family.

"Aa . . . aaa . . . aaa . . . CHOO," I sneezed, five times, pulling out the last record for the day. *The Hobnobbers*. I had never played it and had no idea that it even existed. In fact, it was still wrapped in its cellophane packaging. I threw it in the "terminate" pile with *Spec and the Spiders*, *Heavy Metal Hothouse*, and *Ricky Dee's Happy Sax*.

I was pleased with myself. My apartment had just lost well over a hundred pounds. And it was just past seven. I still had a half hour to get ready before Professor Bloch showed up to take me to the Reinhard Beck opening.

I thought I smelled Karla until I heard the voice.

"You're that lady from television, aren't you?" A boisterous big blonde in a black sequined top and a long black pleated polyester skirt suddenly appeared beside the bistro table where Professor Bloch and I were peacefully standing and nibbling on our buffet snacks. She was wearing Karla's perfume. "Gerda Heenemann, from the Berlin Water Authority," she exclaimed in a booming voice, giving me her hand.

"The American, am I right?" said her husband, a full-bearded fellow in a dark blue suit and aviator glasses. He shook my hand too.

"Carsten teaches English," Gerda Heenemann informed us.

"Oh, how nice," I said.

"Yes, Mrs. Bernstein," Carsten Heenemann said with a heavy German accent, "I am teaching already since ten years in the high school in the Blücher Street."

"Oh, how nice." It was all I could think of to say, although for a moment I wondered if I should correct his English — at least for the sake of his students — and explain that I was a Ms., possibly a Miss, but most decidedly not *Mrs.* Bernstein. But I decided it would take too much energy. Instead, I just suggested that we speak German.

"Oh no, no," Carsten Heenemann eagerly answered in his high-school-teacher English, "It is very good for me to make small talks in English."

"But I'll speak German, if you don't mind," his wife said in a hefty Berlinese. "I'm too excited to think. This is the first time we've been to a gala premiere. My sister-in-law works for the travel agency that booked all the flights for the film." She pointed to a woman dressed like her in sequins and polyester pleats, only in red, standing at a table not far from us.

"Oh, how nice," I said.

"You're repeating yourself," Professor Bloch whispered in my ear. Gerda whipped out her invitation, asked me to sign it, and then proceeded to tell me everything she felt was wrong with the Umberto Bernini interview I had done, which had aired that past Friday. She gave me a list of all the questions *she* would have asked him. What is it about talk shows that makes the viewers think they can handle it better than the hosts? Even *I* have the urge every now and then to give Jay Leno or Oprah a few tips. Once I started to call Howard Stern to bawl him out.

I had to get away from this Gerda person. Her perfume was assaulting me. What was the name of it again? "Well, thank you for your criticism, Frau —" I began.

"Becky!"

Professor Bloch and I turned toward a croaking voice.

"Cheese!" said Ulrike Graurock, the city's most famous roving photographer and gossip columnist.

Flash. Flash.

"Super," she said, pulling a pencil from behind her ear and a pad out of the pocket of her leather jacket. Also known as Frau Grau, Ulrike Graurock was a celebrity in a class of her own, a seventy-year-old dynamo who ran around the city from party to party blitzing the VIPs. "Who's the companion?" she asked, eyeing Professor Bloch. "Paul Newman's brother?" I could tell she liked what she saw.

"Ulrike, he's just a friend," I said, amused. The professor blushed.

"No name?" she insisted.

"Ulrike, we play cards together. My neighbor, Professor Kurt Bloch."

She wrote it down.

"Just write 'Rebecca Bernstein with her escort, the eminent skat champion Professor Blockhead,'" he said, and guffawed. Oh, God. He had had a bit too much to drink again. I really worried about him sometimes. Perhaps he was lonelier than he let on. The professor had many friends, yes. And he was close to his family, yes. He still even went hiking with his sons. In fact, he and his two grown sons and their families ritually cooked up a feast together on Sundays and holidays. But the death of Kurt's wife, only five years before, had left him desolate. I had never met Doro, but I knew he had loved her dearly and buried much of his happiness along with her.

Ulrike Graurock cocked an eyebrow. "Wait a second. Are you *the* Professor Bloch?" she asked. "*Intelligent Cooking* Bloch?" He nodded. "Twenty years ago I bought a wok because of you," she said. "What a waste."

I bet she'd give him a call. She was Berlin's most notorious single.

"Day after tomorrow in the paper," she said, turning back to me. "Becky honey, you're looking fabulous!" She pinched my cheek and then patted my bottom. "Ten, twelve pounds, huh?" And then off she went to the next table, where the ex-mayor of Berlin was standing next to the ex-wife of the ex-president of ex-East Berlin's ex-Academy of Arts and Sciences who was standing next to — omigod, it was my ex-boyfriend Hannes, my Anywhere Chair affair. I hadn't seen him in three years and had no desire to do so now. I turned away and took a sip of my white wine spritzer.

"Becky," Professor Bloch said, "I think I'm cramping your style. If I left you alone for a while you'd have droves of men swarming around you." The professor was sometimes a broken record.

"Professor, that's not why I came here."

"My lovely, I've been inspecting the men. I think it's a good crowd. Okay, so Egon didn't have enough oomph for

you. Don't worry about it. I'm not offended. I've seen some
sensitive-looking types here. Let me point out a few."

"Hey, you're drunk."

"Ridiculous," he replied, brushing my remark aside like
a fly. "Now look at that fellow over there, the tall one with the
silk shirt and those horn-rimmed glasses."

"Professor."

"Don't roll your eyes. Just look!"

I turned around. He was pointing at Hannes.

"Mrs. Bernstein."

Oh, no. Now it was High School Heenemann. I'd forgotten
about him and his wife. They'd been joined in the meantime
by the lady in red.

"My sister-in-law, Gaby Kiesewetter," Gerda Heenemann
said, introducing us. "The travel agent."

"How nice," I said.

"You're repeating yourself again," the professor mumbled
under his breath. "And what's wrong with that fellow over
there? You don't like the glasses?"

"Mrs. Bernstein, I hear you are American. This is true,
no?" It seemed Gaby Kiesewetter knew how to speak English
about as well as her brother.

"*Ja,*" I answered.

"Where from, may I ask?"

"We *can* speak German, you know," I insisted.

"Oh no, no," she said, "it is very good for me to make
small talks in English."

"It seems *everybody's* repeating themselves around here,"
whispered Professor Bloch.

"You too!" I replied.

"Please," Gaby Kiesewetter continued, "where in America
are you coming from?"

"Becky!"

It was Heike with Norbert, her Mr. Right for Now, a tall, gangly sitcom producer with a bored face and a wandering eye. Heike and I hugged. "I can't believe Gerald Jankowitz is here," she said. "I read he'd been detoxed and was drying out in a Swiss rehab."

"Heike, don't you have any gossip about someone we might happen to know *personally?*" I said.

"As a matter of fact, I do," she answered. "I heard from Gerlinde who bought life insurance from your ex-puppy that he's single again. Hildburg left him."

"Serves him right, the lousy bastard."

"He's flying back early tomorrow morning," Gaby Kiesewetter remarked smugly. "I booked his flight to Zurich."

"Who?" I asked. "Who's flying to Zurich?"

"Felix?" asked Heike.

"Felix?" asked Gaby Kiesewetter. "Who's Felix? Aren't we talking about Gerald Jankowitz?"

"We?" Heike said, smiling vaguely, wondering who in the world this lady in red polyester and sequins was. She turned to me. "How'd you like it?"

"What?"

"The movie! What else?"

"Oh, right. I completely forgot we saw a movie this evening. It was okay. You can't expect much from a German comedy. And you?"

"I liked it a lot. I laughed a few times."

A *few* times? God, I thought, how German!

"Oh, we loved it," Gerda Heenemann chimed in.

"I've known about this project for the past two years," Norbert remarked, yawning. "My company turned it down and I'm glad we did. The dialogue's weak. They had to bring in some writer from Hollywood, but I don't think it helped. The timing's off. It's too slow for a screwball comedy."

"But we loved it," Gerda Heenemann repeated. "We adore Gerald Jankowitz. Don't we, Carsten?" She nudged her husband in the ribs.

"Yes, of course," he said, and flushed. He had been off in another world, mesmerized by Heike's good looks.

"Heike, you are ravishing this evening," said Professor Bloch, offering her one of his shrimps.

"Oh, there's one of my writers," said Norbert. This Norbert person had a great talent for using one eye to scan the crowd and the other to converse with us. "I've been meaning to speak with him. I've got to go."

"We'll come with you," I said, seizing the opportunity to get away from the Heenemanns.

"Who is it?" asked Heike.

"Hannes Förster."

Oh no. My ex-Hannes.

"On second thought," I said, "I think I'll stay here and eat some more." Ciao. Ciao. Kiss. Kiss. Heike and Norbert disappeared into the crowd. Maybe if I eat, the Heenemanns will leave me alone, I thought.

"Mrs. Bernstein," Gaby Kiesewetter began. "Mrs. Bernstein, we were asking before where from you are coming exactly in America."

There was no escape.

"New York," I replied, popping a shrimp into my mouth.

"Aahh! Direct?" Herr Heenemann asked, his eyes widening.

"Well, actually I made a quick stop first in Hong Kong to pick up some Chinese food." It's my stock answer to a question I'll never cease hearing in Germany, an answer cultivated over many years of wondering what Germans actually mean by the word *direct*. The Heenemanns and the sister-in-law looked at me blankly. "Yes," I relented, giving in to common politeness, "I come straight from New York City."

"Aahh," said Herr Heenemann. He looked relieved. I guess he really was worried for a moment that maybe I *did* come from Hong Kong. "But where from exactly?" he asked then. "You see, I know New York very well. I have been living there for three weeks two years ago."

Uuhh-oohh. Déjà vu. How many times have I heard Germans say this? Sometimes, of course, instead of saying they had lived in New York for three weeks two years ago, the Herr Heenemanns would say, "I have been living there for two weeks three years ago," or "In three weeks I will be living there for two years." The German language, rich in nouns but suffering from a dearth of verb tenses, infringes in the strangest ways the Germans' ability to express temporal things in English. Anyway, however long they were or will be in New York, the fact remains that these folks always think they really *know* it. But do they? To foreigners, New York is strictly Manhattan, whereas to most New Yorkers, New York is everything *but* Manhattan. Manhattan's just a place where they might work, or take in one of those French movies, or where they go to get weekly allergy shots. Real life takes place in Brooklyn, Queens, and the Bronx. And maybe sometimes on Staten Island.

"Please," Herr Heenemann prodded, "please exactly where from are you coming in New York?"

Okay, I thought, I'll give it a try. "I'm from East New York," I said. "Also Far Rockaway and Forest Hills."

I might just as well have said I was from Hong Kong. "*Where* from?" he repeated.

Gerda Heenemann's perfume, whatever its name, was permeating my brain's headache region.

"Well," I said, "it was very nice meeting you —"

"Mrs. Bernstein," travel agent Gaby Kiesewetter began,

thoroughly ignoring my attempt to leave, "I am very curious. Please, what was the reason why you have first come to Berlin?"

"I'm sorry, but —"

"Were you studying on the university?"

Did I have to answer this question? Why couldn't I just be rude? "I was in love with a Berliner," I said, switching impolitely into German. "But that was a long time ago. And now —"

"So then may I ask what has been holding you here?" asked Carsten Heenemann.

"The museums," I replied. "If it weren't for the Museum Island I would be long gone by now." I smiled, about-faced, and escaped.

"Whew!" the professor said once we were out of earshot.

"Oh, come on," I said, making a huge detour around Hannes, Norbert, and Heike, "they're okay. They're just — I don't know, just — Germans. Germans with strong perfume. I think you're ready to go home, aren't you?"

"Fine with me, my lovely." We turned toward the cloakroom. "But you know, sometimes I too wonder what you're doing here, Becky," he said. "Wouldn't you be better off at home?"

"Right, I should go back to New York and wait tables. Here I'm half a star, there I'm a complete nothing. In New York, girls like me are a dime a dozen. On any corner you're sure to bump into at least nine hundred shortish, dark-haired, fast-talking, wiseacre girls who find world-class museums sexy. I should go back to that kind of competition?" Professor Bloch laughed. "And besides," I added, "I told you what happened to me in New York last summer. I couldn't wait to get back to Berlin."

Up ahead there was a bottleneck at the reception room exit. The guests were queuing up for party favors. At fancy receptions like this, hostesses looking like perky airline stewardesses often distributed designer chocolates at the door, or cigarettes, sometimes even cosmetics.

"And besides," I went on, "in Berlin I have cheap health insurance, buses that run on schedule, relatively safe streets, parquet floors, and a brilliant local language complete with a genitive, a dative, and an honest-to-goodness subjunctive. Whenever I formulate a grammatically correct sentence of fifteen words or more, I feel as brilliant as Thomas Mann. Let's face it, Professor, I don't have any of that in New York."

"My lovely, what *really* kept you here?" he asked. Suddenly he didn't seem at all drunk. And he wanted a straight, sober answer.

"I don't know. I really don't. I think I'm just too lazy to move."

Professor Bloch wasn't buying it.

"I feel comfortable here," I went on. "It's New York *en petit*. It has the edge and tempo of a big city, but it's also kind of old-world charming and provincial. It's like New York, only nicer. It's a nice New York. A humane New York. Berlin is a livable New York."

I remember once telling Grandma Rosie of Flatbush, Brooklyn, originally of Somewhere, Russia, that Berlin was a "nice New York, a humane New York, a livable New York." She almost had a nervous breakdown. I remember her smacking her head with her hand, slapping her babushka. "Baloney!" she screamed and smacked. "Berlin nice? Berlin humane? Berlin *livable?* Did they let *us* live there? *Meshugge!* You make me *meshugge!* To me my own granddaughter should talk like this?" And she was right, of course. Sixty years ago Berlin was not a very congenial place to be. I don't want to even *think* about what might have happened to me, my family, my grandmother Rosie in Berlin sixty years ago. And I'm sure there are people around today, maybe they live right across the street from me or even sit next to me on the bus, who would still want to do to me today what I don't want to even think about.

But these same people live in New York too. In Flatbush. And in Mississippi. In the middle of the Pacific. At the bottom of South America. In the East. In the West. They're everywhere. Even in Switzerland.

So why not stay where life is at least comfortable?

The professor and I had reached the queue near the exit. I was not one for standing on lines. "Whatever they're giving out," I said, "take one for me too, professor, okay? I'll get the coats and meet you out in front."

A few minutes later Professor Bloch joined me at the exit. "I got you a party favor." He was beaming.

"What is it?"

"Missy Ukigumo."

"Missy Ukigumo?"

"*Ukigumo* means 'floating clouds.' It's Japanese. Hold up your wrists," Professor Bloch said, pulling out a pretty little black flacon. "It's perfume." He sprayed it. Sszzcchhtt!

Oh no! Missy Ukigumo? So that was the name. It was — barf! — it was Karla's perfume.

The following day I still had an Ukigumo headache. "It smells like the first floor of Bloomingdales," Barry Sonnenberg said, sniffing the black flacon.

"Just don't spray it on me!" I said. "I'm allergic."

"Ickygumo. Pretty classy stuff."

"*Uki*gumo. And you can keep it. Maybe one of your girl-friends might like it." I poured him a mug of beer. We could hear the dryer working on his laundry in my bathroom; he was two days behind schedule this week.

"Senate. I'll give it to Senate," he said, sniffing the bottle.

"She's new. She works for the Cultural Senate. Does their PR. She'll love this Okaygumo stuff." He took a sip of beer. "I met her a few days ago. I saw her in the subway and then followed her when she got out."

"You're joking."

"I can't believe I had the fucking balls to follow her out of the subway. If it wasn't for her smile I would never have done it. When you follow a girl out of the U-Bahn you're asking for major trouble. Mace to the face, right? But she smiled at me, so I followed her for a couple of blocks, and she knew it, because she kept on turning around. And then we started talking. We hit it off immed —"

"What do you mean you *started* talking? What did you say? Exactly. I want a step-by-step account."

"She turned around and laughed, so I said to her, 'What's so funny?' I said it in English because I figured that would make it exotic from the very start. And then she came right back in perfect English. So I asked her if she wanted to go for a cup of coffee."

"And she said —"

"She said, 'Okay.' So we went to this café near her house and started talking. It was brilliant. It was beyond a blind date. It was ten times more intense than a blind date. I'm telling you, she was nervous, nervous, nervous. Me too. We were both scared shitless."

"Sure she was scared. You could have been a serial killer. A butcher. Barry the Berlin Butcher."

"That's what made it so exciting. The whole time she was asking herself, Is he crazy? And the whole time I was asking myself, Does she think I'm crazy? Because you just don't follow girls out of the subway. But that's why she liked me. Because German guys don't do that."

"And then?"

"We talked for an hour about work and the States, this and that, and then she came to the theater the next night." Barry lit a cigarette and took a drag. "Look, if I was a plumber, I wouldn't have scored. But girls get wet when they see me in all that makeup. And then afterwards we *shtuped* each other to death, death, death."

"Does she know she's not the only one you're *shtuping?*"

"Sure."

"It doesn't bother her?"

"No. I'm not the only one by her. She's in love with some guy in Braunschweig. And that's fine with me. Finally someone who doesn't attach middle-class morality to the world's most natural act. And drop-dead beautiful. The best thing since sliced bread." Barry took another gulp of beer. "God, she's so sexy. She's filthy. And what a turn-out. She has a turn-out like a dancer."

"A 'turn-out'?"

"The pelvis. She knows how to turn it out, out, out. She can mount me when I'm standing up. Now that takes skill. She puts her arms around my shoulders, wraps her legs around my waist, I penetrate, and then we're in business. Up and down, up and down. In and out, in and out. Pump, pump, pump. Shtup, shtup, shtup."

Barry was enjoying his performance. He got up from his chair and started doing deep knee bends in the middle of the kitchen, up and down, his arms wound around invisible Senate's buttocks. "And then I carry her to the filing cabinet," he said, walking across my kitchen, "and flip her down. Wham! The stapler goes flying. And she just *loses* it. She is out of this world. And then I pin her up against the wall and she's begging for more. And more. And more. I do a quick pirouette and then fling her down on the bed and finish the job."

Barry was out of breath. Me too. "Enough already," I said.

"Oh God, she is sooo sexy. What a bonk. Perfect balance —"

"Enough already!"

"Her center of gravity fits right into my center of gravity. That's very hard to find. Very few women have it. I bet your girlfriend Heike has it. Did you tell her I asked about her?" He started guzzling the beer again.

"I sure did. She said you were too young. But that was weeks ago when she was in love. She called this morning to tell me it was over between her and Norbert. It seems they had a skirmish at the Beck party last night. So maybe you still have a chance."

Barry polished off his beer.

"Want some more?" I asked.

He nodded.

"And a bite to eat?"

"Nah, I just ate. I wanted something hot so I went to this café. I got into a beef with the waitress."

"Did you try to pick her up too?" I pulled a beer out of the refrigerator and poured it.

"No, not at all," he replied, indignant. "The issue was bread. Here, listen to this. I ordered broccoli with cheese, right? So right away she brings me this basket of bread. But I'm hungry, so I eat the bread before the meal comes. This can happen anywhere, in cheap restaurants, in classy restaurants, anywhere. When it happens I ask for more bread, they bring it, I give a generous tip and everyone's happy. Okay. So I ate all the bread up and we now have an empty bread basket, right? The meal comes and I ask for more bread. The waitress reluctantly brings me another basket. Ten minutes later, lo and behold, I'm finished with the broccoli but there's a lot of cheese sauce left in the bottom of the bowl that I want to mop up. But no more bread."

"Wait a sec, Barry. How much bread did you get in the first place?"

"It wasn't a lot. They give four tiny slices of French bread to a basket. The size of a silver dollar."

"That's not much. That's nothing."

"That's what I'm saying. So listen! I thought, gosh, wouldn't it be nice to get a little bit more bread? I mean, if I was the chef sitting there in the kitchen and that bowl came back clean enough to go right back on the shelf, that's a great compliment, right? So I asked for more bread. But she starts explaining to me that it was not their policy to give so much bread to one person. One basket, maybe two, but it was absolutely not within their rules to give three baskets to a single diner. And besides, she said, she had never seen anyone eat all their bread *before* the meal actually came. 'That's not the way we do it here,' she said. 'We don't eat all the bread up first.' I told her I would gladly *pay* for the bread. But she got all flustered and stuck to her guns about no more than two baskets. Becky, we're talking about three pieces of skinny bread! It just wiped me out. No one in my whole life, not even my *mother*, has ever told me that I have to *wait* until the meal comes before I start in on my bread."

"So what happened?"

"To listen to this waitress, I'm such a fucking philistine, I think bread's on the table to whet my appetite until the meal arrives. I'm such an uncouth, unrefined bohemian slob, I think bread's there so you have something to nibble on before the meal. I'm such a —"

"So what happened already?"

"I didn't get my bread and I thought it was a real shame to leave all that sauce at the bottom of the bowl."

"You just paid and left?" I asked, shocked. "I would have burned the joint down. I hate that. It makes me sick.

It's so — it's so, I don't know, it's so *German*. It's like my ice cream parlor story. Did I ever tell you my ice cream parlor story?"

"Is this long? My laundry's almost finished."

"Okay. I'll give you the abridged version. I'm walking home from the subway. All of a sudden there's a torrential rain storm, Hurricane Sally–like, and I have no umbrella. I jump into this little neighborhood ice cream parlor, a sidewalk-counter deal with five little tables inside, one of which is occupied by this guy and his girlfriend with sundaes —"

Barry began laughing.

"What's the matter?" I asked. "I didn't get to the funny part yet. There *is* no funny part."

"I can't believe how New York you are. Just the way you talk. You've been living here for twenty frigging years and you still have a New York accent. You're amazing."

"You want me to finish this story or not?"

"Quit the mental prep and get on with it."

"So I order a cone with two scoops and sit down at one of the empty tables," I went on. "There are now three empty tables. Suddenly I hear this voice. 'You're not allowed to sit there.' I look up. The fellow behind the counter is talking to *me*. And I say, 'Why not?' And he points to a sign that says only people with sundaes are allowed to sit at the tables. So I say, 'It's hailing outside. If I go out there with this cone it'll turn into water ices.' He just stands there and says, 'That's your problem. You're not allowed to sit there. That's the rules. You can stand if you want to.' And I say, 'Look, I see the problem. You want to make sure if customers are having a sundae, they can sit down comfortably. I understand. But there's *no one* in here. *No one* wants my seat. There's a major hurricane outside. If all of a sudden a thousand people storm the shop and want to have sundaes, I'll get up, okay?' I was pretty emotional. So this guy probably thought maybe he should just shut up, considering I was this crazy person he didn't want to have to deal with. But then suddenly the snotnose girl sitting there with her sundae says, 'Who do you think you are, talking like that? If that's their policy, that's their policy. Why should he change his policy for you?'

"And *that* is what really upset me. She was a customer like me, but her sympathy was with the stupid ice cream man — the authority figure. Plus, the whole thing had nothing to do with her anyway. What did she care if I sat there or not? These sticklers for the rules —"

"Hey, you're going to get a heart attack if you keep that up," Barry said. "You can't let people like that get to you. There's more of them than there are of you. You're not going to change the world. It's not worth the stress. Do you think that woman is going to change her bread policy because of me? Or that that man is going to change his seating rules because of you? Never!"

The bell on the dryer went off.

"I gotta go," Barry said, jumping up.

"Hey, hold on a second. I'm not finished. Let me ask you something. Give me another minute."

"Okay, one question. One minute." He sat down again.

"Fine. This is my question." I paused dramatically. "Tell me," I said, "what is it with the Germans?"

"That's your question? 'What is it with the Germans?' This you want me to answer in a *minute?* It'd take a *lifetime* to answer that question!"

"Okay," I said. "Then take *two* minutes."

He drew a deep breath. "All right, this is my philosophy," he began. "How many times when I was growing up did I hear from my parents and my school teachers, 'How could the holocaust have happened? How could it have *ever* hap —' "

"Hold on a second." I stood up. "Let me get my Dicta-phone. This sounds like it could be interesting."

"A Dictaphone? What, you wanna blackmail me? What are you doing?"

"Nothing," I said, placing the Dictaphone on the table and switching on the tape. "I just want this for the record. Maybe I can use it for something. Which reminds me. I may be writing a script based on 'Bingo Berlin.' Remember how I kind of based the character of Arthur Zetlin on you?"

"So?"

"So I'll write that part for you in the movie. You'll play Arthur Zetlin. I'll make it at least a ten-day shoot for you, okay?"

"I'll believe it when it happens." He took a swig of his beer. "But it's a smart idea. You're real smart, Becky. One of our smartest. You're the only person I know with an IQ of a hundred and forty-eight."

"Well —"

He tapped the Dictaphone. "Just don't quote me! I'm a member of a prestigious theater group."

"Right, some prestigious theater group. Who ever heard of a prestigious theater group that can't even pay its actors enough so they don't have to come begging for detergent?"

"Okay already. What were you asking me?"

"You were saying how many times had you heard from your parents and from school teachers, 'How could the holo-caust *ever* have hap —' "

" 'How could it have happened? How could a thing like the holocaust *ever* have happened in this century?' That's what they were always asking, right? But I'll tell you something, after living in this country a few years, I know how such a thing could have happened."

I nudged the recorder a little closer.

"They defer to authority," he said. "The Germans defer to authority."

"You're saying an empty bread basket and a no-seat policy for ice cream cones explain how the holocaust could have happened?"

Barry nodded.

"If you said this on my talk show I would say to you, 'Mr. Sonnenberg, that's pretty dark. And pretty simplistic.'"

"But we're not on your talk show."

"So I'll say, 'That makes sense to me.'"

"Exactly! All I know is that I don't ask myself that question anymore. I don't ask myself anymore, 'How could it have happened?' It makes sense to me now. All I know is that the individual does not come first here. They know jackshit about personal liberties. Higher authority comes first. That's why no one fucking jaywalks around here even if there's not a car in sight. Red lights have more authority than their own eyes. And like that girl in the ice cream parlor, they learn to side *with* the authority *against* the individual. In America it doesn't work like that. It's part of our nature to question authority. But here the rules are the rules and to question them is a huge, major effort."

"If this is how you feel, what are you doing here? Why are you in Berlin?"

"Me? What about *you?* You're the one who's been here forever. What are *you* doing here if you have a major heart attack every time you buy an ice cream cone?"

"First of all, I asked *you* the question first. And second of all, I already went through this last night with Professor Bloch. That's why I'm so keen on hearing what you have to say. I need to clarify."

But Barry wasn't in the mood to clarify. He was here to launder his sheets, not to pontificate. He debated a moment.

"Okay, give me that gadget," he finally said, grabbing the recorder off the kitchen table. He cleared his throat. "Testing one-two-three. Testing one-two-three."

"It's already on."

"Ask me the question again."

Boy, was he exasperating sometimes. "Why are you in Berlin?"

"Why am I here? I'm in Berlin because it's the only city in the world where my mother won't come to visit me."

What a character!

"But I'm also here," he continued, "because poor artists can live in Berlin with dignity. Here, an artist, an actor, is treated as someone special. In America you're treated like part of the problem." He put the Dictaphone back down on the table and took a drag on his cigarette. "So that's why I'm here. And also because I think it's important to prove to the Germans that Hitler didn't get away with it. You can quote me on that, but don't make me sound like I'm in the Zionist Action Front. My number's in the telephone book."

"You want to *prove* something?"

"Yes. I'm Jewish and I'm here. They didn't finish us off."

"And that's why you're here? Out of defiance?"

"Hey — this is an intriguing piece of equipment," he said, picking the Dictaphone up again and checking out the details. He cupped it in his hand, like a ball, feeling the weight. "Where can I get something like this? I could use it to memorize lines. You use it for interviews?"

"It's not good enough for that. I just use it to remind myself of stuff. I bought it on my last trip to the States, in the summer." I grabbed the Dictaphone out of his hands and put it back down on the table. "So that's why you're here, to prove to the Germans that Hitler didn't get away with it? Huh?"

Barry gulped down the rest of his beer, stood up, and

leaned forward with both hands flat on the kitchen table. "Bullshit. Bullshit. Bullshit. You want to know why I'm here? I'll tell you why I'm here. I'm here because in this city I score like a fucking bandit. And that is *it*." He sprang toward me, grabbed me around the waist, humped me three times, hump, hump, hump, picked me up, and flung me down on the kitchen table. The Dictaphone went flying. "Sex. Sex. Sex," he cried out. Then he picked me up again and pinned me against the wall. "Hey, I'll be damned," he said. "You really did lose weight. I'll be damned." He let go of me and headed out of the kitchen into the bathroom.

But first he fell over a pile of terminated records I had left out in the hall.

So that's why he was here, I thought as I looked around absentmindedly for the Dictaphone. It certainly wasn't why *I* had decided to stay — alas. Why was it, I wondered, that so many of the men I knew were getting theirs, while the women. . .

The Dictaphone was nowhere to be found. It seemed to have vanished into thin air. And that's when I remembered what had happened to the other one on my last visit to New York, in May. It was enough to make even a Carsten Heenemann understand why I had chosen to live where I did.

The Dictaphone
(May 1992)

I was enjoying my new Dictaphone. I got a kick out of its compact microcassettes and the way the sleek black case fit snugly into the palm of my hand. I held it up to my mouth and spoke. "Okay," I said, "Kaiser's Diner may be gone and with it the perfect vanilla egg cream, but I'm amazed that so little has really changed after twenty years."

It was hot outside. Far too hot for May. And I was panting a little because the hills were beginning to get to me. "Same steep incline and 'BEWARE OF DOG' signs. Same quiet, lazy streets. Green lawns. Neat fences. Sweet little houses," I wheezed. "Amazing! Yesterday morning I was in Berlin, and now I'm gasping for breath on Sixty-seventh Avenue in Forest Hills."

A handsome black maid in a starched white uniform and sensible, squishy shoes walked by briskly pushing a baby carriage. She vanished into one of the mini-mansions and a sleepy stillness settled down again over Sixty-seventh Avenue. Strange how sluggish a street in a busy city could be, in Queens, at the fringe of our hectic universe. The only other person in sight was a janitor in a brown uniform up on top of the hill carrying a garbage bin.

"The question is," I panted into the Dictaphone, "can I or can I not ever go home again?"

Berlin had been fatiguing me. Spring had refused to come that year, and reunification was depressing the daylights out of the city. The skies looked like dirty dishwater, the streets were overcrowded, the buses and subways were running off schedule. And if you tried to get out of the city, you hit traffic jams from Kleinmachnow to Großbeeren. On top of this I was unsure of my future. Media Menzel had lost a few clients, Karla was on my back, the ratings for *Breakfast at Becky's* had dropped. I had started work on "Bingo Berlin," but literature was a rather new and unknown métier for me and I assuaged my insecurity by stuffing my mouth with thick chunks of gorgonzola on Italian white and my head with that Felix nonsense.

The upshot was that for the first time in twenty years I wondered if perhaps I ought to go home. I became obsessed with New York. I longed to attack a real double-thick Dutch chocolate shake at a corner coffee shop, bite into a three-inch-high pastrami sandwich on rye. I yearned to fight for a seat on the screeching, scratchy, shrieking subway. Oh, if only I could take a quick peek at the red brick high-rises looming beside the gray cemeteries that lined the Long Island Expressway, catch a glimpse of the brontosaurus in the Museum of Natural History, feel helplessly lost amidst the cluttered pandemonium of a mom-and-pop grocery store, soil my fingers on the smudgy print of the *New York Times.*

In New York I would feel like a part of things without even trying to fit in, without ever having to explain myself. Hannes's phrase began to possess me: *Home is where you owe no explanations.* Indeed. New York was programmed into my bones, my marrow, my heart. It was me and I was it. We didn't owe each other any explanations.

But could I live there?

"Tell me," I said to Marsha when I called her in New York. "What do you think? You think you can find me the following three things in New York: one, a sunny three-room apartment in a safe neighborhood; two, a boyfriend within a hundred-mile radius of that apartment; and three, a job where I don't have to stand on my feet or on my head all day? If so, I promise to take the first flight back to New York."

"Don't even think for a second you can find a job here," she exclaimed. "The only opening I know of is a secretarial position in my office, part-time, minimum pay, no benefits. Can you type?"

I moaned.

"And a boyfriend!" she marveled. "She wants a boyfriend! Sweetheart, all the men I know are either gay or married. Or both. It's out of the question."

"And an apartment?" I asked meekly.

She guffawed. "Forget it! No one in New York ever gives up an apartment. No one's moving around here except the rats."

"So it's that bad?"

"Of course not! I love New York," she said. "Why don't you come and take a look? See what the city feels like."

I bought the Dictaphone at Heathrow, between planes.

I trudged further up the hill toward Queens Boulevard and the janitor in the brown uniform with the garbage bin. I left the one-family homes behind me. They were replaced on both sides by orderly red brick apartment buildings with canopied entrances and names that made them sound like vacation destinations: the Monte Carlo, Barbizon Gardens, Capri Terrace, El Patio. Opulent chandeliers glittered through the lobby windows.

I was fourteen when we settled down in Forest Hills. At the time it was 75 percent middle class, 85 percent Jewish, 95 percent white, and 105 percent frustrating. My friends' mothers were sparkling housewives. They wore pearl necklaces and cashmere cardigans to the supermarket. My friends' fathers were doctors and lawyers. They barbecued spareribs and sipped highballs out in the backyard on the weekend. And my high school friends were all so special. Anita Klein spoke French fluently, Bobsie Horwitz played the piano like a pro, Elaine Soloman had already performed in an off-Broadway show, Nancy Feldman had been runner-up in the Little Miss Palisades Park contest, Rhoda Weisman won first prize in the National Student Science Fair. All I could do was make people laugh.

"Tacky, chintzy interior deco," I said into my Dictaphone, barely able to catch my breath. Goodness, I'd forgotten how trying it was to climb these hills in the heat. In fact, whenever I had thought about them, remembered them in my mind's eye, I'd always seen them in winter, frozen them into a remembered moment in time when it's always seven-thirty on a frosty February morning on my way to school. The sun is nonexistent, and the steely gray sky is hovering menacingly over the endless rows of Monte Carlos and El Patios. I'm walking beside a girl-friend or two, and the damp bitter cold is creeping up inside my pea jacket sleeves. I'm wearing cranberry penny loafers without the pennies, and my hunter green knee socks keep slipping down. Needless to say, my toes and my knees have frozen to death. Tights haven't been invented yet. Or maybe they have been, but haven't found their way onto the legs of American schoolgirls, at least not on a daily basis.

So the nasty wind is shlepping and shoving us along as we slide on the ice, almost breaking our collarbones or bursting our sides with laughter. And when we finally get to the top of the last hill, when we finally see the tower of Forest Hills High School, our eyes are burning and tearing from the frost, our faces are streaked with black mascara and caked-up base foundation, and under our checkered kilts our naked thighs are red slabs of solid frozen meat. Boy, are we a mess! Yet we feel strangely exhilarated. Let the day begin! Once you've conquered the cruel hills of Forest Hills, you can beat anything — calculus or chemistry or even Aristotle in Great Books, III.

But there I was, walking along Sixty-seventh Avenue in Forest Hills on a hot May day, struggling on the steep incline I had learned to climb more than two decades earlier, when the janitor up ahead suddenly started making a terrible racket. He was banging the metal garbage bin up and down, up and down. I wasn't that far from him, maybe thirty steps or so, and it was deafening.

Suddenly I became aware that to my right, much closer to me than the janitor up ahead, someone else was on the street. A young fellow with greasy hair slicked back in a 1950s pompadour was standing next to a car. It was a good-looking maroon Volvo, but when I got closer I could see that the side window was smashed to smithereens, as if someone had hit it hard with a hammer. Poor guy. Someone broke into his car.

"Well, they didn't get everything," I said to Pompadour consolingly, gesturing toward a leather attaché case on the front seat. He grunted something inaudible and I continued on. I should mind my own business, I thought to myself as I came abreast of the janitor. He was standing stock still holding the garbage bin, as motionless as a wax figure, an expression of anxiety frozen on his face. What's wrong with this one? I wondered. I cautiously walked past him and veered left into 102nd Street, which would take me to Queens Boulevard. I had reached the top of the hills!

And then it hit me. Out of the clear, blue, hot May sky it suddenly drilled its way into my consciousness.

Slowly, ever so slowly, I raised my Dictaphone to my lips. "I can't believe it!" I said. "I just can't believe it! Maybe I'm dreaming, maybe it's jet lag, but if I'm not mistaken, I think a car is being robbed right in front of me at this very second. The janitor must be in on it. He was banging a garbage bin to cover up the noise of the window being smashed. I'm sure of it. Jesus, I could have gotten my *own* head smashed in." And then I realized, maybe I still *would*. I spun around and looked back toward the hills of Forest Hills.

How lovely and lush and still, how hushed, how strange yet familiar. When had I last stood here? How many eons ago? I wanted to dwell on it, drown in the memory, document it all on my microcassettes. But Pompadour and the janitor were standing there, waiting for me to react, say something, call the police, cry out indignantly, throw a rock.

I raised the Dictaphone to my lips again. "Welcome home, stupid," I said into it. And then with a quick flick of my thumb I switched the damn thing off and got the hell out of there as fast as I could.

A few days later I was talking to Marsha at Milton Goldfarb's cocktail party. "He came out of the bagel shop," Marsha was telling me, "and he was amazingly attractive. Tall, dark, handsome, tortoiseshell glasses, impeccably dressed. The works." She burped. "Oh, that onion soup! It's giving me heartburn." Once a hypochondriac, always a hypochondriac.

"Go ahead," I said. She was glaring skeptically at my Dictaphone.

"Do you really promise to change my name if you use this information?" she asked for at least the tenth time.

I nodded.

"Well, all right," she replied reluctantly, looking around stealthily to see if anyone was eavesdropping.

We had retired from the crowd and were sitting in a secluded corner behind the kitchen, somewhere between the maid's entrance and the dumbwaiter. Our host Milton was a film historian whom Marsha knew from her work as a freelance film publicist. His new book, *Hollywood in Deed*, dealing with the last wills and testaments of famous movie greats — who died leaving whom what, why, and how much — had just been published to much hullabaloo. Thus the get-together. Neither Marsha nor I was even remotely interested in dead Hollywood stars, but we had come anyway. Rumor had it that Milton's apartment overlooked Madonna's penthouse and we were anxious to see her sunbathing out on the roof.

"So this great-looking guy walked out of the bagel shop," Marsha continued, "and he was carrying this huge sack of bagels. I've never seen the likes of it. There must have been at least two hundred of them in there. And we were both going up the block in the same direction, pretending not to notice each other, right? Only it was obvious that we were. And I thought, this guy is going to get into a taxi and disappear out of my life forever. Do I want him to do that? No, I do not want him to do that. So I better think of something to say. And fast. But the only thing I could think of to say was to ask him if he needed some lox for the bagels. So I asked him."

"And what did he say?"

"He said, 'No thanks, we have caviar.' "

"And what did you say to that?"

"I said, 'Russian or ersatz? And who's *we?*' And he said, 'In answer to the second question: my friends. I'm giving a brunch.' " Marsha paused a moment.

"And then?" I said eagerly.

Marsha giggled. "You really drill for your data, don't you?"

"It's my job."

"Well, I'm off duty."

I gave her the evil eye.

She gathered her thoughts. "You know that pretty white townhouse across the street from my apartment building? The one with the sign on the garage door that says 'Don't even think of parking here'?"

"Who could miss it?"

"It's his."

"What's his? The sign? The door? The garage?"

"The *whole* thing. All three stories, or in other words about one and a half million dollars' worth. He just moved in. And when we got there, he invited me in. He said, 'Let me introduce myself to you. I'm Alexander Maxwell. Would you like to come in?' "

"And then . . .?"

"And then I went in."

"You went in?" I said, horrified. "Some stranger carrying a sack of bagels invites you into his house and you just go in?"

"I adore caviar. And anyway, he was wearing a Giorgio Armani suit."

Time had been friendly to Marsha Lipschitz. Graceful and slender, she now had stylishly kinky light brown hair, twinkly green eyes (*with* her colored contacts) and a lovely, raspy laugh. She was a well-kept, well-dressed, well-paid powerhouse. She had her nails manicured weekly.

If Marsha were a guy, she'd be the perfect catch. The girls would be lying in wait for her. As it was, she was a woman with a capital *W*, and since most New York men wanted girls with a very small, itsy-bitsy *g*, she hadn't had a real date since Passover, when her mother set her up at a seder with a dentist from Bensonhurst.

Poor Marsha. She was gorgeous and gifted, but single.

Marsha lived alone with her cat Boris, who suffered from delusions of grandeur and fantasies of flying out of their fourth-story window, and her computer Sven, which she protected like a mother hen. "I'll give you the sun, the moon, the stars, my boyfriends, anything but access to my computer," she said to me the very second I walked into her apartment from the airport. She was not serious, of course. No New York woman in her right mind would ever voluntarily give up a *boyfriend*. It could be years, decades, centuries before she found another — especially since the news broke that, according to the latest studies, women born in the 1950s were more likely to be struck by Halley's comet than ever to find a husband. For

Marsha, who had been pushing forty for a number of years, this had been a touchy subject ever since her fateful affair with Lance Lester, one of her independent directors. Lance had turned out to be a little too independent — when it came to women, that is.

But now there was the Bagel Man.

"And suddenly I found myself in Alexander Maxwell's townhouse amidst caviar and champagne and a cook chopping up chives and slicing bagels," Marsha told me and my Dictaphone. "I mean, the setup was terrific. A dream come true, right? So I forgot about my diet and just dove in."

Marsha was graceful and slender, yes, but she did have to work at it. Her TV dinner days, the frozen Salisbury steaks and the glazed hams with macaroni and cheese, were long since gone. In fact, I had a hard time finding anything edible around her house at all: just some cat food, a large jar of iron supplement tablets I mistook for M&Ms, and something that looked like birdseed but was actually her breakfast cereal.

She took a long sip of her mineral-water-and-lime and went on with her story. My Dictaphone was recording every word, every breath and sigh.

"Evidently Alexander got spoiled rich in Chicago, in the commodities market. He's a commodities broker. He put —" She burped.

"A commodities broker?" I said. "You mean he deals in things? Like what? Bagels?"

Marsha giggled. "Bagels! He put his future in soybeans," she said, burping again. "Oh, this damn mineral water. So much gas." She shook her head and went on. "He made millions in soybeans, came to New York, bought the house, and then took me on a tour of it. It's humongous. Beautifully decorated. Very Italian. You should see all the closet space. He opened every door, showed me every nook and cranny. Everything. All twenty-five bathrooms. And then he looked me in the eye and said, 'This is the way I like to live.' "

"And what did you say?"

"I said, 'This is the way I like to live too.' "

Our laughter was interrupted by Milton Goldfarb. "Hey, what are you two doing sitting back here with the garbage?" he asked. "Glenn's looking for you."

Marsha and I rolled our eyes. Glenn was the first male we had met that evening and the last one we wanted to talk to. He was an obnoxious, chubby, flaccid, beady-eyed plastic surgeon with a spastic sense of humor. "I wouldn't mind noseying around her nose," he had said lecherously of a woman standing across the room. Of another in a miniskirt he whispered in my ear, "I'd love to lipo-suck those thunder thighs. Yuk. Yuk. Yuk."

Standing with him was Gwen Mavrick, a cool blonde in white linen, a supermarket romance novelist with a lifeless, lifted face. "My husband is twelve years younger than I am," she revealed with a Southern drawl, "and I wanted to look as young and as fresh as he does, so I went to that honeypie Glenn. And now I appear in *The Face Saver*, his video about cosmetic surgery."

Glenn turned to me and remarked that my nose — which admittedly was no great shakes but nonetheless did its job quite adequately — was okay for now but was the type of nasal fixture that in a few years' time would begin to droop. "But you *can* hinder that process if you choose to," he told me.

"But I don't choose to," I told him.

"Well, just in case you change your mind." He handed me his business card. Dr. Glenn MacKensey, Plastic and Reconstructive Surgery.

"Glenn with a double *n*?" I asked him somewhat facetiously.

"Better a double *n* than a double chin," he replied.

A double *chin*?!

"Glenn's looking for you," Milton repeated.

"Milton," I said, "please tell Glenn we're massaging my chin and can't come out now."

Milton chortled and went back to his party.

"So after the Bagel Man showed me all twenty-five bathrooms I attacked the buffet," continued Marsha once Milton was out of earshot. "I was enthralled, thrilled with life. I stood there nibbling on the caviar, admiring the relaxed cut of his Armani jacket, taking in the beauty of the Rolex on his wrist, stealing a peek at the Jaguar in his driveway, and wondering how many children we would have and what they would look like and who we would name them after, when he came over to me, arm in arm with a very beautiful, young, dark, sultry person."

"Oh no!"

" 'Marsha, I'd like you to meet my boyfriend Luigi,' he said to me, 'Luigi from Milano. He did the house. He's my interior decorator.' "

"His *boy*friend, huh? I figured it was too good to be true."

Milton Goldfarb ran into the kitchen. "Hey, guess what!"

"You've fallen in love with an interior decorator too?" Marsha said.

"A celebrity died and left you millions?" I offered.

"Not yet," Milton said. "But Madonna is out on the roof. Do you want to take a quick look?"

"You bet!" I stood up.

"And do you know what else?" Marsha said, crestfallen. "Do you want to hear the worst of it?"

"Oh no, what? What could be worse?"

"It wasn't even Russian. It was ersatz." She burped. "The caviar was ersatz!"

A few days later I set out to buy some microcassettes for my Dictaphone. This was comforting: I had a goal. I like goals. They make me feel secure. Once I have a destination, once I know where I'm going and what I want, I can deviate from the road, fool around, have another cup of coffee. This goal was simple and realistic: buy microcassettes at Macy's.

I was all the way up in the East Eighties at Marsha's. Should I take a taxi down to Thirty-fourth Street and Sixth Avenue? No — a taxi was too great a luxury during the day. But the subway seemed the wrong choice too. Someone the media had dubbed the Subway Smasher was on the loose. For the past few days he'd been running around the underground bashing in women's heads with a hammer. Frankly, I wasn't in the mood. But neither did I want to walk all the way down to Macy's. I was still a bit bushed from my excursion to Brooklyn the day before. I'd take a bus.

I put my Dictaphone in its case with the original two tapes it had come with and threw it all in my leather sack. Four hours' worth of oral notes were on those tapes. If I had some time later in the day, I might begin transcribing them.

The Lexington Avenue downtown bus was a microcosm of New York life. A round Hispanic woman in a loud cotton dress was nursing her restless baby in the back. Seated next to her was an elegant elderly woman with frosted gray hair in a dark blue silk suit. A gold-chained Chanel bag dangled from her shoulder. She had just finished reading the *New York Times* and was folding it up. Smiling sweetly at the baby, she

pulled a tissue from her purse and wiped her smudgy fingers
clean. Next to me on my right was a schoolboy deep in his
math homework. On my left a fake redhead with hair teased
to the ceiling and dressed in imitation leather and black stilet-
tos slipped a cassette into her Walkman: James Joyce's *Ulys-
ses*. Several passengers were eating: munching on corned beef
sandwiches, drinking coffee out of plastic cups or Cokes out of
cans, spooning out their daily yogurt. The fake redhead spread
a napkin across her lap. On it she placed a large Styrofoam
container. She pulled off the top to reveal an egg roll, three
spareribs, fried rice, what looked like moo goo gai pan, and
two fortune cookies.

In short, I was witnessing a perfectly normal scene on a
perfectly normal New York City bus. But to me, who had gotten
used to living in ultraproper, squeaky-clean Berlin, the scene
was both familiar and exotic. I felt as though, for the first time,
I could see how weird and special and wonderful a place I came
from.

I loved New York. All of it. From "Turty-turd and Turd"
to the Spuyten Duyvil. I even loved the urban badlands I had
visited the day before, when I went and saw with my own
eyes the neighborhood where I first lived, Brooklyn's East New
York.

It was the first time I had been back in thirty years. To be
sure, I had caught glimpses of it occasionally, but always from
a distance. Occasionally, while driving from Queens along the
Belt Parkway to Coney Island to visit Aunt Minnie and Uncle
Morris, or to Flatbush to see Grandma Rosie, we'd pass close
enough to see it. And then for a split second and from a distance of many miles and years I would see the remains of the
Brooklyn housing project where I had grown up, learned to
roller skate, to read, write, fight. But my feet had never walked
its streets again. It wasn't the kind of place you'd go for a visit,

where you'd window-shop or take a stroll. It had become a
dark slum of wild repute. And I was meek.

But I was curious. The East New York of my youth,
surrounded on all sides by furious ghettos — Brownsville,
Bushwick, Bedford-Stuyvesant — had taken on grand propor-
tions in my memory. I wanted to have another look and see
how much was fact, how much fiction. So the day before,
I had rented a car and secured myself a bodyguard — my
cousin Stan, six foot two and streetwise — and together we had
descended into hell.

The corner of Euclid and Sutter Avenues, the corner that
for decades I had envisioned as being the crummiest, cruddiest,
most dangerous and urine-stinking purgatory southeast of the
Bronx, was, though poor and run-down and far from comfy,
surprisingly tame. No one threatened us or harassed us. I didn't
see one rat, one cockroach, one dead body.

The trees had grown; they were fuller and greener. The
drugstore, where I once stole a bottle of Evening in Paris cologne, had been transformed into a Korean green grocery, and
Sarah's Bakery into an off-track betting center. Crack vials
lined the gutters. They had replaced the discarded Popsicle
sticks we used to find in the street when I was a kid. In those
days, we'd comb the gutters looking for pop sticks to construct
makeshift houses for our Barbie dolls. Did the neighborhood
kids these days collect the crack vials? What could they make
with them? Could they be recycled like our pop sticks?

Just a few blocks from the housing project, the neighborhood had for the most part become an open, festering wound,
a war zone. Street peddlers with anxious, darting eyes banged
on our car windows. "Hey, you need a knife? Want a knife?"
they cried out like newsboys selling the evening paper. They
held out vendor's trays displaying fifteen-inch butcher knives
and a shocking array of sharp and jagged razorlike implements

with points glistening menacingly in the sun. Stan and I locked the car doors.

As we drove on toward Far Rockaway, the pretty, thriving, middle-class neighborhood of my puberty, we drove past clusters of men drinking from brown paper bags, and young boys sitting drugged-out and bleary-eyed on front stoops. The wasteland of Far Rockaway almost made East New York look like East Hampton, so overwhelming were the gloom and deterioration.

But our old Rockaway apartment building stood amidst the rubble, tall and proud; a large sign informed us that condominiums were in the offing.

"You here to see them apartment, lady?" a dark-skinned doorman asked me.

"No, not really," I said. "But can I see the roof?"

"What you want with the roof? No way!"

The roof overlooking Cornaga Avenue — my secret hiding place, the open, windy spot where I had learned to smoke, where I had run away to be alone — was locked, off limits, shut tight, and no form of persuasion, no bribe, no nothing could convince the fellow to let me up.

"Look, lady," he said. "I no care when you live here or who you are. If you're the Queen of Sheba I no let you up. That's what management say. We no want junkies!"

Despite the emotional impact of being jolted back thirty years in time, despite the sheer joy of remembering, recalling, *knowing* that this was where I began being who I had become, this reconnection with my past did not bring me any grand revelations. I made no earth-shattering discoveries — except perhaps the realization that, though most of my childhood haunts were gone, had vanished from all tangible existence, it didn't really matter. It didn't matter that the steamy, cluttered Chinese laundry was gone, or the Sugar Bowl where we went for five-cent Cokes after school, Dan's Supermarket, or the only synagogue in the neighborhood, an orthodox one down the block with the ladies' section upstairs and the men's downstairs. It didn't matter that they had disappeared, for they all actually did exist, as they always had, deep down in the far regions of my memory, where they loomed as large and bright as ever.

On the Lexington Avenue bus, the leatherette redhead sitting next to me had finished off the moo goo gai pan and was already on her fortune cookies. The boy and his math homework were gone, but now a huge man carrying a large manila envelope was standing in front of me. His two front teeth were missing. He was muttering softly to himself. What are they always muttering about? I wondered.

"I gotcha!" he suddenly cried out, startling me and half the bus. He peered at the address on the envelope for a moment or two, ducked down, glanced out the window, stood up straight again, smacked the envelope with the back of his hand as if he were bashing in someone's face, and exclaimed, "That'll teach ya!"

A few moments later he repeated the entire procedure.

This was not the type of person you want standing in front of you in a bus. I wondered if the mutterer might really be a compulsive serial killer. The Bus Basher I'd call him. Or maybe he was the Subway Smasher himself, checking out new turf. Or perhaps he was a sicko, crazy but harmless. Yes, he was probably just an ordinary schizo, the kind you meet up with at least 99½ times in an average week in New York. It wasn't worth worrying over.

I glanced out the window, saw Fifty-fourth Street, jumped out of my seat and off the bus. I had one short stop to make before Macy's: the Museum of Modern Art.

Picasso's goat was still out there in the sculpture garden. In

my memory, where it was forever the goat I had leaned against
when I fell in love with Jürgen, it stood on a pedestal, watching
over the garden like a pagan god of love. But now I found it
resting on a block of stone but a few inches from the ground,
munching lazily on the grass. Two children walked over to it
timidly and stroked its head, giggling. It was far, far smaller
than I had recalled. And I couldn't imagine leaning against it
anymore.

The garden and the museum had gone through many
changes. Much had been built, rebuilt, torn down, added. I
wondered if the very spot where Jürgen and I first glanced at
each other was where the dirty food trays were now stacked in
the cafeteria.

But it was getting late. And I had a goal. I continued down
Fifth Avenue on foot toward Macy's.

Fifth Avenue — I remembered it from way back when.

I remembered Fifth Avenue from before the United Colors
of Trumpton had gotten hold of it.

I remembered Fifth Avenue before it became an open air
flea market, an outdoor five-and-ten. I remembered the fine
shops and how people used to stop you on the street, smile
nicely, and ask for directions or a light or the time. Now, when
people stopped you on the street, they wanted a quarter from
you, a cigarette, drugs. Peddlers screeched at you, "Buy this
map. Here's your fresh-squeezed orange juice. Hot roasted
chestnuts! Men's ties, two for one, real cheap. What? You don't
want? Well, fuck you, lady!"

I remembered Fifth Avenue before people began wearing
Walkmen to tune out the pleas of the beggars, the muttering
of the Crazy Eddies, the cries of the peddlers, and before they
began wearing impenetrable dark glasses to block out the ultra violence on the streets, or the sight of the homeless, or the
young men dying of AIDS in front of Tiffany's.

I remembered Fifth Avenue when it was safe to park your car there at night. Now you had to put signs in the window that read NO RADIO AND NOTHING IN TRUNK.

"Look at that filthy cup!"

I was about to turn west onto Thirty-fourth Street. At the corner with Fifth Avenue a resolute woman of sixty was yelling at a beggar who was holding up a soiled Styrofoam cup.

"What a filthy cup! Why don't you invest something in your career, you creep!"

"Shit, lady, I ain't planning on this being my career!"

"And I don't plan on giving you any money," she growled back.

He stood there, dumbfounded, helpless. The people of New York had been asked too long and too often to be charitable. They were getting testy, feisty, hostile. And the beggars had nowhere to go. They simply turned around and walked away, muttering under their breath.

As I walked into Macy's, I wondered how it had come about that after two weeks in New York I had remained relatively unscathed. The Subway Smasher hadn't smashed me, my taxi drivers hadn't caused an accident, I hadn't gotten stuck in an elevator in the World Trade Center, no one had jumped me from behind and thrown me into the bushes. I was a survivor.

And I had almost achieved my goal. I was standing in the electronics department buying microcassettes for my recorder.

On one of my last trips to New York a few years earlier I had been at the exact same spot, checking out the CD players. I remembered standing there debating with myself whether to get one or not. I often was indecisive about buying electronic equipment, afraid that the day I finally surrendered my money someone would go and invent another model that was even better and cheaper.

So I was standing there, wondering whether to buy a CD player or not, when my thoughts were interrupted by a news bulletin flashing across the screens in the neighboring TV section. A reporter was standing in front of the Brandenburg Gate. "Good evening," he said. "I'm Dick Breslaw and what an historic night! The East German government has just declared that East German citizens may now pass into the West beginning tomorrow morning, no restrictions. I'll have complete details shortly, live from the Berlin Wall at the Brandenburg Gate on the late night news. Stay tuned!"

Huh?

It took a moment for it to sink in, but when it did, I was shocked. I was flabbergasted. I was blown away. But even more than that, *I was indignant.* For half of my life I had lived and sweated it out in Berlin, and on the day the Wall fell, I wasn't there. Reporter Dick Breslaw, the creep, was there, but not me!

A crowd had gathered around the televisions. "Omigod!" I exclaimed as I saw a Trabi, East Germany's feeble answer to the Volkswagen, squeeze past a border control.

"Oh, look at those cute little cars!" a woman standing next to me remarked.

"That's Checkpoint Charlie!" I cried out. "My God! It's Checkpoint Charlie."

The woman eyed me. She probably thought I was a schizo. Maybe I was. She edged away without taking her eyes off me. But what did I care?

A triumphant group of East Berliners streamed by perplexed border guards, storming the West, weeping, shouting, guzzling down champagne with beer and tears. It was easy to recognize them in their ski jackets and stone-washed jeans and their white running shoes, the women with their hair curled in perms and cut in 1970-ish shags.

"The news broke at 7 P.M. Central European Time," the newscaster's lead-in began. "Despite the late hour and the cold November weather, the word spread like a wildfire."

I looked at my watch. It was almost 9 P.M. Eastern Standard Time. It was 4 A.M. in Berlin. Macy's would be closing in a few minutes.

The reporter came into view. He was standing with a crowd at Checkpoint Charlie. "How does it feel, sir, as an East Berlin citizen, walking through the border like this?" he screamed above the din.

The camera inched around him, bringing the man he was interviewing into view. For a fraction of a nanosecond the only thing I took in was a classy Scottish tweed blazer with a smart, silk paisley scarf resting comfortably under the collar. This was an *East* Berliner?

"It is a great moment for everyone in the city, both East and West," said the man in the classy Scottish — Omigod! Oh no. This wasn't possible! It was Jürgen! *My* Jürgen. My ex. What was he doing on American television? And since when was he an East Berliner?

I must have gasped, because the people standing around me in the TV department all backed away from me. And then I must have cried out, because now the crowd was decidedly giving me the evil eye.

"Can I help you, miss?" asked a salesman. He gripped my elbow as if to lead me back to my psychiatric clinic.

"*Ich bin ein Berliner,*" I said, smiling lamely.

"Oh, I see," he replied, not at all seeing.

I called Jürgen long distance the following day. His explanation seemed perfectly reasonable. When he heard about the Wall, he was sitting in the café-bar he and his partner

Ulf owned in the building across from Checkpoint Charlie he had refurbished two years before. He and Ulf took a bottle of champagne out of the fridge and, with an ever-growing group of West Berliners, they walked across the vast neon-lit control point grounds to the barricades on the eastern side. The East German guards, at first unsure of the situation, refused to let them through. So they stood and waited, watching the crowds growing on both sides. Eventually, with one joyous thrust, the throngs on the East side broke through to the West. Jürgen about-faced and retraced his steps in their midst, only to be greeted by an entourage of reporters thinking he was an East Berliner.

But standing there in Macy's on a late Thursday evening in early November 1989 watching the Wall fall and my ex-boyfriend squirt champagne into a television camera, all I had been able to think was, *Why aren't I there? How the hell could this have happened without me?*

Thirty months later my visit to Macy's was not punctuated by any fast-breaking historic events. I paid the salesman for the microcassettes and reached into my handbag for my Dictaphone. I was eager to slip in a new cassette, as the others were full and I had gone the whole day without taking any oral notes. I wanted to tell my built-in microphone about the Bus Basher and the Styrofoam cup.

My hand came up with my wallet, my passport case, my makeup case, my hairbrush, a floor plan of the Museum of Modern Art, a bus transfer, a crumpled Hershey Bar wrapper, a small bottle of aspirin, my keys, and a perfume atomiser. It came up with everything, with everything except my Dictaphone and the two cassettes I had already taped.

It was gone. My Dictaphone was gone. My cassettes were gone. The history of my last two weeks was gone. All my notes, gone, gone, gone, stolen from under my nose!

I had a goal. One goal and one goal only: to get the hell out of New York as fast as I could.

As I left Macy's, if you came up real close and weren't wearing a Walkman, you may have possibly heard me muttering softly under my breath.

Chapter Seven

Sunday, November 15
Diet Week: 6
Day: 7
Weight Loss: still 12 lbs.
Late morning

" 'Why does coffee often taste like green beans?' "

I was reading Heike an invitation to a museum opening.

" 'What does the color yellow sound like? How bright are our darkest dreams? Where does the fourth dimension meet our seventh sense? Come join us to celebrate the opening of Germany's first Sensory Museum and help us find answers to these questions. Experience the music of erotic poetry, savor the taste of the whitest of wines, breathe in the subtle fragrances of the changing seasons, yield to the touch of tangible —' "

"That's enough," Heike said on the other end of the telephone line. "I'm not up to it this evening. Museums are your obsession, not mine."

"I promised Martin I'd go. His new boyfriend works there. It starts at seven." Heike was in an agoraphobic phase, still mourning her decision to ditch Norbert of the Wandering

Eye. I detected a sigh. "Martin tells me everyone gets to taste astronaut ice cream," I added.

"Another reason not to go," Heike replied dryly.

Well, then, I'd go myself. I hung up and turned my thoughts back to my tasks at hand. Either I'd begin the day finishing off the rest of my record collection, or I'd grit my teeth and get down to the outline for the new show.

I knew the answer. Brandenburg beckoned.

Karla Menzel was expecting my outline on Wednesday. It was only a matter of putting together the bits and pieces we had gathered over the previous few weeks. I'd include what Patrick and I had picked up on Thursday and Friday: Count von der Lühe de Labomté; the ghost town at the edge of the mines; the two manager types. I had three stenographer's pads chock full of sloppy, haphazard notes and quotes.

I put pen to paper and wrote *Becky Goes Brandenburg* across the top of the page.

> The camera pans in on an arid landscape in gray-brown tones in a brown coal mining region southeast of Lübbenau in Brandenburg. Towering sand dunes. Piles of muddy earth. Not a tree or bush, plant or flower in sight. Above we see the merest sliver of an overcast, threatening sky. All in all, a desolate, unsettling scene.
>
> Suddenly something moves at the edge of the picture. It's Becky on a bicycle, bumping along past the craters and dunes. What in the world is Becky Bernstein of Brooklyn doing in a Brandenburg desert? Her face registers fatigue, loneliness, irritation. She's not happy about being here. In fact, she hates —

I faltered. How could I begin an upbeat television pilot about Brandenburg on such a negative note? I crossed out everything

I had written with such vehemence the paper ripped. I crumpled it up, tossed it into the wastebasket, and whipped another sheet out of the drawer. I slapped it down on my desk. My pen diligently went to work again — doodling.

I watched my fingers draw, fascinated. I often found that my doodles, like my dreams, gave me a clue to some strange inner life of mine that I hadn't yet tapped into. What were my fingers creating? Whatever it was, it was wispy. Circular. Spindly. Puffy. Was it dandelion fluff? A fleck of dust? A spider with a hundred legs? I was a particularly unskilled artist, so I imagine it could have been any of those things. For all I knew, it was a rubber Kooosh ball or the skull of a hairy ape. But no, none of those things made sense to me. It was — it was — It hit me. It was a pompom. An exploding pompom.

My pen wrote the word *pompom*. Once, twice. And then all over the page. It printed it in block letters, large, small, in cursive writing, slanted to the left, upside down. *Pompom*. And then I watched as it scribbled "gone with the pompom." It sounded nice. What other rhymes could I come up with? "Mom and the pompom." "Bomb the pompoms." "Upon the pompom." Wait a second. How about "Once upon a pompom?"

My heart began to race. Adrenaline poured into my veins. I grabbed a fresh piece of paper and wrote:

Once upon a Pompom.

Not bad for a title. So what now?

One fine day, many many years ago, back in New York City, all the way back in the early sixties, in the days when I still wore scabs on my knees and a ponytail down my back, at a time in history when television was black and white and things always went better with Coke —

I was flabbergasted. A story was emerging. My pompom story had finally found the nerve to pop out of me and plop itself down on paper.

I jumped up from my desk. I *had* to finish the Brandenburg pilot before getting caught up in something else. The pompom story was a ploy, a way to sabotage Brandenburg. I had to be disciplined and box my way through the muck.

I paced through the apartment. I went into the kitchen, poured myself a cup of coffee, and then traipsed off to my bedroom. How many times had I come in here to take another peek at my new bed? Almost as many times as I had walked up to the mirror to get another glimpse of my new hair. Pedro had done a good job. Thanks to Ruth's coloring kit, which I had persuaded him to use, the gray had been miraculously transformed into chestnut red highlights. The bed looked lovely too, the way the mattress rested on the low, sleek, modern wooden base. I loved sliding the two adjustable back rests to the right and left, watching them glide along the rim of the frame. A brilliant invention. I didn't have to put my bed against the wall anymore. I could prop a pillow up against the back rests and watch television, read, do a headstand.

I lay down on it. What was it about the Brandenburg project, I wondered, that was making me so edgy? Why was I so overwhelmed? I rolled onto my side. The mattress was hard, but pliable. I could almost feel the flexible slatted frame adapting to the shape of my body.

The telephone woke me. I grabbed for it, but it had vanished. It took me a moment to realize that I had fallen asleep on my new bed and the telephone was no longer on the bottom step of the wooden base but on an adjustable shelf attached to the bed on the right. By the time I had figured all of this out, the answering machine in my office had already taken over.

I turned to look at the alarm clock. It read Sunday, November 15, 12:05. I'd been sleeping for thirty minutes. Oh well, a half hour less to write my outline.

My outline — uugghh. Almost nothing had gone right on the fact-finding mission Patrick and I had made to Brandenburg the week before. Perhaps I should get my record collection out of the way first. Hard Rock Richie, the fellow who sold used records at the flea market, was coming the next day to pick up my rejects. I wanted to make sure he got *all* of them. I wouldn't need more than an hour or two to go through what was left. It would clear my head for writing, and I'd have plenty of time to work on the outline before going to the Sensory Museum.

I pulled myself out of bed, trudged into my office, and switched on the answering machine. It was Marsha, in New York. "With bad news," she said. I began flipping through my records as I listened to her taped voice.

It seems that the week before, Boris, her cat, finally fulfilling his dream, had flown out of their sixth-story window and landed in a convalescence clinic. To make matters worse, the heating in her apartment was on the blink and Sven, her computer, had caught a virus and gobbled up *Forever Fassbinder*, one of the press packages she was putting together for a nationwide retrospective on contemporary German cinema. And then, on top of all this, she had finally agreed to a date with the dentist from Bensonhurst who'd been bothering her since Passover. She was hoping it would give her some respite from her troubles. But it turned out that his idea of having a good time was to take a sniff of laughing gas and then show her slides of a trip he had taken with his mother to Atlantic City. "Furthermore," Marsha went on, "Milton Goldfarb is being sued for slander by the heirs of a dead Hollywood star, Dr. Glenn MacKensey was sued yesterday for malpractice, and the Bagel Man disclosed that he was moving to Milano with Luigi, his interior decorator. I thought you'd like the info."

In short, Marsha's life was desolate.

"Tell me, Becky," she said to my answering machine with great urgency in her voice, "please, tell me. Do you think you can find me the following three things in Berlin: one, a heated apartment no higher than the second floor; two, a man who could possibly by some small stretch of the imagination be interested in women. And I don't mean his mom; and three, a well-paid job so I can pay for Boris's hospital bills? If so, I promise to take the first flight to Berlin."

Poor Marsha. She was gorgeous and gifted and getting terribly, terribly desperate. When she signed off there was no doubt in my mind that I could never really go home again. So I went back to my neat little nest instead, back to my records, back to my past, and the last of my quit-the-chaos trash.

I was pleased with myself. The major junk was gone, the colossal clutter, the accumulated detritus of a woman in midlife. My mother would be proud of me come Christmas.

One by one, I pulled the last of my dust-infested discs out of the record shelves, taking the unwanted ones and whisking them onto the "terminate" pile.

"Aachoo," I sneezed.

And then the phone rang again. It was Felix, the lousy bastard, which didn't surprise me a bit — especially after Heike had told me the other night that his ex-girlfriend Hildburg was now his ex-ex-girlfriend. I knew that sooner or later he would try to wiggle and wangle his way back into my life. "The Umberto Bernini interview was super. You did a good job," he said cheerfully.

It had been six weeks since I last spoke to him. A lot had

happened since then. I was a different woman now. Cooler, calmer, twelve pounds lighter. Hey, I had straightened out my life. Felix would never again possess the power to move me.

"Thank you," I answered noncommittally, almost graciously. There was a silence in which he cleared his throat. He knew I was waiting for him to continue.

"He's an excellent actor. He was great in *Morning on Mars,*" he put in.

"Yes."

He had expected more. Again he cleared his throat. Then there was silence.

"I was wondering," he said finally, "if you happened to find a pair of longjohns hanging around your apartment?" Longjohns? He wants his *longjohns?* "I'm missing a pair."

"Well, actually, Felix, I've been cleaning up the place, and I did happen to find a pair of angora undies a few weeks ago." My voice was strong, almost jovial.

"Oh," he replied eagerly, "may I come by later and pick them up? We can have a glass of wine together too. I could explain things."

"Thanks for the offer, but I'm afraid it won't be necessary." Indeed, I really was above it all. My coolness surprised even me. "It won't be necessary, Felix, because your longjohns don't exist anymore. At least not in a form that could be of interest to you. I cut them up and made them into rags. Angora's excellent for dusting, you know."

I could hear him inhale deeply. "I suppose you're going to hang up on me again," he finally said.

"You're under a misconception, Felix. I never hang up on people. I simply replace the receiver in its cradle." I replaced the receiver in its cradle and returned to my record shelves. Indeed, Felix had lost the power to move me.

The phone rang again.

Why, the nerve of that pipsqueak, that creep, that weak-bladdered bastard, that — I lunged for the receiver. "Listen, you SONOFABITCH!!"

"Excuse me?"

I was taken aback. "Felix?" Silence. "Is that you, Felix?"

"Uuhh, no. This is Benno. Benno Fabian, back from vacation. I — uuhh — I guess I caught you at a bad time."

"Oh, Benno. No, no. No problem. I — uuhh — I was only throwing out some old records. And an old boyfriend. No. No problem." We spoke briefly. I told him about "Bingo Berlin" and the kind of illustrations we needed. He told me he'd like to show me his work but was loaded down with assignments at the moment. I promised to send him a copy of the story anyway. He explained that his English was terrible, but he'd try to read it. I asked him to please keep me informed about his brother's third divorce. We said goodbye.

I went back to my record shelves and pitched the last remains of my deejay career one by one into oblivion. Amazingly, I had reached the Zs. I decided to preserve all the Zappas but get rid of some Zeppelins (which should have been alphabetized under "L" anyway) and was pondering what verdict to pass on the Zombies when I felt another sneezing attack come on. The dust was really giving me a beating.

I remembered reading somewhere that "dust" was composed of a variety of interesting odds and ends: particles of fabric, the remains of dead insects and food and plants, itsy-bitsy spores of mushroomy substances and diverse microscopic single-celled organisms. But surprisingly enough, I learned, most of the icky, fuzzy, grayish fluff actually came from two other main sources: the dead skin and hair of human beings, and disintegrated meteorites, oodles of which fell to the earth every day. In other words, the gray fuzz that hid behind my kitchen cabinets and infiltrated the grooves of my records came from none other than little ol' me and a big black hole. More precisely, I said to myself, it comes from parts of me and parts of the universe that are no longer living. That is to say, dust is nothing more than cosmic and human decay. To be exact: dust is death.

As I kneeled there, watching the records sail across the room, it occurred to me that sneezing was probably no more than a defense mechanism, my own little futile attempt at fending off death — in the same way the vacuum cleaner and the broom were my mother's preferred weapons in *her* battle against decay. It was like holding up garlic to scare away Dracula.

I packed the rejected records in cartons and carried them into the hallway. My War on Junk was over. There was nothing left to do but return to my desk and Brandenburg.

I picked up my pen and read the page lying on my desk:

Once upon a Pompom

One fine day, many many years ago . . .

All right, I thought, I'd let myself work on it for *ten* minutes. And when the ten minutes were up, I'd go back to Brandenburg.

I reread the paragraph. It was far too busy.

I began again.

One fine day, back in the early sixties, all the way back in New York City, in the days when television was black and white and things always went better with Coke, my best friend Marsha Lipschitz and I were walking down our red and gold tree-lined street.

This was fun. The writing didn't come easy, but at least it came.

It was a brilliant and crisp autumn afternoon. Royal blue sky, puffy white clouds, bright, stark sunlight. The street —

And that's when the telephone rang again. It was Benno Fabian. Again.

"Oh, did your brother's divorce come through already?" I asked.

Benno chuckled. And then shyly, modestly, he said, "You mentioned before that you were getting rid of some old records."

"Yes."

"I collect them, or rather record *covers*. For my work. For ideas. I was wondering if, before you throw them out, I might come over and see if you have anything for me. I could show you my portfolio at the same time."

"Sure, why not. But someone's picking them up tomorrow, so you'll have to get over here soon if you want first choice."

He said he'd come at six.

I shouldn't have agreed to it. It was already two-thirty and I was getting nowhere with Brandenburg. I sat back down at my desk. Once again I wrote *Becky Goes Brandenburg* on a blank sheet of paper. I stared at it.

The paper wasn't the only thing that was blank.

"I'm stuck," I said, summing up my predicament for Professor Bloch in his kitchen a few minutes later.

"I thought you'd be," he replied. "You're stuck. And I'm busy." He was wearing an apron and cooking up a racket. "Popcorn. Manni and Bea are coming over with the kids later."

Besides the popcorn, I saw a pot roast sweating in the oven, soup bubbling away on the range, and sliced and diced greens sitting in bowls waiting to be dumped into simmering water. Professor Bloch handed me a few carrots. "Make yourself useful," he said. "They match your hair." He reached over and threw me one of his state-of-the-art peeling gizmos. He whisked the pan of popcorn from the stove and turned his attention back to a pot full of polenta. He began to stir it.

"I have a knot in my stomach," I said.

"That doesn't mean you can't wield a peeler. Chuck it."

"Chuck it?" I looked at the gadget. "How do I 'chuck' it?"

"Brandenburg, Becky. Chuck Brandenburg."

I knew he'd say something drastic like that. "I can't 'chuck' it. Karla would sue me."

"She's not going to sue you. She'll kill you, but she won't sue you. Of course she might not pay you for the work you've already done on the project. But you can deal with that."

"And she'll never make a movie of 'Bingo Berlin.'"

"So someone else will."

"She'll throw me out of *Breakfast at Becky's.*"

"You're her bread and butter. She won't throw you out." He looked over his shoulder at me. "The TV station might throw *her* out if the ratings don't pick up, but she won't — Hey, what are you doing to those carrots? I asked you to *peel* them, not whittle them out of existence."

"But, Professor, it's the chance of a lifetime."

"You'll have another chance at fame and glamour. I'm not telling you anything you don't already know." He was right. He wasn't.

"It's not just that," I said. "It's —" Well, what *was* it? "It's just not in me to give up. I can't give up."

The professor stopped stirring the polenta and turned toward me. "My lovely, you've got to give up. Stop making yourself miserable. Who said you have to do everything? Who said you have to be perfect? You're allowed to goof up. And you goofed up."

"Well, it's not just *my* fault. Nothing fits into place. I couldn't even find a boyfriend there."

"If you really wanted Brandenburg, you would know what to do. Becky, it's not for you. You don't care enough about it. And that's the truth of it."

"But I could *learn* to care, couldn't I?"

"Why put in the effort? There are more important things for you to do." He was right — again. Didn't I care more about exploding pompoms than I did about the Germans' obsessing over the relationship between the two halves of their country? He looked me square in the face. "My lovely, all you have to do is say no. *Capisce?*"

I looked down at the carrots.

"And do me a favor," he said, turning back to the polenta, "if you intend to cry, take the carrots away first. I don't want any salt on them."

I pushed the carrots away. "You and your amateur psychology," I managed to say just before the dam broke.

"You have to have patience for polenta," Professor Bloch told me. "It needs your undivided attention. You stand at the stove like a slave and stir for at least half an hour. If you don't, it clumps up."

I wiped the tears from my eyes, blew my nose.

"Plenty of patience," he went on. "It was one of Doro's favorites. Polenta was one of the first things I ever cooked for her. She told me she fell in love with me watching me smoothing out the clumps. 'That's what I need,' she said to me, 'a man with patience and a strong arm.' " He took the polenta from the stove and flipped the mixture onto a floured wooden board. "Want to stay for dinner?"

I shook my head. "A museum opening."

The professor molded the polenta into a rectangle. "How are those carrots doing?"

I tried smiling. "Better." I exhaled deeply. "I'll call Karla tomorrow. First thing in the morning. She's going to kill me." I made a gesture as if to slit my throat. "I can already see the headlines. BECKY TO BRANDENBURG: DROP DEAD."

"She's a real witch, that Menzel." The professor was washing out the polenta pot.

"Oh, she's all right. She's got a great laugh. Anyone who laughs like that can't be all that bad. She's just very career-oriented." I finished peeling the carrots. "Do you want to celebrate? I have some raspberry schnapps in the refrigerator. A remnant from what's-his-name."

Professor Bloch turned to me. "What *was* actually his name?"

"Felix."

"Ah! So you can say his name out loud these days?"

I smiled. "Should I get the schnapps?"

"Sorry, my lovely, I'm off the booze." I narrowed my eyes. "Alcohol and I don't agree with each other," he went on.

"Since when is this?"

"Since I've been drinking too much of it," he replied wryly. "Since Doro died, I guess. But I've been thinking about it more and more."

"Have you really?"

"I look at you, Becky, and I think, if this little snotnose can go on a diet and stick to it, I can stop drinking."

"Professor, I'm touched." I really was. I was getting all choked up again.

"And I look at 'Bingo Berlin' and I think, if this little

snotnose can write a story like that, she can write more, too."
He paused. "Becky, forget Brandenburg. Write. That's what
you should be doing."
    "What? Become an artist? You want me to starve to
death?"
    "You've done a pretty good job of that already these past
six weeks."
    He had a point. Maybe he even had *two* points.

When I got back to my apartment, it was past five o'clock. The
temperature had dropped drastically, and it was already dark
outside. I could feel winter coming. When I moved through my
rooms, a veil of cool air seemed to envelop me, but surprisingly
enough I was all warm inside, strangely at peace, cleansed,
emotionally unfettered.
    It was time to start living again.
    I slipped into black sheer stockings, gray suede pumps,
a low-cut black silk blouse, an over-the-knee gray cashmere
skirt. I applied the bare essentials of eye makeup, blusher, and
my recently rediscovered Scarlet Passion lipstick. I dabbed a
mild perfume behind my ears, on my wrists. I ran my fingers
through my hair for a natural, windswept look, pleased with
the way the plant-based highlights twinkled.
    I inspected myself in the mirror. Something was missing.
    Reverently, ceremoniously, I took my father's gray pin-
striped suit jacket from its hanger. It had been modernized,
tapered and shortened to size. I slipped it on and buttoned it up.
    I looked again in the mirror.
    I liked what I saw. Under my skirt my hips still bulged
a bit and my thighs still shook like jelly, but what of it?
My waist was back, and my belly was flat. I had to admit I
would never again fit into my brown mini, but I was tired of

counting calories. It was time to come to terms with this body of mine.

So there I stood, the swindler's daughter, the lumpy sum of some forty years and so many lives and loves. And I felt just fine.

And then the doorbell chimed.

Benno Fabian, tall, skinny, and not as thin-lipped as Heike had described him, arrived on time, with tousled hair and a battered trenchcoat. He handed me his portfolio. In return I gave him "Bingo Berlin" and a glass of water. Then we got down on our knees and began flipping through my records. I sneezed, and Benno reached into his pocket and gave me his last tissue. As I blew my nose, I wondered why Heike had never mentioned those kind, wise eyes. Nor the smile that graced his face. It was a kid's grin. It surprised me to find the gentle, trusting grin of a child on the grown-up face of a man.

Soon thereafter Benno left with an enormous sack of record jackets.

And I left with him.

In the Sensory Museum we feasted on astronaut ice cream and coffee that tasted like green beans. We danced to the sound of the color yellow, and let the subtle fragrance of poetry blind us. In the Ebony Room, under the bright lights of our darkest dreams, we lost our sense of direction and wandered out into the Berlin night.

It was dark and damp outside. A soft breeze, sprinkled with rain, tickled our faces. The air was pungent with autumn, the promise of frost, wet earth, the oozing sap of broken twigs. It stung my nose. There were trees above us, and under our feet were crisp fallen leaves. We heard them crackle and crunch. Hundreds of them. Thousands. There was a whole sea of them out there. A deep red sea of autumn leaves. We waded through them, knee high, crushing, kicking and squashing, running and scrunching. My heart cried out with sudden happiness. Benno must have heard it, for he reached out and took my hand in his.

We crunched on together.

And have remained together since.

Epilogue

Autumn 1994
Evening

Benno is an angel. To say the least. And believe me, I'd love to say more. I'm dying to let you know in very exact, precise terms how I really feel about him.

But I won't.

And you know why?

Because this is not his story. Just like it wasn't Felix'x. This is a story about me and my apartment, about what happened to us when we went on a diet. The fact that Benno happened to come along at the tail end of our diet, that concluding my tale with his entrance ties everything up into a neat and tidy package, does not warrant going on and on about him. Hey, this is a story about clutter and calories. As far as I can see it's not about love. Some other time I'll tell you how we ran off to Venice and swooned under the moon in a lagoon one afternoon; how amazed I am every morning to wake up and find this perfectly wonderful, tall, skinny person next to me; how Benno and Professor Bloch devised a jogging program for me, so even if I do give in to gorgonzola on white or roast suckling pig, I can knock the fat off the next day on a run; how we now play Doppelkopf every Monday night; how Benno inherited his great-aunt's house, a rambling, spacious villa with *sooo* much space to keep all our possessions arranged and orderly; how it turned out, to my sheer horror, that his great-aunt's house is situated southwest of Berlin, right outside the city, smack in the middle of Brandenburg, of all places; how we only recently moved in and everyone joined in to celebrate. Martin came with a kneeling chair and Jürgen with architectural plans for our new, roomy, perfectly organized walk-in closet. Barry Sonnenberg made an appearance with Marsha Lipschitz. They're an item now and have been since Marsha's last visit to the Berlin Film Festival. ("Do you love her?" I asked him. "Part of me loves part of her," Barry answered. "Oh, and dare I ask *which* part of you loves *which* part of her?" Barry just shook his head and laughed. "Well, that's an improvement in any case. Did you at least *tell* her so?" I pressed. He nodded. "Was it the first time you ever told someone that?" I wondered. "No," he told me, "but it's the first time I ever really meant it.") Heike made the party too, with Hannes, whom she met at that Reinhard Beck premiere. They gave us a gift to put in the guest bath, Hannes's recent nonsense best-seller *Quotes for Dopes*. Even Karla Menzel came. We were enemies for about six months, but then "Bingo Berlin" brought us together. Shooting commences in six weeks, and Barry has the male lead. He'll finally be able to buy his own washer and dryer.

And my mother blessed us with her presence, too. You should have seen the way Professor Bloch pranced around the kitchen cooking couscous for her and how fast she knit him a headband for winter jogging. She even sewed in one of her MADE ESPECIALLY FOR YOU BY GLORIA BERNSTEIN labels. The two of them — boy, it's really a riot. In fact, it's *all* a good story, really, and I promise to tell it some day, okay? It just doesn't belong *here*, that's all. I like to keep things in their place, if you know what I mean.

Now, I'm aware that some of you may be thinking that I'm swindling you into accepting an ending that's a bit contrived, that it didn't really happen quite like I say, that it would be far too great a coincidence that exactly on the day I and my apartment go off our diet, I meet the man of my dreams, my life begins anew, and everything falls into place. Well, what can I say? This story could no doubt have any number of endings, but for a reason unknown to me it simply chose to end itself this way.

However, if it's any consolation to you, I would like to add that the end is not quite as perfect as you may think. It's happy, but not perfect. And you know why it's not perfect? BECAUSE BENNO IS THE BIGGEST SLOB I HAVE EVER MET IN MY ENTIRE LIFE! I'm talking *major* mess: candy dishes with rancid mints and rotten nuts moldering under piles and piles of old newspapers; torn envelopes, unpaid bills, old love letters, forgotten bank statements floating in the bathtub. Benno's socks never match, his teacups are chipped, he stores silverware in the utilities closet, stamps in the medicine cabinet, and shoes with the linens. And what did I trip over this morning in the little vestibule connecting his office space with mine? Five cartons stuffed with hundreds of dusty old record jackets! I couldn't believe my eyes: there were *Ricky Dee's Happy Sax Party*, *Spec and the Spiders*, *Heavy Metal Hothouse*. I started to sneeze, my eyes teared up, my throat got all scratchy.

"Help!" I cried out, near hysterics.

And suddenly he was there. Benno rushed to my side, wrapped me in his arms, and held me tight. And when I had calmed down he gave me a tissue to blow my nose.

"Oh, sweetheart, where would I be without you?" I sighed.

"I guess you'd be out there looking for me," he replied.

Indeed, Benno is an angel. To say the very, *very* least.